ULTIMATE ABUSE

S. J. RITCHEY

www.trafford.com

North America & international
toll-free: 1 888 232 4444 (USA & Canada)
phone: 250 383 6864 ♦ fax: 812 355 4082

ACKNOWLEDGEMENTS

Sincere gratitude to members of Blue River Writers—Judy Beale, Carter Elliott, Lesley Howard, Susan Huckle, Joe Maxwell, and Paul Poff for their honest critiques, helpful suggestions, and unwavering support throughout the development of this manuscript.

This is a work of fiction. Names, places, and institutions are the product of the author's imagination. Any connection to an actual person or place is unintentional.

CHAPTER 1

The offices of Watson, Attorney At Law, and Randle, Private Investigator, hummed with activity on a Tuesday morning in late March. Established two years ago when the two partners had agreed pooling talents and resources made more sense than continuing with their informal consulting arrangement, the firm now had a growing client base.

Jennifer Watson had returned to Chester, a growing city of over a half-million in the Midwest, after several years with a large law firm in New York. Tired of dealing with huge egos in the corporate world, she intended to set up a small practice focused on helping ordinary people with legal problems. She'd met Dave Randle, a former Marine with experience in special forces, as he started out as a private investigator after tiring of the typical retirement activities of golf, fishing and watching television. Rented offices on the same floor of a downtown office building had led them to a common coffee area, idle talk about the weather and local affairs, and then to more serious discussions about how to assist each other. The advantages of forming a lawyer/private investigator partnership led them to a formal agreement.

The firm had grown from struggling to meet the cost of a small two-office suite to a facility of three offices, conference room, and reception area. As the number of clients increased, they'd brought in Eleanor Blackwell known to colleagues as Ellie, a paralegal who now acted in support of Jennifer in preparing court documents, doing background work for cases, and a host of other jobs. In her spare time Ellie was pursuing a law degree through the local university.

But more than professional responsibilities had pulled at Jennifer and Dave. Fourteen months ago, they had married after trying to ignore growing feelings for each other. They'd promised each other their private lives would not interfere with their professional responsibilities and thus far, the sailing had been smooth.

On the phone to a potential client, Dave glanced at the woman who limped into the reception area of Watson and Randle and said something to Helen Knight, their receptionist/secretary who'd been with the firm for three months. Though Dave recognized Miriam Reading immediately, everything about her had changed since he'd last seen her. Once a slender vivacious person always dressed to perfection for her marketing position at Channel 14 Television, Miriam had gone to hell. Her face, almost bloated beyond recognition, was partially hidden beneath a mop of lifeless blond hair covering her ears and drooping to her shoulders. Her navy pantsuit bulged at the wrong spots. Still not believing he'd once asked her to marry him after several months of an intimate relationship, he nodded to Helen's signal to come to the conference room. He completed the phone conversation by confirming an appointment with the caller concerned about a son who'd gotten involved with a drug dealer.

Dave followed as Miriam dropped into a chair at the table as though she could not tolerate a standing position. Jennifer was shaking Miriam's hand when he came through the door. Jennifer said, "Dave, you remember Miriam?"

Miriam smiled at Dave, revealing a missing tooth, reached to take his hand, and said, "Life has changed since I last saw you."

Dave asked, "How are you doing?" He could tell she wasn't doing well, but didn't want to ask what had gone wrong this early in the session. The fact that she was in their office confirmed she had problems.

"I need help and I thought about the two of you." Her eyes swiveled from Dave to Jennifer, both now sitting across from her. "And I apologize for not making an appointment but I wanted to get this started as soon as possible."

Jennifer asked, "What kind of help?"

Meeting their eyes, Miriam said, "First, I want to sue a pharmaceutical company for maiming my child. I'm convinced the medication I took during pregnancy caused my child to be deformed and brain-damaged. She will never be normal and may not survive until her first birthday. It's all their fault."

"What does your physician think?" Jennifer asked, as she looked at Dave.

"He thinks I'm off-base, but he prescribed the stuff and probably got some payoff from the company to side with them. I no longer trust his judgment in the matter and am taking my child to a pediatrician in a different group."

Jennifer asked, "Have there been other reported cases of birth defects after the use of this medication?"

"I haven't found any, but I'm looking as I have time." She paused, rubbed her hand across her face as though trying to erase problems. "But that's why I need your help."

"What is the medicine?"

"According to the gynecologist it's a new product called Plertex. The company claims it has been approved by the Food and Drug Administration and will soon be available widely."

Jennifer said, "We'll need as much information as you have to give us a starting point. Bring in a container with the name and if you have the formulation, that would help. Also, the name of the doctor who prescribed it for you."

She pulled a sheet of paper and a plastic vial from her jacket pocket. "This is what I have."

As she placed the items on the table, she continued, "The second thing is my husband. He's become so abusive I'm hiding from him." She rolled up a sleeve of her top to reveal deep bruises along her upper arm, and added, "That's where he hit me four days ago. For a while I couldn't move my arm at all. I thought he'd broken a bone. I could show you more, but I'd rather not disrobe."

Dave asked, "You reported this to the police?"

Miriam nodded. "Of course, but they seem unable to do much. I obtained a restraining order, but that doesn't phase him at all. For the past three days, my daughter and I have been in a shelter for battered women, but I'm afraid he'll find us."

Jennifer said, "The authorities are better able to deal with this than we are."

Miriam shook her head. "On paper that's true, but I remember how Dave dealt with guys like my husband."

"Are you divorced or moving in that direction?" Dave asked. He shifted in his seat to ease the throb in his leg he'd injured in a recent scuffle with a man now in the city jail.

Shaking her head, she said, "He won't buy into a amicable split and threatens to kill me if I pursue divorce. I talked to one lawyer who insisted I get counseling before filing any legal papers. I want your help in moving the divorce process forward."

When Helen opened the door and nodded, Jennifer said, " I'm sorry to rush you out, but my nine o'clock appointment is waiting. But we'll begin work on your behalf." She stood. "We'd like you to complete an information form and pay a small retainer fee. That will give us the legal right to pursue your concerns. Then give Dave details of where you're living and the security arrangement."

Dave waited at the table until Miriam shuffled into the outer room. "I couldn't believe how she's changed."

Jennifer nodded, her face glum, "Neither could I. She was once the sexiest woman I knew and had you wrapped around her little finger."

"I remember. We had a solid relationship and talked about marriage, but Miriam insisted I was too much in love with you to take the chance." He stood and touched her arm. "She knew more than I did about feelings."

She touched his hand and said, "So who did she marry?"

"Some guy who works as a sports announcer for Channel 14. He'd been a professional football player for the Broncos. I read the wedding announcement in the *Register.*"

"I don't remember seeing that."

"You were immersed with the trial against those guys at Black and Redfield and didn't look at any news for days."

He passed Jennifer's next appointment on the way out. Miriam was engrossed with the paperwork, but looked up as he entered his office.

Ten minutes later, she rapped on his door and came in to take the chair in front of his desk. She eased into the chair in front of his desk as though the movement pained her. A grimace contorted her face for a second. She brushed hair out of her eyes. She asked, "What else should I tell you?"

"Where are you staying?"

"The Fourth Street Shelter. It's run by a group of churches who've joined together to support homeless or battered women. They're watching my baby while I'm here."

"Any security there?"

She considered for a moment. "Not much. Two older men take turns during the day, but if someone really wanted in, they wouldn't be able to stop them. They'd call the cops, but by the time a patrol arrived, the woman would be taken or beaten or both."

Dave made notes on a pad, then asked, "Your husband?"

"Billy Cranford. I met him at the station and we hit it off quickly and got married. Everything was great for a few months, then he came in drunk one night and for some reason became irate and knocked me around. By then I was pregnant and thought I had to stick it out."

"Things didn't improve, I take it?"

Shaking her head, Miriam said, "For a while, they did. But he goes into terrible tantrums and always hit me, no matter what I did or didn't do. A few weeks ago, he cracked me across the face, damaged a tooth so badly, I had to have it extracted. I intend to have a bridge soon, but I haven't had time."

"Did you ever discuss counseling with him?"

Nodding, she said, "He refused. Finally I concluded it was hopeless and if I were to survive, I had to get out. I left four days ago and a friend took me to the shelter. But I'm concerned Billy will find me."

"He ignored the restraining order?"

"Called it a bunch of crap. That was earlier when I'd gone to a friends house and got the order. Billy broke in their back door and dragged me and Melanie back to the house."

"Tell me about Billy. I remember he played pro ball and got into broadcasting after he retired. I saw the wedding announcement and the pictures. You looked happy then."

"I was. He's nice looking, intelligent, makes a good salary, and seemed to be kind and thoughtful. Before we were married, he treated me like a queen." Her eyes clouded for a moment. "After the beatings started, I tried to please him as much as I could, but nothing worked. As you might guess, men who spend their lives in contact sports believe everything can be solved by violence. They're larger than most people and have the mind-set that they can't be challenged without lashing out." For a moment Dave thought about himself, a special forces trained killer who worked to control his instinct to revert to those lethal tactics when provoked or challenged. Being with Jennifer had helped and he knew he'd never harm her. But it was a constant struggle, somewhat like conquering an addiction to drugs or alcohol.

Dave asked, "Is he doing well at the station?"

"They like him. He has this persona that draws people to his segment of the news. He's remembered as this fierce linebacker, not an ex-jock going to pot. Viewers have increased since he came to the sports desk and that makes management happy. And all the local athletes and coaches view him as the star he once was. It's akin to worship."

"Did you resign your position at the station?"

"I took a three-month leave just before the baby was born. If I can solve all my personal problems I intend to return. I'll need the money for sure and I enjoyed the work."

"Even if Billy is still there?"

"Yes," she nodded. "We work in different parts of the operation and our paths seldom cross."

"Anything else we need to know?"

Miriam shook her head. "Just help me get past these things. File for divorce and get Billy off my back so I'm not walking around in fear all the time."

"I'll start by talking to the cops and to your physician."

"All the addresses, names, etc., are listed on the form I gave to your secretary." As she stood, she smiled, a crooked semblance of her once beautiful lighting of her features. "By the way, your receptionist is pretty sexy."

"She's Helen Knight who worked in Congressman Hankins office before joining us. She's very good at meeting people and keeps the office organized."

"I remember reading about the problems Hankins had and Knight being abducted."

"You gave me good advice about marrying Jennifer," Dave said, "but it took a while for me to figure it all out."

"I'm glad it worked out for both of you."

Dave called Bill Rasmussen, Chief of Detectives, Chester Police. They'd become friends and frequent allies, an unlikely alliance between professionals who often were on opposing agendas in their worlds of crime and justice. They seemed to have an inherent sense of when not to interfere into the other's domain. After two years of interactions a solid sense of trust existed between the two. Neither intended to damage that relationship.

Rasmussen said, "Haven't seen you in awhile. Doing okay?"

"Good, but I need advice. How about meeting for lunch at Gibbons? I'll buy."

"Can't turn down a free meal. Twelve okay?"

They arrived within a minute of each other and were directed to a back booth by the head waiter who knew they desired as much privacy as possible in a busy restaurant without private rooms. The place was filling rapidly as downtown office workers rushed in for a quick lunch. Aromas of food pervaded the space. A waitress dropped menus on their table.

Dave glanced at the menu. "We've been retained to look into the wife abuse problem of Billy Cranford. There's a restraining order, but she says he's ignored it. I don't want to become involved if you guys are dealing with it."

The waitress returned to take their orders for the daily special, a bowl of clam chowder and a tuna sandwich. Both asked for coffee.

As he returned the menu and focused on his response, Rasmussen's round face clouded. He leaned forward and lowered his voice. "I don't know what to tell you. We got the word from above to ignore any complaints from the wife. I can't figure out who's been influenced but the directive came from the Mayor's office. No one will confirm the rationale, but you know politicians."

Dave said, "You think the television station contacted the Mayor?"

Rasmussen leaned back and sipped his coffee. "Don't know, but that'd be a good bet. Cranford jerked his wife and child out of a neighbor's house while the order was in force. The neighbor called us, worried the wife could be in danger, but before we could respond, the hold order came down. Between the two of us, I was pissed. So was the Chief."

"So you're going to allow this guy to beat up on his wife until he puts her in the hospital or kills her and maybe the child?"

"I know," Rasmussen muttered, "but the Chief is afraid to ignore the order."

"What about the judge who issued the order?"

"The Chief doesn't have the guts to stir the waters and get in trouble with the Mayor. And as you know, the judge wouldn't get involved again until Cranford is hauled into court or we notify her of Cranford's ignoring the order."

"Who was the judge?"

"Anita Chandler, the one who married you and Jennifer."

They waited while the waitress placed their meals, then gave attention to the chowder. The restaurant had filled to capacity and people were waiting in a short line at the door. Aromas of broiling meat and French fries mingling with body odors had become more pronounced.

Rasmussen said, "I assume the wife was the one who requested your intervention?"

Dave nodded, putting aside his spoon. "She's been knocked around and is now in a shelter, but Cranford will find her."

"They always do. It's almost impossible to provide protection short of putting the woman in jail. Police departments don't have the manpower to guard victims. All we can do is run routine checks and those usually don't work out." Rasmussen hesitated and looked at Dave. "Between the two of us, you should do what you can to help her. I can run a background check on Cranford. See if he has a history of violence."

"That might be useful. These guys often lose control of their emotions and get in trouble. Start in Denver. He lived there several years."

"I'll let you know."

Wiping crumbs from his mouth, Dave said, "I'll talk to Cranford as a starting place."

Rasmussen nodded. "Don't do anything to set him off."

"I know." But deep inside, his instincts were to confront the bully and hope he tried something physical.

They consumed their sandwiches and sipped coffee, conversing about the upcoming Congressional race and the fate of the Cardinals as they prepared for the season opening.

CHAPTER 2

After the last client had departed and Helen and Ellie had left for the day, Jennifer came into Dave's office, sat in the chair across from his desk. "Rasmussen any help?" She rubbed her eyes as though she was weary at the end of a lengthy spell of concentration on a legal matter. She raked a hand through her brown hair.

"He's stymied by this order from the Chief, but he'll run a background on Cranford. That may tell us something." He told her about the political interference with the restraining order issued by Judge Chandler.

Jennifer stared in disbelief at him for a moment, then said, "That's out of bounds by someone. I wonder if she knows."

"Rasmussen doesn't think so. The Chief hasn't told her."

She walked around his desk and gazed out the window overlooking Main Street, filled with traffic as downtown workers made for home. Pedestrians lined up six-deep at the crosswalks waiting for the light to change. Eyes still on the street, she said, "Suing the physician on Miriam's behalf may be a reach. Those charges are difficult to prove unless there's obvious negligence and now with this recent wave of restraints on suits, it could be hopeless. But we need to know more about the drug and the physicians role. He's supposed to know the risks before prescribing it."

"I made an appointment to visit her gynecologist tomorrow afternoon, but I haven't thought through my approach yet—accuse him first thing or beat around the issue."

"Maybe just get a feel for his reaction—see how defensive he is or if he refuses to discuss the case. Might tell us something."

"Let's have Ellie dig up what information there is about this drug. May not be much yet, but it'd be a start."

Dave left his desk and stood next to her, slipped his arm around her waist. "You ready to go home?"

"Sure. Let's go for a run, maybe the trail by the creek."

"Good idea, but I'll start the charcoal first. We can do those steaks you bought yesterday. Use every good day we have." Early in their marriage they'd discovered their mutual love of the outdoors and spent much of their limited free time jogging, walking, picnicking along the creek. They'd even discussed a vegetable garden but hadn't done anything yet. But with spring approaching, Dave was eager to put their plans into action.

Dave approached the receptionist in the offices of Dr. Edward Stafford and two other physicians, all specialists in Obstetrics and Gynecology. Late in the afternoon, the waiting room had only one pregnant woman waiting for her appointment. But the debris left on the floor and the disorderly arrangement of chairs suggested there'd been a crowd earlier. Toys from the kids play area had been scattered throughout the carpeted space.

To the middle-aged woman at the desk, Dave said, "I have an appointment with Dr. Stafford." He handed her a business card.

She checked the appointment schedule. "He'll be free in a few minutes. Please have a seat and I'll call you."

Three minutes after a woman left, the receptionist called to Dave, "He's ready now. Through this door and second office on the left." She pointed to the door to the right of her desk.

Stafford, medium build, balding, ruddy complexion, was flipping through a set of papers clipped together when Dave rapped on the door. "Come in," Stafford said, "have a seat. I understand this is about Miriam Reading's child." He sat behind his desk and raked a hand across his face. He hooked a pen into the pocket of his white coat.

Dave said, "She's retained our firm to represent her in a possible suit against both you and the pharmaceutical company for the damage done to her child."

Meeting Dave's eyes, Stafford said, "I'm not surprised after our last discussion. She was very upset when the baby was born with multiple defects and I'm sympathetic to her feelings. But I'm confident I acted in good faith."

"Miriam indicated she received a new drug that hasn't been widely used yet."

"That's true. Miriam experienced significant difficulty early in the second trimester of pregnancy and developed the classic symptoms of preeclampsia, including hypertension, loss of protein in the urine, severe cramping, nausea, some bleeding. I thought she was going to abort the fetus. This drug developed by Frasier Pharmaceuticals had been reported to relieve the very symptoms she was having. As luck would have it, a regional representative had dropped off samples of the drug with the usual pamphlets touting its effectiveness. With her consent I administered the recommended dosage. Her problems disappeared and as prescribed by the company, I continued the treatment. There were no apparent problems with the fetus until we did a routine scan a month before delivery."

Stafford leaned forward. "Gross developmental abnormalities were obvious. One side of her face was not developing properly, her nose seemed disfigured, but we couldn't tell about internal problems. Against my recommendation, Miriam decided to let the pregnancy proceed though she was devastated when the baby was born with those abnormalities."

Dave asked, "What's the prognosis for the child?"

"Frankly, I don't expect her to survive very long." Stafford shook his head. "There are too many defects. The facial abnormalities can be improved by cosmetic surgery but it's too soon to try those. The more severe issues are with the kidneys and heart. I'm concerned those organs will not develop as they should and could fail quickly."

"I assume you had faith in Frasier?"

The middle-aged physician nodded. "Although small in comparison to the major companies, they have a solid reputation. They take risks their products will fill a unique niche, areas not usually tackled by the better known organizations because the problem is too difficult."

"Any concerns they cut corners or don't fully check out the products before putting them on the market?"

Stafford eyed a set of papers momentarily. "I must admit this experience with Miriam has tainted my feelings. Prior to this drug, I had used three or four of their formulations with good outcomes and without problems."

Liking the candor of Stafford, Dave smiled. "How did you learn about the drug?"

"Through Frasier's representative who comes by at regular intervals. He told me the drug had been approved by the Food and Drug Administration after comprehensive trials."

"Do you have confidence the representative would reveal any reported problems?"

"You know how salesmen are," Stafford shrugged his shoulders. "Representatives from all the pharmaceutical companies visit routinely, leaving samples with the hope we'll favor their product over their competitors. And sometimes we do without serious review because our patients are pleased with the outcome." He shook his head and added, "And because we're too busy with patients and paper work."

"Did the Frasier rep attempt to convince you about Plertex?"

"Nothing beyond the usual spiel. You may know, Mr. Randle, some of these new drugs work well at first, but over time prove to be harmful under certain circumstances. I've thought about this case a lot and I'm reasonably well convinced that's what happened here. It could be a combination of factors that were present in Miriam's genetic background that weren't seen in the early trials. Mass usage may uncover the truth."

"Have you considered that the drug may be less effective than the company proclaims?"

Stafford nodded, a deep frown on his face. "Yes, I probably should have checked around more before using it. But physicians take the word of those reps, especially those who visit regularly and those companies we've had good experience with. I take some responsibility for what went wrong with Miriam, but I want to blame Frasier for putting this drug on the market before it had proved beyond doubt its safety."

"Could you give me the name of the representative from Frasier?"

Stafford hesitated, then pulled a stack of business cards from the middle drawer of his desk, sorted through them, and handed one to Dave. "Here. His name is Jeffrey Short. You can reach him faster using the cell phone number because he's always on the go."

Dave stuck the card in his shirt pocket and said, "Miriam has another problem. Her husband is abusive and knocks her around. Could physical abuse have created the problem with the child?"

Stafford shook his head. "I wondered about bruises on her shoulders and back, but she wouldn't discuss it, only saying she'd fallen. No, I doubt battering created the damage to the fetus. Severe trauma caused by outside force might have resulted in abortion, but the abnormalities with this baby were either genetic, drug related, or a combination of the two."

Dave said, "Dr. Stafford, you've been helpful. We'll continue to check out Frasier and their drug development program. It's hard to know where that might lead." He stuck his pad in his coat and stood.

Stafford came around his desk to shake Dave's hand. "I'll understand if Miriam pursues legal action. I might do the same under similar circumstances. My malpractice insurance will cover me and my practice, but I hate to waste time in the courts and with lawyers. It's counterproductive for me. Frankly, I'd rather spend my energies finding out what went wrong and how to prevent the same problem for another mother and child."

Stafford walked through the now empty reception area to the outside door with Dave. "I'll lock behind you, then do some paperwork for a while. Let me know about Miriam."

Driving home Dave reviewed his conversation with Stafford. The physician had been forthright and seemed concerned about Miriam Reading and her child. Suing Stafford was something he and Jennifer had talked about. They intended to avoid gaining a reputation for suing on shaky grounds just to make money. But their job was to find out what had gone wrong with Miriam's pregnancy and perhaps obtain some compensation for her.

Drops of rain spattered the windshield, then a downpour caused him to increase the speed of the wipers. The weather forecast for early evening showers had been on target. Now he'd have to alter his plan for a jog around the property. Jennifer had a dinner meeting with the Chester County Bar Association, so he was on his own for the evening meal. He'd miss their exercise followed by a drink together on the porch of their log house three miles from the downtown. But the rain curtailed that anyway.

But this might be a good time to revive his martial arts skills he'd not practiced since leaving the service. He'd been thinking about those defense mechanisms since his reliance on his gun was under scrutiny by the police, although he'd used it only to wound and slow aggressive antagonists. But with appropriate control, the power thrusts of arms and legs could be just as deadly. He knew because of his experiences in resisting enemies under conditions when the noise of weapons was not allowed. He'd never told Jennifer about this part of his former life, but soon he'd have to come clean. Maybe she'd be interested in joining him, particularly during the meditation phase. But he hoped she'd become intrigued enough to gain some skills in defensive tactics. Their work, seemingly void of physical dangers by any reasonable examination, presented challenges he'd not anticipated. He wanted Jennifer to be prepared just in case some idiot attacked her.

Ellie came into Jennifer's office at mid-morning. "I found a few articles about this experimental drug from Frasier."

Jennifer stood. "Get Dave and tell us both."

In the conference room Ellie opened a folder and started. "Tests have been ongoing for years in attempts to create an improved medication to relieve conditions of bloating, cramping and nausea during pregnancy and to avoid spontaneous abortions of healthy fetuses. Most companies had abandoned the search, but Frasier persisted and is convinced Plertex is the answer.

"Preliminary trials went okay. The drug relieved the symptoms without adverse side reactions. That report was based on twenty women who'd volunteered through their physician and were dosed under controlled conditions with constant medical supervision and checking. Then Frasier reportedly conducted a much more exhaustive trial with two hundred women, but I couldn't find any report of the outcome. According to Frasier those results confirmed the initial trial."

"And there were no reported problems?"

"None." Ellie continued, "I'm getting the information from the FDA on which they gave permission for general human usage. If they followed the usual protocol, Frasier did experiments with animals prior to the first human trial although I'm not sure they could replicate the human pregnancy. That information should be in the transcript. And they should have reported any unusual outcomes among those women in the tests."

"Unless," Jennifer noted, "they didn't include the negative data in their submission to the FDA."

As Ellie turned to leave, Jennifer asked? "How're your studies going?"

"Good. I have three more courses and a case study to complete. I could be done by the end of next spring."

"I still hope you will stay with us after you've passed the bar." As the firm had grown and clients were added, the need for an additional attorney had become evident. One young man had not worked out and in the interim, Jennifer decided to tough it out until Ellie gained her license. Even as a paralegal, she had done much more than the typical hire. She was bright and efficient, a bit on the stocky side, but she'd masked her body mass with loose fitting clothes. Jennifer knew she'd tried to lose weight but as with many, her efforts hadn't paid off.

"I'd love to do that," Ellie said, a smile breaking across her face. "I've thought I would ask for a two-month leave when the time comes to study for the bar exams. That would be next summer if I can stay on track."

"We'll work that out somehow."

As he entered Rasmussen's office, Dave said, "I got your phone message about Cranford."

Rasmussen handed a sheet of paper across the desk. "This is what we found. He was arrested twice while in Denver for use of excessive force and abuse. The first time he knocked a guy down during an argument in a bar. They held him overnight and nothing ever happened. Either the man refused to bring charges, or someone squashed the incident. A year later the cops brought him in for abuse of a woman he was living with, but she refused to file charges. Six months later she was admitted to the hospital with broken ribs and a bruised shoulder. Again, she refused to file charges."

"Sounds as though he always gets special treatment."

"Or threatens the opposing party with even worse damage if they persist. Prior to Denver, he has a history of minor scrapes with the cops, but nothing to cause arrest."

Dave scanned the report. "You're right. But it's always about his use of physical force to gain his way or relieve his frustration."

"It's ingrained into his personality. Likely goes back to early in school. He was probably bigger and stronger than his peers and bullied them. They either fell into line or else. And they were afraid to snitch to teachers who may have been able to curtail his meanness."

"Thanks Bill. This helps us get a handle on Cranford. His abuse of Miriam is not an isolated event."

"Guys like Cranford never change. They may spend time in jail, but within days after their release, they revert to former habits. Sometimes I believe they practice their skills while in confinement."

As soon as he returned to the office, Jennifer and Ellie came into his office. Standing in front of his desk, Ellie said, "I went to the shelter to get Miriam's signature on the divorce papers, but she wasn't there. She'd gone to the hospital with her child. I found her there in the room for family members of patients, got her signature and then I filed the papers with the court. But Miriam is terrified her baby isn't going to live."

"What happened?"

"The baby had some kind of seizure this afternoon, was struggling to breathe, and screaming with pain. The volunteer nurse at the shelter took them to the emergency room."

Jennifer said, "We'll go by the hospital on the way home. I assume she's there alone?"

Ellie nodded. "She is. And she said there's no family near, but a friend is coming after work to be with her for a couple of hours."

"Has she heard from her husband at all?"

"I doubt she's told him anything."

They found Miriam huddled in a corner chair in the waiting room of Chester General Hospital. Late in the day only two other people sat among rows of chairs and sofas. Vending machines hummed away from their location along one wall. The typical smells associated with hospitals lingered in the air.

They eased into chairs near Miriam and Jennifer asked, "How is Melanie?"

Through a stream of tears, Miriam murmured, "She died thirty minutes ago. A nurse came to tell me. The physician will do an autopsy." She wiped her face with a tissue and sat straighter in the chair.

Taking Miriam's hand, Jennifer asked, "Can we do anything for you?"

Shaking her head, Miriam said, "A friend is coming soon to take me to the shelter. She offered to let me stay with her, but I don't want to get her caught in the middle of my troubles. The people at the shelter will take care of the essentials."

"Have you called Billy?"

Shaking her head, she said, "He'd only cause problems."

"Have you seen him at all?"

"No, but he knows where I am. One of the security men told me he'd seen Billy in front of the building. No doubt he's seen my car in the lot. He'll wait until his rage overwhelms his judgment and then he'll crash the place."

Dave said, "Maybe you should move before that happens. I can get you into a safe house for a few days. You won't be bothered there."

Miriam seem to think about the offer, then said, "That might be best. Can I get into it by tomorrow?"

Dave said, "I'll need to make a call, but I'm almost certain that would work."

"So you know," Jennifer said, "we filed the divorce petition this afternoon."

"That'll upset Billy, so I need to be out of the shelter before he's notified."

Dave said, "I'll be in touch first thing in the morning."

CHAPTER 3

After they left the hospital, Dave went by Gibbons Bar and Restaurant, an increasingly popular establishment in the downtown area owned and managed by Antonio Gibbons who had a reputation for ties to the mob. He and Dave had become friends, at times allies, after an early altercation related to a break in at a retirement village. They relied on each other for information not available through the police or other sources.

Antonio manned the cash register as the early evening crowd, primarily workers who stopped in for a drink before heading home, paid their tabs, turning to talk with friends creating a steady drum of voices. Dave waited until the line had disappeared and approached Gibbons, the usual white towel draped across one shoulder.

Seeing Dave, Gibbons grinned, his crooked teeth showing. "Hey, haven't seen you lately. Doing okay?"

"Really busy but I'll get by for lunch soon. Now I need advice and help."

Gibbons turned to a middle-aged woman who'd worked at the place for years. "Anna, watch the register for a few minutes."

He motioned for Dave to follow him through a small hall into a dark office in the rear of the building.

"What can I do for you?" He remained standing behind his desk filled with stacks of papers. A desk lamp provided the only illumination. The aroma of pipe tobacco grabbed at the nostrils.

Dave explained the situation with Miriam and her husband. "I want to hide her out somewhere for a few days. I've heard you refer to a safe house and thought it might work for her. Or perhaps you could recommend a different place."

Gibbons picked up the rotary phone and dialed. He waited for a few seconds, then said, "I need to place someone in your facility for a few days. A woman who needs privacy and protection."

He listened for a few seconds, his free hand shifting papers from one stack to another, then said, "A friend of mine will bring her by tomorrow morning. Thanks." Gibbons dropped the receiver and scribbled an address on a note he handed to Dave.

Maintaining their running joke, Dave said, "Thanks. My tab must be getting pretty big."

"Don't worry. I'll get even one day." Gibbons eased toward the door to the restaurant.

As they traversed the short hall, Dave asked, "How're things with Helen Knight?"

"Good," Gibbons replied, his face breaking into a grin. "I introduced her to my kids who loved her. But I can see in their eyes they don't understand how such a gorgeous woman would spent her time with a reprobate like me."

"Some people think that about Jennifer and me."

The next morning Dave arrived at the Fourth Street shelter just after eight. Miriam waited near the front door, two suitcases and an overnight bag stacked by the entrance. An elderly man, one of the security team, nodded and returned to reading the newspaper.

Miriam looked rested and had regained some of her facial color. "Thanks for doing this." Her black slacks and lavender blouse fit better than the outfit she'd had on yesterday. She'd begun to regain her slim figure that captured the eye of every male.

"You need to go by the hospital or do anything before we go to the new place?" He wasn't sure what to call the safe house and he didn't want to give out an address in case Billy Cranford confronted the shelter people.

"No, I'm set. Should I leave my car here?"

"Either that or park it at your house. If you must travel, use cabs."

"I'll leave it here." She picked up one of the suitcases.

Dave grabbed the other two bags and led her through a side door to a parking lot.

As they emerged onto the street, Dave said, "The place I'm taking you is used by some seedy characters hiding out until it's safe for them to resurface, but you'll be okay. Antonio Gibbons is my contact and he wouldn't put you in danger." As he pulled away from the parking spot, Dave tried to observe any cars tailing them although no one suspected Miriam would be moving from the shelter. He made a couple of unnecessary turns and timed a traffic signal to make the amber light just before it turned red.

"I remember him. That's the place you confronted those guys who were coming on to me and he threatened to throw them out."

"Yeah and if you have problems, give him a call. Here's his number." He handed her an index card on which he'd written Gibbons office phone.

They drove through a neighborhood of middle-class homes that had not been well maintained. Some needed painting, porch steps and eaves had pulled away, and the yards were filled with weeds and litter tossed from passing cars and walkers. At 2450 Bullard Street, Dave turned into a drive and stopped at the rear door of the old three-story brick structure. "Let me check first. Be right back."

A heavy-set man with shoulders and mangled ears of a boxer waited for Dave to enter, then said, "You bringing the broad Gibbons wants hidden away?"

"Right. I assume it's still okay."

A crooked grin creased his face and emphasized a scar running across his cheek. "If Antonio wants it, we do it. I go by Monk." He stuck out a gnarled hand, one finger not aligned with the others.

Dave grasped Monk's hand, introduced himself and handed Monk a business card. "If she needs anything or if there's a problem, give me a call."

Monk glanced at the card. "Yeah, I've heard about you. Gibbons trusts you a lot."

"It's a mutual feeling."

Dave led Miriam into the building, introduced her to Monk, the caretaker, guard or whatever his duties were. They took her bags to a second floor space, a sitting room with a television and phone, a small bedroom and a tiny bath. The rooms were clean and the lights worked. Through the window one could see Bullard street.

His eyes on Miriam, Monk said, "Food is available in the dining room on the first floor at the usual meal times. If you need anything, I'm in my apartment in the basement. My number is on the front of your directory. No one should bother you, but if anyone does, let me know."

She asked, "I assume there is a charge?"

Monk nodded, "Hundred a day, but if you have problems, we'll work out some deal."

"Sounds okay and I'll pay when I leave if that's okay."

Dave said, "I'll check back tomorrow, but call if anything comes up."

She leaned against him, reviving memories of their closeness. "Thanks, Dave. I'll need to call the hospital and begin to arrange services for my baby." A tear crawled down her cheek. Her hand trembled when she wiped it away.

"Would you like me to drive you there?"

"That's okay. I can manage by phone."

"I'm sure Monk will help if you need assistance."

Dave eased away, stamping down any concern he'd put Miriam in a dangerous situation. An attractive woman could become the target of characters who were street smart, thought little about consequences, and had limited contact with attractive females. But Cranford wouldn't get to her without raising the ire of Monk and his buddies.

From the office, Dave telephoned the Frasier representative. Jeffrey Short answered on the second ring of his cell phone. "Short here."

Dave explained his interest in Frasier and about the Watson/Randle partnership, then said, "I'm like to meet with you the next time you're in Chester."

"I'm in Chester now, but not sure I can help with the problem."

"Let's give it a try anyway."

"I could meet for a drink around 5:30."

"How about Gibbons?"

"I know the place. Meet you at the front entrance — 5:30."

Jennifer and Dave waited in the entry of Gibbons. Jennifer said, "He'll be well-dressed, probably young, and good-looking."

"How do you know that?"

"From some reading I've done on those sales reps. They're energetic and fit the stereotype I described to make a good impression on medical people who aren't easily influenced."

"Then there's our guy," Dave said, as a thirty-year-old man hustled through the front door, his eyes ranging across the cluster of patrons waiting for seating.

Dave walked toward the man, asking, "Jeffrey Short?"

"Yep, and you're Dave."

Dave introduced Jennifer. "We're partners so I thought it'd be okay to have her join us. And they're holding a place for us."

Settled in a booth toward the back of the bar area, they ordered drinks — a martini for Jennifer, Scotch on the rocks for Jeffrey, and a Killian draft for Dave.

Short asked, "What can I tell you about Frasier or about this new drug?"

Jennifer explained the situation with Miriam and Dave filled in his conversation with Stafford. Then Jennifer asked, "Have there been other reports of problems with the medication?"

Short hesitated. "Not to my knowledge. As best I know, Dr. Stafford's patient is the first to complain, but I'm out of the loop for most of those issues. They are handled by our attorneys and administrators. But since I was coming here and will see Stafford, one of our administrators alerted me to the case. Our research people discount her story and chalk the problem up to something else, more likely a genetic aberration or strange dietary habits."

"Based on what I know about human genetics," Jennifer said, "that could take a lot of testing and checking at great expense and she still may not know what went wrong. And she tells us her diet is pretty normal."

Their drinks were placed. They sipped for a few moments. Then Short said, "You have to know issues of safety and function are beyond my responsibility and expertise. My job is to make physicians aware of our products. I depend on our research group for reliable information and I have a lot of confidence in their judgment. Then it's up to me to convey the potential benefits of the product to those who treat patients."

Dave asked, "How long have you known Dr. Stafford?"

Short sipped his drink. "Roughly five years. I met him the first time I came to Chester, but he'd been on Frasier's contact list prior to that time. The company was changing its approach of interacting with medical personnel. It used to be nothing more than drop in, leave samples and information sheets, and move on. Now we're expected to get to know the physicians and administrators on a personal basis."

"For example?" Dave asked.

Short grinned, rattled the ice in his glass. "We take them to lunch or dinner, arrange for groups of physicians and sometimes hospital administrators to spend time at up-scale vacation spots, try to know their families, any way to build relationships."

Jennifer smiled and said, "And that makes them trust you and your products more."

"Sure, that's the game. And I've enjoyed doing it. Meet a lot of great people, visit exotic places and get paid for doing it." He glanced at his watch.

Jennifer asked, "Could you send us the packet of information about Plertex you distribute to physicians?"

"Better still. Follow me to my car and I'll dig the stuff out for you. Sorry to cut this off, but I'm meeting a group of public health physicians and nurses for dinner at the country club, so I need to get going. I like to check things out before others arrive." He picked up the check as they left the booth.

Short's rental car was parked in the lot across the street. He popped the trunk of the Buick, opened a cardboard box, and pulled out samples of the drug and pamphlets extolling its features and giving details of its chemical composition.

Dave said, "Thanks for your help. We may wish to talk again later as we learn more."

Shaking their hands, Short said, "Anytime. I'm in Chester every month. Give me a call and we can arrange a time to get together."

As Short drove away, Dave said, "How about dinner at Gibbons?"

"Suits me. Avoids our cooking when we get home."

Reentering the restaurant, Dave said, "Short can't really tell us much. He wows these doctors who spend all their days looking for symptoms and filling out insurance forms. They're easy marks. They don't have the time to research every new formulation."

"I've read articles about the efforts and the amount of money these organizations expend courting physicians and their staff. It's mind-boggling and no doubt drives up the cost of health care."

Jennifer leaned back in her desk chair as she scanned the printout Ellie had assembled about Plertex. According to the information, Frasier had completed extensive testing with animals, both mice and monkeys, then had done a trials with small numbers of pregnant women followed by a larger study before applying to the FDA for approval. They had reported no complications or side effects of the medication. But the raw data were not included in their report, thus the reader was left to take their opinion.

The panel of FDA scientists had questioned Frasier for several hours and asked for raw data from the human tests. Frasier had complied, but one member of the panel had questioned whether the company had been completely forthright. In the heat of an argument, she accused Frasier of selective reporting. The company had denied the charge.

Information of the composition of the drug had not been included. As with any pharmaceutical house, Frasier had to protect its investment. Jennifer shoved the paper aside, thinking she wouldn't understand the complicated chemical information anyway. But, she knew a competitor with intimate knowledge of the science might be able to reproduce the medicine, costing Frasier a bundle.

She stared out the window, her mind on the problem of Miriam, when her door was shoved open with such force it banged against the wall. A huge man burst in, his face red, his fists raised and balled as though ready to strike. She started to rise, but when he leaned across her desk into her face, she was forced to remain seated.

She felt trapped but yelled, "Get out."

Still leaning across her desk, his face inches from hers, the intruder screamed, "You goddam bitch. Filing divorce papers for my stupid wife is going to cost this fly-by-night firm." He banged a fist on her desk, sending pencils and papers flying.

Jennifer rolled back her chair and stood. "Get out. I'm guessing you're Billy Cranford. No matter, you're way out of bounds charging in here." She reached for the phone.

Cranford grabbed her wrist. "Try calling for help and I'll crack your damn head."

From the doorway, a firm voice. "Touch her again and I'll kill you."

Cranford whirled to confront Dave. "Who the hell are you?" He smirked when he saw a shorter man, maybe six feet, one hundred and eighty pounds—not a problem for him with a height and weight advantage.

"She asked you to leave twice. Now get out."

Cranford stepped toward Dave, then reached for him, intending to grab his jacket or shirt.

Dave sidestepped the thrust and rammed stiff fingers into Cranford's side below the rib cage hitting a bundle of nerves.

The big man's mouth gaped open, a gasp escaped from his throat, his face went red, then ashen, before he collapsed to his knees. His arms clutched his midsection as though trying to relieve intense pain.

As Cranford began to regain his alertness, Dave grabbed a place beneath his collar bone and pressured it until Cranford screamed. Dave released the pressure and watched as the pain subsided.

Dave shoved him onto his side and waited. Three minutes later, Cranford stirred and sat up, his blank stare telegraphing his confusion. Beads of sweat appeared on his face and neck.

Dave said, "Now get out. The next time you threaten her, an ambulance will haul you out, if you're lucky."

Cranford struggled to his feet, his arms still holding his mid-section. He wobbled out, a shoulder banging against the door frame. Both Helen and Ellie watched with open-mouths as Cranford stumbled through the outer office.

Dave followed him to the elevator and waited until he saw the signals indicating Cranford had reached the ground floor.

Jennifer, who had trailed along, asked, "Good Lord, what did you do to him? I thought he was going to die before our eyes."

Dave asked, "Are you okay?"

"He scared me to death. I thought for certain he was going to hit me. But you didn't answer my question."

"I'd rather not give details, but I'll tell you I used tactics learned years ago. I'm afraid to employ it because you can easily kill the person, but just now I reacted without thinking through my options. Cranford could hurt both of us if he wasn't neutralized quickly."

"But what you did looked so mild."

Dave took her hand. "It's taught in those martial arts defense classes. I'll tell you more when we get home. But Cranford will think twice before he storms in our office again."

"Or he'll hire some killer to come after you—or both of us."

"I doubt it. He's one of those guys who gets his way by physical threats. His very size overwhelms most and they cave in."

"No wonder Miriam is scared to death of him."

CHAPTER 4

As they changed into sweat suits at home, Dave said, "You want to know about my tactics with Cranford. Let's go to the exercise room and I'll tell you more about it." Their workout area was actually a storage shed built by the former owner. Dave had cleaned it up, painted it, and moved some weights into the space before they were married. Jennifer had added a treadmill, a stationary bike and two mats.

Standing on a mat and facing her, Dave said, "You already know I learned about martial arts during my days with special forces. When we weren't on a mission, we worked at it on a regular schedule — building strength, refining techniques, sparring with other guys, until we could maintain our proficiency. Although I've used the stuff occasionally, it's been off the cuff. I haven't kept up my skills, but I intend to start working on them again. That episode with Cranford reminded me of the advantages. "

"And you want me to learn this stuff?" Her look and hand-on-hips stance suggested he was crazy.

"I'd like to show you the basics, then you can decide how much, if any, you'd like to perfect. It includes periods of meditation which the service instructor didn't do much with. The approach I learned focused on exercises to strengthen your arms and legs, before we ever attempted to use techniques of defending yourself."

"Or attacking someone," Jennifer grinned, seemingly spooked by the whole idea.

"It's whatever you wish to do." Dave picked up a manual from the table. "Here's an introduction I dug out of my gear. This describes the meditation and basic methods." He rushed on as she thumbed through the manual. "You'd soon look forward to doing this. It relieves stress and worries. Clears your head of all the clutter you think about and can't control. But as I said, in the service we didn't dwell on that phase."

"I've heard of this, but thought you needed lessons from a licensed instructor."

"Going to a professional instructor would be better than my guiding you. I've never taught others and could lead you into habits not the best."

"I'll think about it, but now could we run along the creek for exercise." She placed the manual on the treadmill and started for the door.

"Sure, but remember our stretching exercises." He dropped to the mat on his back and raised one leg. Jennifer followed the routine she'd done numerous times.

Dave said, "There are Tai Chi and other classes in Chester. We could go together."

She rolled to one side and pulled one leg against her chest. "I'm not sure I wish to spend time doing that. I'm too busy now without taking on another activity." She turned her head to grin at him. "Plus, I might become too aggressive."

The Wilson Chapel seemed almost empty as the memorial service for Miriam's child started at 11:00 a.m. Jennifer and Dave were the only occupants in a pew designed for ten. A dozen of Miriam's friends and co-workers were present along with a woman Dave had seen at the shelter. The service, conducted by a minister employed by the funeral home on those occasions when the deceased had no connection to a church, consisted of a hymn, prayers, and a brief eulogy about the innocence of the very young and their special place in heaven.

As the benediction ended, Dave reacted to movement behind him and turned to see Billy Cranford leave the rear pew and exit the door. He nudged Jennifer who nodded her awareness of Cranford's presence.

They waited for Miriam in the foyer as others hugged her and left, their faces reflecting the somber mood of the occasion.

As an elderly woman departed, Jennifer took Miriam's hand and said, "You look lovely in spite of the grief I know you're experiencing." Her black dress, a single strand of pearls, high heels, her blond hair falling around her face yielded a sophistication they'd previously associated with her but had been missing as she struggled through her recent ordeals.

"Physically I feel better, but it'll take a while to get past this. I had so looked forward to being a mother." Her attempt at a smile faded into a frown.

"You're getting along okay at the safe house?" Dave asked.

"It's been strange being the only female among a bunch of guys hiding out for one reason or another, but Monk has taken me under his wing. Makes sure I get things I need. He drove me to my house yesterday afternoon so I could get clothes appropriate for this service. Then I retrieved my car from the shelter."

"Stay on the alert," Dave said. "Billy came in late and rushed out during the last prayer. I guess he didn't wish to be seen."

Miriam said, "I'm not surprised he came. Despite our differences and his tendency to bully people, he wanted to be a father and felt bad when our baby was so deformed." She paused and grimaced. "But he blamed me, screaming I should have taken better care of myself."

Jennifer asked, "Can we do anything for you?"

Shaking her head, she said, "I'm okay. I'm going back to work, but live at Monk's place for a while. Work will take my mind off my problems and help get my life back to some normalcy."

"I understand," Jennifer said, "but do you think it's wise to get near Billy?"

"I'll be careful. Our paths seldom cross at the station. If he follows me, Monk will take care of the situation. And you should know the physician completed the autopsy."

Dave said, "We'll talk with him. It could be essential to any suit against Frasier and Stafford."

As they walked out the door onto the sidewalk, Jennifer said, "Keep in touch with us. We'll need to consult with you as we move forward."

"Thanks for coming today. I was concerned I'd be the only person here." She turned toward a black sedan waiting on the street. Dave recognized Monk when Miriam opened the passenger door.

Jennifer introduced herself to Dr. Benjamin Riley, the pathologist who'd done the autopsy on Miriam's child. Riley shook her hand and watched her settle into a chair before he returned to his desk.

"Thanks for meeting with me," Jennifer said, suddenly aware that Riley's eyes were probing as though visually undressing her. In spite of her sudden discomfort, she said, "As you know from our telephone conversation, I'm representing Miriam Reading in a possible suit against Frasier Pharmaceuticals and another physician." Riley looked too young to be a physician and she wondered if he'd been a child prodigy or if she was aging faster than she wished to admit. But it was obvious he was interested in women.

Nodding his head, Riley said, "I wanted to confirm with Miriam your interest and relationship, but I've been unable to find her." He grimaced. "You can never be too careful these days. I don't want to give out personal information if there's a chance she might object."

"I understand and I can get a telephone number for you. The bottom line is she's hiding from her husband," Jennifer said, " but I hope you can trust me enough to tell me about the autopsy."

Riley looked at her for a moment as though sizing up her true intentions. "I did look up your business address and know you are a reputable attorney. I'll take the risk you are acting on Miriam's behalf and hope this doesn't come back to haunt me."

He opened a folder and glanced at the contents for several seconds. "I'm reasonably confident the underlying cause of death was kidney failure. The accumulation of fluids plus hypernatremia are clear signs the kidneys were not functioning."

Jennifer smiled. "I believe your medical term means excess salt in the body fluids."

"Correct." Riley grinned, revealing an engaging smile. "Sorry, but we fall into the habit of using physiological terminology." He continued. "At any rate, the load of fluids and sodium overtaxed her heart which in itself had not developed properly. There was likely no remedy for her condition as she would not have been able to withstand the rigors of a transplant. And I'm not sure the hospital would have approved a transplant under the conditions of multiple deformities."

"Was dialysis a possible approach?"

"I'm sure Dr. Stafford considered that, but according to the records, by the time she was brought in, it likely wouldn't have worked."

"Meaning she would probably have died anyway?"

"It's always difficult to predict, but the prognosis would not have been good."

Jennifer asked, "Could you speculate as to the cause of her flawed development?"

"If you're asking about this new drug the mother used, I wouldn't take a guess. But it's worthy of further examination and testing before other women use the medication."

"I understand the company is conducting tests in a wider population. That might reveal something."

Riley shook his head. "Maybe, but honestly, I don't have a lot of faith in what these guys do. They're looking for predetermined answers and I'd bet they'd skew the data to demonstrate positive outcomes."

"But," Jennifer said, "they could find themselves in multiple lawsuits."

"In my experience they usually settle out of court for a pittance. The money they make is astounding, so a few settlements don't phase them."

"Sounds like you have bad experiences."

"In my practice, I usually don't see patients directly but I know patients are damaged by medications. Some sue the company, but nothing has happened to cause significant changes in the way drugs are tested and approved. These companies buy off regulatory officials and Congressmen who throw their weight around until FDA approves the product."

Jennifer asked, "Have you had experience with Frasier before?"

"I heard of a patient who'd used one of their drugs to treat a thyroid condition. It didn't solve the problem and but worsened the malady. The attending physician was wise enough to drop it. He prescribed another medication that worked."

Jennifer stood, award Riley was staring at her knees when she uncrossed her legs. "We're trying to get the transcripts related to the FDA hearings about this Frasier drug. Maybe that will tell us something. I may wish to get your opinion if there seems to be anything unusual."

Riley came around his desk to shake her hand. "Let me know." He seemed reluctant to release her hand. After an uncomfortable moment, she pulled it away.

Jennifer left Riley's office confident she'd made an ally in the battle if for no other reason than his attraction to her, but Riley might be so distrustful of the pharmaceutical industry he couldn't be reliable. His continual perusal of her face and body suggested he would make a more conspicuous pass at her under the right circumstances. Then there was the holding of her hand, pressure gently increasing, until she broke the contact. She wondered if Riley had a history of unseemly interactions with female patients. Then she smiled thinking she was still attractive to men.

When Dave answered the telephone, a female voice inquired, "Would you hold for Dr. Stafford, please? He'll be right with you."

As he waited, Dave flipped through pages of a preliminary report he'd prepared for a client who'd hired the firm to search for a missing relative who'd disappeared under odd circumstances.

As he marked an error on page three, Stafford came on. "Thanks for waiting. Is this Mr. Randle?"

"Yes, how're you doing?"

"I wanted to give you some information related to the incident with Miriam Reading. I attended a medical conference in Chicago last week and got talking to an old buddy from med school. The upshot of our conversation was he'd had a patient who'd gone through the same thing Miriam had. During the middle of her pregnancy, she started cramping, bleeding, severe pains. My friend gave her that drug a Frasier representative had dropped in his clinic. The symptoms cleared but her child was born with severe abnormalities and only lived ten days after birth. His description of the deformities matched those of the Reading child. If I'd not known differently, I would have believed he'd seen my notes."

"And you're certain the drug he gave her was Plertex."

"That's right." Stafford responded without hesitation.

"Would he be willing to talk to me about his experience and maybe set up a meeting with the family of the deceased child?"

"I'm sure he'd talk to you, but I can't say about the family. But it would mean traveling to Kansas City."

"I could arrange that," Dave said, "but would you suspect there are more of these incidents associated with this drug?"

"Likely. I'd be willing to try to find out or put you on the right track."

"Thanks, we may wish to take you up on that offer. But for now, give me the name and address of your colleague in Kansas City."

CHAPTER 5

In Jennifer's office, Dave said, "You won't believe this, but Stafford ran across another incident that matches Miriam Reading's."

"Here in Chester?"

He related Stafford's story and said, "His friend practices in Kansas City. We should follow through and get as much information as possible. I'm going to call for an appointment and I'll fly there tomorrow if he's available."

"Sounds good. If there was an autopsy, get those results too."

He paced across the room to glance out the window to watch cars along a side street as they stopped to enter Main. "I bet there are a bunch of those women, but neither they nor their physicians have made the connection to Plertex. They just chalk it up to bad luck."

Hiram Bently, the attorney for Billy Cranford, sat across the conference room table from Jennifer. He started as soon as they'd settled into chairs, none of the usual how're-you-doing stuff that goes on between professionals doing the same kind of jobs and competing with each other in court cases and for clients. Clearly on edge, Bently tugged at the sleeve of his shirt until it showed from his coat.

"Ms. Watson, this divorce thing with Cranford is tearing him apart. He wants to find grounds for reconciliation. He'd like for you to make his wife come around, at least talk to him. He's tried several times to contact her but she's refused to talk. More recently, he's not able to find her at all."

Not surprised by the opening, Jennifer said, "Your client refused to try counseling early in their conflict. Things progressed to the point I doubt she'd attempt getting together now. Also, based on his past actions any contact with him could put her life in jeopardy."

"Billy has changed. He's sworn off violence and vows he'll never hit her or anyone again. This divorce has shaken him to the core, like nothing else he's ever experienced."

"That's hard to believe, Hiram," Jennifer smiled, trying to put Bently more at ease. "He stormed in here last week and threatened me if we didn't drop the divorce proceedings. People don't change life-long habits overnight. In good conscience, I can't advise Miriam to get back together with him."

"Would you go so far as to suggest they go to counseling together? I can convince Billy to give it a try."

Jennifer said, "I can tell her what you've told me and let her decide. However, I'd be concerned for her safety if she's near him without someone to protect her."

Hearing what he'd wanted to hear, Bently stood. "Thanks for that much. I want to avoid a nasty divorce trial that drags everybody through the gutter. Let me know her reaction." He pulled a business card from his coat pocket and handed it to Jennifer. "Call me and I'll take it from there." He left the door open as he left.

Jennifer scanned Bently's card. He was a partner in a small firm of three attorneys who specialized in personal injury litigation. She'd seen their ads on television inviting potential clients to bring their grievances to them for rapid and fair settlements. She'd met him at the Chester Bar Association meetings but they'd not interacted on cases before.

Then she realized she had no idea how to contact Miriam. She smiled at her own confusion. With Dave out of town, she'd have to contact Gibbons, something she'd never done before.

Dave rented a car at the Budget desk in the Kansas City airport. The woman attendant gave him a map and assisted him with directions to the clinic where Donald Givens practiced.

An hour of driving and getting lost a couple of times brought him to a rambling two-story brick building on the outskirts of the large city. He parked in the only vacant visitor's slot and thought again about his approach to Givens who might be protective of client records. But Stafford's promise to alert Givens should open the door.

In the crowded reception area filled with pregnant women and small children Dave waited thirty minutes until the receptionist called him. "He's fitting you in his schedule, but he has to be at the hospital in an hour." Dave realized she was telling him to be quick about his business.

Givens, tall, balding, dressed in the typical white coat over a blue shirt and khaki pants, was waiting as he came through the door and invited Dave to a chair in the corner of a employee lounge. Two nurses were sipping coffee at a table on the other side of the room. Aromas of food reminded him he'd not eaten since an early breakfast at home.

"I apologize for the lack of privacy" Givens said, "but we really don't have offices here. All of our contacts are done in the patient examination rooms and I thought this would be better." He glanced at his watch.

Dave said, "I appreciate your fitting me in and if Dr. Stafford called you about my coming, you know what I'm seeking."

Crossing his legs and seeming to relax, Givens said, "He did call soon after you'd made an appointment. And you know we had talked about two patients who'd had the same problems after we'd administered this drug put out by Frasier Pharmaceuticals. He faxed me the records of his patient. The symptoms and reactions to the medication were much the same. Both women had children severely malformed. And the problems with the children were remarkably similar. Thus, we became suspicious that the drug either caused directly or exacerbated the some unknown condition present in both mothers. Both children died within two weeks of birth."

Again, Givens looked at his watch and handed a manila folder to Dave. "Here are the copies of the files of my patient. I've blacked out names to protect their privacy, but if this leads to anything you wish to talk to them about, I'll act as a contact person. I believe they'd be open to discussion and perhaps legal recourse against the company."

Dave asked, "Was an autopsy done on the child here?"

Givens nodded. "The pathology showed severe kidney malfunction, retention of fluids and elevated sodium levels in the fluids. We concluded the heart, also not completely functioning, could not tolerate the excess load of fluids and electrolytes. We were preparing to try dialysis but I doubt it would have worked. The infant wasn't strong enough to deal with that additional stress. All that is in the file."

"Are you certain the family plans to sue for damages?"

"I don't know. Both parents are coming in tomorrow night to talk with me. I expect their lawyer will accompany them, but I'm not certain of that."

Givens stood, saying, "I'm sorry for the rush, but I must be at the hospital for an intestinal operation in thirty minutes. Let's talk as I go toward my car." He scanned the items in his coat pocket as though to be certain he had necessary articles.

Threading their way out the rear doors of the building, Dave told him about Miriam and her plan to sue Frasier, then added," My partner, who is the attorney for Dr. Stafford's patient, believes any suit against Frasier will be stronger if there are multiple plaintiffs. We'd like to coordinate with your patient if she proceeds with a suit."

"Stafford told me about that and he's worried he'll be found liable for the death of that child. You know, Mr. Randle, physicians are giving up their practices because of the exorbitant insurance necessary to shield them from lawyers and suits. In these cases, I think Frasier is the culprit, but it'll be almost impossible to hold them responsible. The pharmaceutical companies retain high-powered lawyers who spend their careers in litigation, fighting suits, and producing expert witnesses who will testify to anything supportive of the organization and its products. But I agree with the notion of joining forces. That moves the argument away from the company yelling about some revengeful individual out to gain money."

Nearing the parking area reserved for physicians, Dave asked, "Have you utilized Frasier products before?"

"On a couple of occasions I gave patients samples the Frasier representative had brought by. Those seemed to work okay."

Givens stopped walking at the rear of a Buick sedan as Dave asked, "You recall the name of the rep?"

"Not off the top of my head, but he was young and aggressive. Invited my wife and me to dinner but I never accept those deals." He shook his head and grinned. "Makes you feel beholden to them and they press every advantage."

"Does the name Jeffrey Short ring a bell?"

Givens smiled and nodded. "Yes, he's the person who dropped off the wonder drug from Frasier." He turned toward the car. "Let me know how this goes."

Dave found the rental car, reviewed the map again and drove out, hoping he could get an earlier return flight to Chester.

Jennifer and Helen Knight entered Gibbons Restaurant just before noon. Jennifer approached Gibbons who recognized her and grinned. "Well, good to see you. Finally got rid of that bum who hangs around with you and brought another sexy woman. Helps my business." He came around the counter and took Helen's hand. They smiled at each other as though they shared some secret.

Trying to keep the mission on focus, Jennifer said, "Dave's off on a trip and I need a phone number from you—the safe house where Miriam Reading is staying."

He motioned with a gnarled hand. "Come with me." He led them to his small office in the back of the public area and looked at a list near his phone. He scribbled the number on a pad and ripped off the sheet for her. "She in any kind of trouble?"

"No, I just need to get in touch and didn't have the number."

"Good to know she's okay. Monk likes having her there. Says she brightens up the place."

Jennifer turned toward the dim hallway. "Thanks for your help."

"My pleasure. You staying for lunch?"

"Helen and I will have lunch. Maybe in a back booth if one's available."

As they settled, Helen said, "I haven't been here since I was with you and Dave after the Hankins trial." She opened the menu.

"I'm glad we could do this," Jennifer said. "We seldom get to talk in the office to learn how life is treating one another."

Taking the signal, Helen said, "Actually, I'm doing well. It's been a relief to be away from the political life and I enjoy the office and your firm. I hope I've met your expectations."

Jennifer smiled, "You've been a good addition. Ellie has been freed up to do more background searches for us and is doing more of the routine work I did before."

The waitress took their orders and returned almost immediately with iced tea. Jennifer said, "As you know, we're in the early stages of filing a suit against a pharmaceutical company and may want to gain access to files the FDA has about a new drug. Is there any way we could get that information through our Congressman's office? We could use the Freedom For Information ploy, but I'm concerned that will provide only the minimum information. Or they will drag out their response with bureaucratic blocks until we give up."

"I'm out of the loop, so to speak, since resigning from the representative's office after Hankins folded and decided not to run again, but I could make a contact there if you like. I know the woman who replaced Hankins and I believe she'd try to help."

"I'd appreciate your inquiry and will go with you if a meeting is necessary."

Steaming bowls were placed and they gave attention to the lobster bisque for a while. Then Jennifer said, "It's really none of my business, but I take it your relationship with Antonio is progressing well."

Helen wiped her mouth with the napkin. "It's been strange. I worried about his gruff manner at first, but I've discovered he's quite gentle and even refined in social situations. We've been to dinner several times now and it's been enjoyable. Now I'm glad I didn't allow my reservations to prevent my seeing him in social settings."

She let the conversation shift back to the drug issue, but after seeing their interactions at the front door, Jennifer suspected the relationship had gone beyond dinner and holding hands.

As soon as she was back in the office, Ellie brought in a stack of papers for Jennifer. "Here's what I've found about

Frasier and about this new drug. Some of this comes off the internet but a transcript of the FDA hearings is there too."

"Anything jump out at you?"

Ellie sat in the chair in front of Jennifer's desk. "The hearings were long and apparently contentious. I don't know how accurately the transcript reflects what truly went on, but a couple of scientists on the panel were adamantly opposed to any use of Plertex. They worried about the mode of action of the drug and expressed concern about the lack of rigor in the trials. One expressed doubts Frasier had brought in all the data."

"What do you mean?"

"She accused Frasier of selecting outcomes from subjects that reflected the results Frasier desired and didn't include information from those persons who'd experienced side effects from the drug or perhaps hadn't responded at all. I don't know how she would have known this, but she refused to concede. As a result of her argument the scientific panel voted not to release the drug for general use until additional test data became available."

"What about the trial of two hundred subjects? Any reference to the outcome?

"I don't believe so."

"Then how did Frasier get around the recommendation of the panel?"

"The FDA administrator overrode the recommendation from the panel and allowed Frasier to release the drug with the stipulation that the company bring back more data in a year."

"Did someone influence him?"

Ellie smiled. "Probably, but the transcript wouldn't reveal that."

"And in the interim, Miriam and likely several other women delivered malformed babies."

Ellie said, "There's a lot in the transcript I don't understand. You will want to read it to be sure I've interpreted it correctly."

"We'll probably need consultation from a physician or pharmacologist before we move forward."

Remembering her promise to Hiram Bently, Jennifer called the number given to her by Gibbons. A gruff male voice responded on the third ring. "Yeah, Monk here."

"I'm trying to locate Miriam Reading. She's been staying at this address."

"Who's calling?"

"Jennifer Watson. I'm acting as her attorney. My partner, Dave Randle, brought Miriam to your place several days ago."

A significant pause ensued before Monk responded. "Look, Ms. Watson, I've been trying to find her myself. She left here yesterday afternoon and didn't return last night. She'd gotten her car from the women's shelter and was running errands. She came back here for lunch, then left for another chore."

"And you were expecting her to return for the evening meal?"

"Yeah. She said she wouldn't be gone long."

"Any idea of where she was going?"

"Nope, but she was talking at lunch about returning to work next week. I thought maybe she'd gone to the TV station to check in and arrange for starting back."

"Did you contact the police?"

Silence for several seconds, then Monk said, "I didn't want them to know she'd been here. Too many others here need their privacy. If investigators came snooping around, I'd violate my agreement with them."

Jennifer said, "I understand. Thanks for your trouble. We'll make some contacts and try to locate her."

"Let me know if that bastard husband has grabbed her."

CHAPTER 6

Realizing she had to be in the court soon but concerned about Miriam, Jennifer called the information number of Channel 14. She waited through a recorded response until she heard an extension number that sounded promising. She punched the two digits and waited while soft music played some tune she was not familiar with. She retrieved her briefcase from the credenza as she tune continued.

The music stopped and, after several rings, a female voice asked. "Human Resources, may I help you?"

"I'm trying to determine if Miriam Reading was in the station yesterday. I didn't know who to ask but thought you might be the right office. I understand she's planning to return to work and would likely need to check in at your office."

Silence for a moment, then, "Let me look at her file. Just a moment."

The voice on the phone asking, "May I ask who is calling."

"Jennifer Watson, Miriam's attorney."

A delay while the clerk considered the information, then, "Ms. Watson, Miriam came by yesterday to sign papers reinstating her. She plans to resume work next Monday."

"Can you tell me what time she was there?"

A pause, then, "I wasn't the one who met with her and don't have that information. Sorry."

Jennifer thanked the woman, hung up, and leaned back in her chair. Miriam was likely in the station early afternoon, assuming she went directly there from the safe house. Now she'd been missing eighteen hours, but Jennifer didn't have time to search further. She had an appointment with Judge Barrett regarding an appeal of a previous case. She considered calling Rasmussen, but realized the police wouldn't know about her missing and would not have mounted a search. She left a message on Dave's desk, hoping he'd be back in time to follow leads to Miriam. She asked Ellie to call the hospital to be certain Miriam had not been in an accident. She left the office with only minutes to spare if she were to be on time.

Dave found Jennifer's note at 5:30 when he returned from Kansas City. He called Monk who had not heard from Miriam but had two guys out looking for her. Then he called Channel 14 and asked to speak to Billy Cranford only to be informed that Cranford was out of town on an assignment.

Pressing the woman on the phone, Dave asked, "It's important I locate him. Can you tell me when he left and where he went?"

"According to the schedule I have, he left Chester on a Delta flight at 9:30 last evening and was headed for Denver. I don't know the specific assignment, but he's due back in time to do the sports segment on the evening news tomorrow."

"I need to find him as soon as possible," Dave said. "Can you give me his home address?"

"I'm sorry. We're not allowed to give out that information."

"Thanks. I'll find him some way."

Dave called the Chester police. The dispatcher had no knowledge of Miriam's being missing and the station had not been alerted to look for her. After Dave told the dispatcher Miriam had been missing almost twenty-four hours, he promised to inform his shift supervisor.

On the slim chance Miriam had gone to Denver with Cranford, he called the Delta desk at the airport. The clerk confirmed that Cranford was on the flight, but had no record of Miriam or any companion for Cranford but admitted they likely wouldn't know that anyway.

Dave called the Fourth Street shelter, thinking she might have gone there again, but they'd not heard from her since she checked out several days earlier. And he didn't know the name of the friend who'd tried to protect her before.

Having exhausted his sources, Dave went home, tired from the all-day travel and ready to relax. But the question of Miriam dogged his mind. He wasn't sure where to turn next but a plan was forming in his mind.

After completing a three-mile run around the property, Jennifer was pacing the front lawn, their usual cool-down activity spot, when Dave arrived home in the semi-darkness. She walked to him and they embraced.

She smiled up into his face. "Be careful. You'll get all wet." She backed out of his arms and pulled her sweat top on.

"I've been wet before." His arm circled her waist as they moved toward the front door. "Even though it's late, let's have a drink on the porch while we talk about Miriam. I saw your note, called around, but came up blank."

Conversation stopped while they made drinks and found their usual rockers on the veranda. The sun had disappeared behind the trees on the west side of their land, a ten-acre square with a creek cutting across one corner. A rabbit hopped into their view, stopped to look around, then disappeared into the woods. Leaves were lush and green as spring came into full flower. Tulips along their porch front poked their colorful heads toward the sky.

Dave said, "I figured Cranford had grabbed Miriam, but according to the station, he left for Denver yesterday. She didn't go with him if the airline gave me correct information."

"My initial thought was he'd encountered her at the TV station, talked her into leaving with him, had beaten her up and left her in a motel somewhere. I had Ellie call the hospital, but she'd not been admitted."

Dave said, "I have one other idea about finding her, but it'll have to wait until tomorrow and Billy's return. Let's have dinner and call it a day. I'll bring you up to speed about my meeting with the doc in Kansas City while we eat." He stood.

"I put that leg of lamb in the oven before I went running. Can you get the vegetables ready while I shower?"

"Sure, plus I'll do a salad."

From the office the next morning, Dave called the airline about flights from Denver. The arrival of a direct flight at 2:45 this afternoon was the logical one for Cranford's return. That would give him time to get to the station and prepare for the evening broadcast. He called Monk who'd not heard anything nor had he been able to locate Miriam. Neither had the Chester police found a link to Miriam.

Following his instincts, Dave waited in the lounge of the Chester airport until he saw Billy Cranford emerge from the gate area. A leather garment bag across one shoulder, Billy waved to a couple of admirers and hustled through the terminal. A Channel 14 van picked him up from the 5-minute parking slots.

Dave trotted to his car, parked illegally in the bus drop-off area, and followed. The van sped through the airport exit without slowing and onto Airport Road headed into the city. Dave remained well behind, but kept the van in sight.

When the van turned onto Thirty-fifth street, Dave relaxed a bit but maintained his vigil. His initial hunch was rewarded when the van swung onto a side street and two blocks later, stopped in front of an apartment complex on Hodge street. Dave eased to a stop a block away. Cranford emerged, hurrying to the front door of the end unit. But the van waited, something Dave hadn't counted on.

Rethinking his options, Dave drove past the van, turned right onto an intersecting street and parked beneath a huge maple. He walked to the corner and waited behind a large ornamental shrub in the corner of a well-kept yard, hoping the owner wouldn't call the cops about a vagrant loitering in the neighborhood. Ten minutes later, the Channel 14 van did a U-turn and sped away. Cranford was in the passenger seat.

Dave walked to the apartment, rang the doorbell and stepped aside from the peephole. Twenty seconds elapsed before the door cracked. A deep voice growled, "What'd you forget?"

When Dave didn't respond, a burly figure pushed the door wider. Seeing Dave to one side, he muttered, "What're you selling? We don't want any."

"I'm looking for Billy Cranford. This is the address I was given." Dave moved so he could see inside. A faint noise of someone moving about a rear area of the unit solidified Dave's instinct he was on the right track.

"He ain't here and if he was, he wouldn't let you in. Now get moving." The guard glanced over his shoulder as though to muffle the sounds.

Dave said, "I'd like to leave him a message if you don't mind getting a piece of paper."

The guard hesitated, then said, "Call him at the station." He stepped back and started to close the door.

Dave shouldered into the door, catching the man off-guard as he stumbled to retain his balance. Moving fast to keep the advantage, Dave rammed his hand into the man's chest, sending him stumbling backward against a recliner.

By the time the man had regained his equilibrium, Dave had his gun out and pointed into his chest. "Don't move again. I'd hate to shoot you and leave blood all over this new carpet. Now where do you have Miriam Reading?"

"You're crazy," the man responded, his eyes on Dave as though waiting for an opportunity to charge him.

Motioning with the gun, Dave said, "Open that door there."

"Screw you, it's none of your business."

"Kidnapping is a major crime and you're aiding your buddy Cranford. So come clean and let's see who you're holding. Or I can call the cops and let them bring a warrant for a search."

The man shuffled toward the door. "You'll be sorry you ever messed with Cranford." He turned a key in the lock and opened the door.

Miriam rushed out of the room to lean into Dave. She screamed, "These bastards have held me here for three days." Her finger, shaking with fright and relief, stabbed toward Cranford's ally.

"We'll leave in a second, but first I want to tie up this goon so he doesn't alert Cranford for a while."

"Just lock him in here. He won't break the door down or Billy will kill him."

"Good idea." He waved for the guy to go in, who hesitated, staring into Dave's face, looking for some weakness. When he couldn't detect any, he backed into the space. Dave locked the door and left the key in the lock.

Looking closely at Miriam, Dave asked, "How are you? You need to go the hospital?" There were no obvious bruises and her clothes had not been torn, although she appeared frazzled with dark circles around her eyes. Her hair was tangled into dangling strings.

"I'll be okay. Billy knocked me around some and forced me to have sex, but now I just want out of here."

As they exited onto the sidewalk, Dave asked, "How'd he grab you?"

"I went to the station to sign papers for reinstatement. He saw me and waited near my car with this buddy. They manhandled me into Billy's van and brought me here. The rest you can figure out."

"Who's the buddy?"

"Billy called him Hank. They played football together in Denver."

At Dave's vehicle, he said, "I'll take you to the Chester police. You must file charges against Cranford for kidnapping."

"It'd be a waste. Billy has the authorities believing he's within his rights."

"I can't believe the police will ignore this episode. I want you to talk to Bill Rasmussen. He'll give you good advice and if nothing happens, we'll alert the media. They always like a good story of corruption in city administration."

She touched his arm. "Go with me tomorrow morning. Now I want to get my car and get to Monk's shelter. I need a shower and clean clothes."

"Okay, but you can't let this slide or that will only assure him he's beyond the law."

She shifted in the car, fingered the seat belt, and said, "Okay. Pick me up at 8:30. Maybe I'll get Monk to take care of the issue and get it done with."

"He might, but it could put him in the sights of the cops, something he tries to avoid. Let's try my approach first."

Knowing the meeting would evolve into legal issues, Dave was relieved when Jennifer's schedule could be modified so she could accompany them to the Chester administration building. A call to Rasmussen had produced a promise to meet them with a representative from the City Attorney's office.

As they settled around a rectangular table in one of the conference rooms, Assistant City Attorney Stuart Channing opened the discussion. "My understanding from Detective Rasmussen is that Ms. Reading was forcibly taken to a private residence and held against her wishes for three days. Further, Billy Cranford has been identified as the person responsible for this alleged abduction."

Jennifer spoke up. "That is correct and you must be aware that on several occasions Cranford has ignored a court order to stay away from Ms. Reading. She intends to file charges for kidnapping, rape, and violation of a court directive."

Channing leafed through a thin folder on the table. "This record shows the court order, but there's nothing about Cranford's violation prior to this latest episode."

"That's because," Jennifer said, a semblance of a smile crossing her face, "someone in the city administration quashed the complaint filed by Miriam Reading."

"Are you accusing this office of . . . .?"

Leaning forward, elbows on the table, Jennifer said, "I don't know who to accuse, but the City Attorney needs to investigate the matter. And I intend to let Judge Chandler know her order was somehow swept under the rug by someone protecting Billy Cranford."

"We'll look into the situation," Channing said, "but now I'd like to hear Ms. Reading's version of this abduction."

In a monotone voice with little expression either of bitterness or anguish, Miriam reiterated the events as she'd told Dave the day before. Finally, she said, "If Dave Randle had not found me, they would have held me forever."

Rasmussen said, "We are picking up Cranford and his buddy as we speak, charging them with kidnapping and rape. I doubt we can hold them very long, but we intend to investigate both this crime and the breaking of the court order."

His eyes on Rasmussen, Channing said, "Let's talk to the City Attorney before you get into the court order problem."

CHAPTER 7

In the parking lot outside the city building, Miriam, Jennifer, and Dave stopped under the greening elm. The sun was bright and traffic noise precluded normal conversation near the front entrance but the building blocked some of the roar to this side. Plus, the structure protected them from the direct blast of exhaust fumes coming from the idling vehicles at the traffic signal.

Miriam said, "Thanks for being here. I'm glad that session is over. Each one of these seems to become more tense." She shifted her feet and rubbed the back of her neck as though releasing the tension that must be there.

"Will you be okay?" Jennifer asked.

Shrugging her shoulders and staring into the distance for a moment, Miriam said, "I'm hoping this arrest will get Billy's attention. And Monk has offered an escort to and from his place when I need to run errands."

"We're moving ahead with the divorce and making progress with the suit against Frasier," Jennifer said, as they began to edge away. "But let us know if you need help."

"I appreciate that, but I'll be fine, although I need to move out of the so-called safe house pretty soon. I don't want to abuse Monk's support. I might need it again someday and it's expensive. I intend to return to work on Monday so I must get ready for that."

"If you need to do some shopping, I'll be glad to go with you," Jennifer volunteered, knowing her schedule would be in tatters, but thinking Miriam didn't want to be alone.

Miriam smiled and took a step away. "That's kind of you, but it'll be okay."

"Keep in touch with us," Dave said. "Let us know if there's a problem."

As Miriam turned toward her car, Dave said, "I'm going to visit with Rasmussen and maybe see how this arrest went."

"I have a meeting with a client in a few minutes," Jennifer said. "Can we meet for lunch?" She shifted her briefcase to her left hand and turned toward the sidewalk.

"Gibbons at noon." He touched her shoulder as they took different routes away from the city building.

Dave found Rasmussen hunched over a file folder, his brow furrowed with concentration. Dave waited a few seconds before rapping on the door.

When Rasmussen looked up, a frown on his face, Dave said, "You look busy. I'll come back."

"No, it's okay. I just can't figure out these notes an arresting officer left for me."

Dave eased into the chair in front of Rasmussen's desk. "I'm interested in how the arrest of Cranford went."

"Pretty routine. Both Cranford and his buddy, some guy named Hank Willard, were surprised and didn't resist or do anything stupid. Of course, as soon as they were brought in, Cranford called his lawyer and refused to talk until he arrived.

They're meeting with Stuart Channing and the arresting officers now."

"So they'll be released on bail?"

"If they're actually charged. You know Cranford will argue that Miriam went with him voluntarily and without any witnesses to the actual abduction other than his buddy, it'll be hard to prove otherwise. It'll be his word against hers."

"Even though she was being held captive?"

"He'll find some way to wiggle out of that. We have your account of how you rescued her, but again, it might not be enough. Cranford and his smooth-talking lawyer will say they were dealing with a hysterical female. You know how it goes."

Dave asked, "What about Cranford ignoring the court order to stay away from her?"

Rasmussen's face clouded, his eyes narrowed. "Something is going on that involves Cranford, the Mayor, and someone at Channel 14. Between the two of us, Channing told me the Mayor had intervened on Cranford's behalf. Forced the Chief to drop the charge against Cranford."

"So if Cranford is charged with kidnapping, the politician will come to his aid again."

"Could be. Before you ask, Channing doesn't know what Channel 14 has on the Mayor to influence his decision. It's still two years away from the next election but he would shun any negative publicity at any time."

"Maybe I'll scout around, especially if Cranford is not charged this time."

"I'd like to help but my hands are tied. The Chief has let us know we're not to poke around in the Mayor's affairs. Bottom line, the Mayor could fire the Chief and then the entire department is in shambles."

Dave stood. "Thanks. I'll call later to find out about Cranford's charges."

"Probably be on the evening news."

Rasmussen came around his desk to stand near Dave. "The department can't be involved in any investigation of the Mayor's office, but if I hear rumors, I'll let you know."

He closed the door to the hall. His voice dropped to almost a whisper. "A clerk, Sadie Turnbolt, in the city administrative offices has helped us in the past when there've been little indiscretions that hint at illegal acts. She seems to discover a lot of stuff that doesn't appear in the usual rumor mill. But don't let people know you're talking to her. Call her at home—number is listed under S. Turnbolt."

"Thanks, I may try her. And you know I'll be careful. I don't want to cross swords with those city hall guys and place our firm at odds with the politicians. But it might be useful to let the Judge know her restraining order was ignored or overridden by the Mayor or someone close to him."

"The Chief is almost certain it's the Mayor himself. And you could nose around Channel 14. I don't have a contact there, but maybe Miriam can help."

"It's a possibility, but I'd guess the people there are pretty close-mouthed about their co-workers. But, whatever I do, I'll keep you posted."

"You don't need to until you discover something we can act on." Rasmussen returned to his desk chair to respond to the ringing telephone.

Dave arrived first at Gibbons and was led to a booth toward the back. Three minutes later, Jennifer came in, her eyes scanning the room for him. He half-stood and waved. He watched her weave through the crowd, her figure subdued by the dark suit, but males eyed her as she passed, causing Dave to acknowledge how beautiful she was and how lucky he was to be married to her. One guy turned to examine her legs.

She slipped into the seat opposite him and asked, "How it'd go with Rasmussen?"

"Channing was still with Cranford and his lawyer when I left, so I don't know. Rasmussen gave me a tip on a possible informant in the administrative offices."

Jennifer waited until the waitress had taken their orders before saying, "I'm concerned about Miriam. She thinks this arrest will stop Cranford, but I suspect it might send him over the edge and he'll do something stupid."

Dave sipped coffee. "If he follows his pattern, he'll play it quiet for a few days until he thinks the cops aren't watching him, then do something. Or I'd hope he'd accept her decision and move on."

"They never do," Jennifer said, as their food was placed. "You look at the history of batterers and most don't stop until they kill their victim or they're jailed for life. Even those who serve long sentences often return to begin their attacks again. It's something about control or ownership of their victim."

"I recall an instructor in a class talking about the issue. What you say matches his analyses." He twisted his plate to a different position His mind remained on Cranford as he considered how they might steer him in a different direction. Or how they might give Miriam more protection even if she didn't want it. Nothing reasonable jumped into his thinking.

Sadie Turnbolt lived in an older house on 39th Street with a spacious front yard filled with shrubs and flower beds arranged under several large oaks. Dave had called her around six and she'd agreed to meet him at 8:30 that same evening. He eased into the long driveway.

She responded immediately to the front bell as though she'd been waiting just inside. She invited him in, saying, "Thanks for being on time. I hate to wait when I have something pending." Tall, almost gaunt with few of the typical feminine features, she had her brown-gray hair pulled back in a bun. Her mid-calf brown skirt and tan blouse suggested someone who paid little attention to current fashion.

She led him into a large room with couches and soft chairs that were decades old and arranged in conversational groupings. Dave scanned the high ceiling and paneled walls. Sensing his interest, she said, "I inherited this place from my parents fifteen years ago but have made only a few changes during the time I've owned it."

Dave sat in a chair next to her. "You don't see many like this anymore."

"It's a wonderful place, but as you might guess, the plumbing and wiring are outdated and sometimes pose problems. I suppose soon I'll be forced to replace all those things, but how may I help you?"

"I didn't tell you very much on the phone," Dave said, "but my interest in meeting with you has to do with recent events related to Billy Cranford, Channel 14 Television, and the Mayor. I understand you may not even be aware of the circumstances, but a friend in the police department thought you might help me piece together what has gone on." He recapped the recent events involving Cranford, Miriam and the police so she'd understand the background of his request.

Turnbolt's eyes riveted on his face as she seemed to be assessing his character. "Mr. Randle, I agreed to meet because I've heard about you and your partner. I'd been impressed by the way you assisted those people in the retirement community and the fact that you stand up for the underdogs in our society. Too often these elected officials forget who put them in office and only kow-tow to the rich and well placed." She paused and tugged at the sleeve of her blouse. "My father was a physician, one of a dying breed of doctors willing to assist those who couldn't pay or had no insurance. He always thought working people were trampled by those in power or who thought only about how to beat them out of money."

Hoping to turn her aside from her digression, Dave said, "My suspicion is your father would be interested in what has apparently happened with Cranford and the Mayor's influence."

The semblance of a smile cut across her face, easing the sternness inherent in her personality. "He would have been outraged." She touched her glasses as though adjusting the frame across her nose. "Around the office I do my work and never ask questions, but if you stay alert to what's going on around you, you can learn a lot. Mr. Randle, there's no doubt the Mayor intervened on behalf of Billy Cranford either at the request or demand of the owners of Channel 14. But there the certainty ceases and the rationale for his actions remain unclear. I've heard rumors that the news people at the TV station know about some event in the Mayor's background that allows them to wield their influence over him. Sooner or later, the specifics will emerge as they almost always do in these situations."

Dave said, "I agree. However, I'm not in a position to wait for things to play out in the usual way. We're interested in the welfare of this woman who has been abused by Cranford and want him to stop his criminal acts."

"I've read in the papers that the station managers have high regard for Cranford because he's elevated the ratings of the station. And you know, this increases their advertising rates and they make more money."

"Maybe," Dave probed a bit, "there's a personal relationship between the Mayor and Cranford. Often politicians foster connections with sport figures."

"That's true, but in this case, I suspect there's some dirty deed in the Mayor's past that makes him vulnerable to manipulation. At any rate, I'll do my best to discover more but it may require some time." She seemed to think about her next statement and asked, "Is your client vulnerable now?"

Dave stood and reached to shake Sadie's hand. "She seems safe for the moment, but I'll appreciate any insights you can share. We're not so intent on knowing about the Mayor's past as we are in getting Cranford out of the life of our client."

Turnbolt struggled from the low chair and led Dave to the front door. "Thanks for coming here. I am careful with my contacts. I'll call you in a few days to report any progress."

She followed him to the front door and waited there until he backed out of the drive. Dave drove away thinking he'd made another valuable ally and he grinned as he thought of the dour Sadie as a spy in the heart of the political center of Chester. Her very personality made her effective.

The morning edition of the *Register* contained no mention of Billy Cranford's arrest. As they scanned the inside section for any note about the incident, Jennifer said, "It appears that even the news media have been influenced."

Turning another page of the paper spread across his desk, Dave said, "Or more likely, the City Attorney's office somehow failed to release any information."

"But what about the reporters assigned to cover police activities? Surely they would recognize and have some curiosity about Cranford being hauled into the station."

"Something is going on that we haven't seen before."

Jennifer said, "I'm having lunch with Anita Chandler today. I'll let her know her order regarding Cranford has been ignored or worse."

"What can she do?"

"Throw Cranford in jail for ignoring the order and maybe file contempt charges against those who interfered with the police. I don't know how far she'd push the matter."

"Any chance she's become involved in this scheme to protect Cranford?"

"I'd be flabbergasted if she were." She turned toward her own office.

CHAPTER 8

Jennifer met Judge Anita Chandler in the dining room of the downtown Marriot. As they scanned the menu and ordered lunch, they talked about the last Bar Association meeting and the speaker who'd reviewed the implications of the Sarbanes-Oxley legislation for attorneys who represent small businesses and non-profits. They reminisced about their days in law school and wondered about the location of a classmate. Anita told Jennifer her cancer had not returned in this third year after treatment and she felt confident about the future. In addition, her creamy smooth skin and upbeat tone in her voice testified to a renewed vigor.

As their salad plates were removed, Jennifer said, "The reason I asked to meet has to do with your restraining order for Billy Cranford to stay away from Miriam Reading. We represent Reading in both her divorce and in the probable suit against a drug company."

"I remember the case. Is there a difficulty?"

"The problem is Cranford ignored the order and was arrested, but the police have been overruled and instructed to leave Cranford free to do whatever he wishes. We believe the

Mayor's office intervened and forced the Chief of Police to desist from his normal procedure. There seemed to be an underlying threat of dismissal if the Chief ignored the Mayor."

Chandler's jaw dropped, her face twisted into a grimace. She seemed to consider the situation for several seconds, her eyes exploring Jennifer's face. "Are you certain Mayor Ridley is involved? I've known him for several years and have never suspected any wrong-doing on his part."

"Not absolutely, but the directive to the Chief came from the Mayor's office, certainly implying Ridley wanted Cranford protected."

Jennifer decided to fully inform her friend of the actions of Cranford. "Since your order to keep his distance, Cranford kidnapped Reading, held her for almost three days, was arrested again, but released without any charges being brought. The City Attorney isn't talking, but we believe someone at Channel 14 through the Mayor's office caused the dropping of charges. And there was never an official report of the arrest. Police reporters either didn't know about it or were forced to ignore it. I suspect they never knew. From our perspective, something dirty and illegal is going on."

Chandler looked at her watch. "I'd like to discuss this further, but I have to be in court for a two o'clock session. But I'll have my clerk look into the situation and if you're correct, I'll do something about it."

As they waited at the cashier stand, Chandler asked about Dave and the marriage she'd performed for her friend from law school at Northwestern.

Jennifer waited for change and said, "We're doing well. There've been fewer bumps than I anticipated when two people who'd lived alone for years establish a common household. And I've come to love this house in the country. I never knew how quiet the world could be away from the bustle of the city."

Chandler smiled. "I thought it would work out well."

In the foyer, they touched hands, then hugged.

Helen Knight came into Jennifer's office mid-afternoon Thursday. She pushed the door closed and perched on the edge of the chair in front of the desk. "I talked last night to Tom Ware in the Congresswoman's office about the possibility of her meeting with you regarding those FDA hearings. He'll try to set something up for Saturday when she'll be in the district office for a few hours."

"Tell me a bit about the Congresswoman. I know you have high regard for her, but I've not interacted with her at all."

Knight settled into the chair and crossed her legs, reminding Jennifer of the effect Helen could exact on men. "Marilyn Womack has been active in local party politics for ten years or more. She was willing to do anything to help the party be successful and worked hard for Hankins while he was the representative. When he decided not to stand for reelection, everyone urged her to run. And she was elected.

"I'm sure she's still becoming acclimated to the Washington scene, but she's a fast learner. I have great respect for her and know she refuses to become involved in anything remotely dirty or unethical. Now whether she can obtain what you want from FDA is another question but I'm certain she'd try, especially if she can be convinced something occurred that had the smell of wrong-doing. Her deep interests include health issues and protection of the public from environmental hazards. This thing involving infant deaths would grab her attention."

"Thanks, Helen. I assume Tom will phone us if a time can be established."

"He'll let you know either way, probably by late tomorrow."

"I like to keep weekends clear, but I'll bend in order to see her."

Standing in front of the desk, Helen added, "Just to keep you in the know, Hankins sold his house and left the area. Rumors are he couldn't stand the publicity that was bound to occur if people found out about his new living arrangement." The former Congressman had admitted his gay orientation and many knew he now lived with a male companion.

Jennifer met Womack at the Congresswoman's local office at 1:30 on Saturday afternoon. Offices and a conference room were located behind a reception area filled with two desks, several comfortable chairs and a magazine rack. Photographs of Congresswoman Womack, the Speaker of the House, and the President adorned the walls along with a couple of paintings by local artists. Jennifer waited ten minutes for Womack to complete a session with another party. Unable to sit without doing something, she flipped through the latest issue of *Time*, thinking about her plans with Dave to work on their garden project. They hoped to get some vegetables planted in the space he'd paid a neighboring farmer to plow for them rather than spend money for a small tractor or spend hours digging with a shovel.

Womack followed a couple out of the conference room and moved toward Jennifer, reaching to shake her hand, saying, "Come in. I'm sorry to be behind schedule, but things always take longer than we think." She looked tired, her eyes in deep hollows, even her shoulders seemed to sag under the weight of the dark suit jacket. A small compact figure, she moved quickly as though time was her most valuable commodity.

Jennifer said, "Thanks for meeting with me. I know these local issues take all your weekends, so I'll be brief."

Scanning a sheet in front of her at the table, Womack said, "I've heard of your firm and your practice through my friend Helen Knight. And how is she?"

"She's doing well. We're pleased to have her with us. And she seems to have weathered the ordeals she experienced, but I know very little of her life beyond the office." Jennifer felt she shouldn't reveal Helen's relationship with Antonio Gibbons yet. Those who knew Gibbons by reputation only and had not interacted with him would reach a wrong judgment.

"I tried to persuade Helen to take a position in my Washington office, but she turned me down. I think she wanted out of the political spotlight after the ordeal with those people trying to obtain revenge on Hankins."

"You're correct and I hope we can keep her. She's become a real asset because she knows the local political scene so well."

"I've been impressed the things you have accomplished in a relatively short time. But tell me about the problem with FDA and how I might help."

Jennifer sketched the problem of the experimental drug issued by Frasier and the damages it had apparently caused in pregnant women. She revealed the rationale for her interest. "We're likely going to sue Frasier for damages on behalf of Miriam Reading and possible other victims. To prepare for that I'm trying to determine as much as possible about the approval process for new drugs. Our review of the transcripts of the Food and Drug hearings about this drug, available under the name of Plertex, raised some concerns." She paused while Womack scribbled on a notepad.

"The hearings were contentious with a couple of the scientists accusing Frasier of not revealing the entire truth about the initial human trials. As a result of their questions and arguments, the scientific panel denied Frasier's request and asked that additional trials be conducted. But somehow, the drug was approved and released for general use. Rumors are that the FDA administrator ignored the advice of the panel and gave the go-ahead. If this is true, it could be an important consideration in our case against Frasier."

Womack put her elbows on the table. "I'm not surprised at this position taken by the Commissioner. The present Administration has appointed people into important positions with little or no background or experience with the issues they're confronted with on a daily basis and the Congress has rubber-stamped the requests. I'm afraid they deal in never-never land and ignore reality. If it's politically expedient, those appointees often ignore the advice of expert panels and witnesses. It's as if they don't care about the safety or welfare of the public. Anything goes if a political ally benefits." She frowned and added, "Not to mention big donors to their campaign chests."

A bit surprised by the harshness, almost bitterness, in Womack's statement, Jennifer said, "I suppose it's possible the reviewers were split down the middle and the administrator felt he could justify his call."

"Maybe, but I'll try to discover more, although this may take some doing. Since I'm in the opposition party, anyone in the agency will be reluctant to discuss the matter. But I have a couple of people on staff who know the career people and how to get around the political hurdles in Washington."

Jennifer stood. "Anything you can find could be useful. This entire thing might blow apart and never progress to a trial phase, but I like to be prepared."

Womack stood and the two moved toward the door. Womack asked, "Are there others in addition to your client who've been impacted?"

"We know of one other but intend to search more extensively. I won't be surprised if numerous women have been affected. The problem of eclampsia is common during pregnancy and this Frasier drug seemed to be the needed treatment."

Womack shook Jennifer's hand and said, "We'll get back to you as soon as possible. Likely Tom Ware will be the messenger." She turned toward two women waiting for their appointment.

Jennifer drove home optimistic Womack would delve into the matter and with considerable more respect for the Representative from her district. Then her thoughts turned to Dave and the garden they intended to get started over the weekend.

On Tuesday morning Dave had a message on his machine asking that he meet Sadie Turnbolt at her home that evening. The call had been left at 8:30 the evening before. Dave smiled, knowing Sadie was taking no chances of being overheard or have her messages recorded at the city administration office.

As on his previous visit to Sadie's, she met Dave immediately and led him to the same room. Without any preliminary discussion, she said, "I poked around a bit more than usual in finding out about the Mayor and his call to the police chief." She smiled, if one could characterize a fleeting glint of pleasure across her face and a parting of her lips a true smile, and said, "The Mayor's Executive Assistant has been in that position for about six months and isn't as close-mouthed as those before her. She talks to others in the office and I overheard her telling this young clerk about calls between the Mayor and Channel 14's President, Arthur Zabrisky. And she revealed he'd called the Chief of Police about this Cranford person."

"Then it's clear the Mayor made the call himself?"

"Yes. I don't doubt it for a minute."

"Was he doing Zabrisky a personal favor or did the station have some scuttlebutt of a personal nature the Mayor couldn't afford to become public?"

Turnbolt eyed Dave for several seconds. "I can't be certain of his rationale in protecting Cranford by yielding to this Zabrisky person."

Leaning forward in the chair to ease the jabs from a broken spring in the old chair, Dave asked, "Has there been a history of Ridley cutting corners and getting involved with shady deals? There's nothing known by the public, but you never know what's just below the surface."

Again she hesitated as though unsure, her lips in a tight line. "Most of the citizens regard him above reproach, but like most public officials, he has his weak spots. I know he ignored the recommendations of his Planning Commission and pushed through City Council a request to rezone a tract of land along Route 36 for a developer. Rumors of a payoff persisted for some time in the office, but never became public knowledge. Now as for Channel 14 or Zabrisky specifically, I don't truly know."

"Is it reasonable for you to probe some more or you think you've reached the limit?

"I'm not good at skirting around the edges of problems. I usually just wait until someone blabs something out of line. Then I may ask a question or two, but I attempt to disguise my true interest." Again, her smile, then she added, "Most around the office regard me as out of touch with the modern world. Sometimes that gives me an advantage."

"Tell me more about the Mayor's Executive Assistant. Is she approachable and could I rely on her confidence?"

Turnbolt straightened in her chair, crossed her ankles. "She'd talk to you, but soon everyone would know about the conversation. Her name is June Skinner. She worked in Human Resources before Ridley chose her for her position. There were several applicants because of the increased salary and some wanted to be closer to the center of power. Everyone was surprised when he selected June."

Dave grinned. "Did you apply?"

"Lord, no. I'm content to remain in my present position and work until I can retire."

"Is there something personal between June and the Mayor?"

Turnbolt leaned forward as though prepared to convey some inner secret. "Rumors are they're having an affair. And if the hints are correct, it started before she came to the present job while she was still in the HR department."

"Could this be the issue Zabrisky at Channel 14 is holding over Ridley's head?"

An actual smile creased Sadie's features. "I bet it is, but I can't be sure. Only he and the TV people know."

Dave stood, saying, "I'll look further and ask that you continue to be alert to any tidbits that could lead us to the truth."

Turnbolt extricated her self from the old chair. "I'm always alert, but my colleagues don't volunteer things to me."

Friday afternoon brought an unusual lull to the office. Not a single client had an appointment and walk-in traffic had ceased as people took advantage of the warm weather to participate in outdoor activities. Or no one had a legal problem. Ellie went to the University law library to search for information about an ancient law that Jennifer thought might apply to a case. Jennifer read through a backlog of law journals. Helen used the down time to straighten files. Dave completed a report to a client and decided to leave for the day.

He went into Jennifer's office. "I'm going home since nothing urgent seems to be on our docket. Work on the garden while the weather is right."

The telephone rang on Jennifer's desk. She responded and listened, then said, "No, I don't think we've heard from her recently. Any reason for concern?"

She listened again, then said, 'We'll check around. Let you know if we find anything."

Punching the off button on her phone, Jennifer said, "That was Channel 14 Marketing Department. Miriam hasn't been at work for two days and they're calling people who might know about her." She walked around the desk to stand near Dave. "We should have been more aggressive in keeping up with her, but she seemed not to want close monitoring of her movements."

"You know Cranford has kidnapped her again. I'll swing by his apartment on the way home."

CHAPTER 9

Dave stopped in front of Cranford's apartment, surveyed the street for a moment, waited for a car to pass, went to the front door and pressed the bell. No one responded. He banged on the door. After two minutes of pacing and watching the street, he walked around the building, but couldn't detect anything unusual nor see inside the apartment. He tried peering inside, but the shades were drawn on all the windows and no sounds emanated from the interior. Two pre-school age kids were in a sandbox next door, too intent on their castle to notice him. He heard a car enter the drive in front and started that way expecting to find Cranford entering the front door.

As he turned the corner to the front of the structure, he collided with Cranford's buddy, Hank Willard. Without a word, the huge guy grabbed Dave and threw him to the ground like a sack of grain. He aimed a kick at Dave's head, but only connected with a grazing blow to the shoulder as Dave rolled away. Hank pressed his advantage, jumped forward and kicked again. Dave grabbed Hank's ankle as the thrust narrowly missed contact with his chest. He jerked hard, throwing Hank off balance and sent him crashing onto his back. By the time

Hank recovered and scrambled up, Dave stood waiting and wishing he had his gun.

Holding up his hands, palms out, Dave said, "Enough of this crap. I'm looking for Miriam and know you and Cranford have kidnapped her again."

His features contorted into a deep scowl, Hank growled, "We don't have the bitch, but I'm going to teach you once and for all to stop poking around in places that are none of your goddam business."

He shuffled forward, his arms cocked, his fists closed, ready for another assault. He had the stance of a fighter, no doubt a throwback to his youth or his days in the football world. Dave edged away from the left hand, knowing Willard would first throw a jab, then follow through with a right in the tradition of most boxers.

Hank jabbed a left. Dave ducked under the punch, but slammed Hank across the throat with a backhand. The big man's eyes bugged out, his hands grasped his throat as he struggled to breathe. Dave punched him in the nose, blood gushing out of the broken veins running through the cartilage.

As Hank tried to recover, Dave said, "Stop before you get hurt really bad. Just tell me where Cranford's holding Miriam and I'll leave you be."

A mumbling response through a bloody hand holding his nose, "She ain't here. That's all I know." Hank had regained his upright position, but he wobbled as he moved.

"You're lying. Let's go inside."

"Screw you."

Dave kicked him in the gut, dropping Hank to his hands and knees, gasping for breath, his face red. Dave reached inside Hank's pants pocket and pulled out the keys. When he had the door open, he glanced back to see Hank still on his knees and not prepared to rush Dave again very soon.

A quick walk through the unit proved Hank right. Miriam was not in the Cranford apartment. Outside again where Hank had rolled onto his back, he said, "I could force you to tell me where she is, but you might die. Somehow I'll find her, then I'll be back." He tossed the keys on Hank's stomach and turned to his vehicle.

Dave delayed in the Blazer until Hank rolled to his stomach, struggled to his hands and knees, then gained a standing position, and made it inside. While Dave tarried, he called Rasmussen on his cell phone. He waited until the dispatcher tracked him down.

When Rasmussen responded, Dave said, "I wanted you to know Miriam Reading has gone missing again. I suspect Cranford, but his buddy Hank wouldn't talk. She's not at Cranford's apartment."

"Maybe he's not involved this time."

Ignoring Rasmussen's attempt to ease out of the situation, Dave said, "She's been absent from work two days. If she had to be away for some personal reason, she would have let her boss know. They're concerned enough to call us. I hope you can mount some effort to find her."

Rasmussen hesitated, then muttered, "You know the restrictions we're operating under. I'll talk to the Chief, but I don't dare go off on my own. Could get the Chief in hot water with the Mayor."

"Do anything you think possible," Dave said. "It's going to be a major scandal if she comes up dead and the press learns about the Mayor's little game."

"I know. Don't do anything rash." The line went dead.

Dave accepted the police weren't going to look for Miriam. He uttered a curse at the games being played by the politicians. He eased away from the curb.

By the time Dave got home, his shoulder throbbed with pain. The shoulder of his coat had been dirtied and ripped by

Hank's battering shoe. He tossed it on the chair and pulled off his shirt.

Jennifer arrived home from the office as he was putting ice cubes into a plastic bag. Her eyes focused on his efforts. "What happened?"

He told her about the confrontation as he zip-locked the bag and placed it against his shoulder. He wrapped a towel around the edges to collect any drippings or condensation. He dropped into a chair and pressed the ice against the bruise. The cold penetrated almost immediately.

"Maybe you should see a doctor. The blow could have broken a bone." She arranged the towel around the bag in places difficult for him to reach then brought another towel to tie the bag in place.

Shaking his head, Dave said, "Let's wait until morning. See how it is then."

"What do we do about Miriam?"

"I called Rasmussen, but his hands are tied by this order from the Mayor. The only thing I know to do is track Cranford. He'll lead me to her. But by now Hank has alerted him to be on the lookout for me or anyone else."

Jennifer paced across the room. "We could call Monk. Maybe some of his boys could look for her or maybe he knows where she is."

"I hate to get those guys involved, but with cops on the sideline, it's our best alternative. You have his number here?" He shifted in the chair to find a more comfortable position.

Jennifer smiled. "I do and I'll call." She grabbed her purse from the end table and went into the kitchen.

Three minutes later, she came back where Dave was sprawled across the couch, the ice pack clamped tightly.

"Monk hasn't heard from her. I didn't know, but she moved to an apartment on Monday. The address is 1204 Melrose Place.

I think it's in that new development of condos and duplexes. I tried the phone number he gave me, but no answer."

"I'm surprised she didn't let us know she'd moved, but she wanted out of Monk's place. It's not normal living, especially for anyone not evading the cops. And for a single woman mixing with guys living on the fringe is doubly strange, maybe even threatening when you know your housemates are suspicious characters and could be dangerous."

"I can imagine her discomfort there, perhaps concerned she'll be sexually assaulted at any time. Nevertheless, Monk plans to send a couple of guys on a so-called scouting mission."

"That won't be healthy for Cranford if those thugs locate him." He shifted to reposition the ice contraption.

"Is the pain subsiding?" Jennifer held his coat up, twisted it around.

"Too cold to tell, but think so. It'll be black and blue by morning. And too stiff to move."

"Your coat is beyond repair. Gives us an excuse to upgrade your apparel."

Jennifer brought him his usual beer and sat beside him on the couch. Automatically their hands came together. After five minutes of silence as each thought about Miriam and the things that could happen to her, Jennifer said, "I'll get dinner, then you can get in bed and rest your shoulder."

"Better to stay up, plus this ice pack will only wet our sheets."

The regular television programming was interrupted at 10:15 that evening by a solemn voiced reporter. "Breaking news. A body has been found in the Case Street canal by two homeless people living under an overpass near the scene. Police have not yet identified the body of a Caucasian male, but we have learned he'd been badly beaten and shot in the head. We'll update you as we learn more."

Dave sat up straight from the couch. "I'd bet it's the work of Monk's guys. Probably killed Hank who wouldn't reveal where Miriam is being held."

Jennifer's face blanched a pasty white. "My God, Dave I shouldn't have called him. I had no idea they would go this far."

He pulled her closer. "It was the right thing to do under the circumstances. And the positive outcome is it'll get Cranford's attention and send him the message he's next. Only a matter of time. Monk and his kind can be relentless."

Twenty minutes later as they were dressing for bed, the telephone rang. Dave answered to hear Rasmussen, "I don't like to do this, but we want you to come into the station in the morning. The City Attorney wants to talk about the death of this guy found in the canal."

"Have you identified the body?"

Rasmussen paused, cleared his throat. "I can't tell anyone yet."

"Am I under suspicion?"

"Could be."

As Jennifer came out of the bathroom, he told her, then added, "That was Rasmussen. They want to talk to me. They believe I killed this guy which in my thinking confirms the corpse is that of Hank Willard."

"I'm going with you."

"Rasmussen told the attorneys I'd called him or they wouldn't connect me to the scene. Or he went to the Chief who blabbed."

"Maybe they had no choice."

"Or maybe they're passing the buck to stay out of the spotlight. Bottom line is I should not have alerted Rasmussen."

Rasmussen and Stuart Channing were grim-faced as Jennifer and Dave settled around the conference table in the City Attorney's suite. Rasmussen couldn't meet Dave's eyes. When Channing reached to switch on the ever-present recorder, Jennifer said, "I object to this being taped. I want this conversation to be off the record. And I don't want anything we reveal to come back in another forum. Our only reason for participating is to help the authorities determine what went on with Mr. Willard and locate Ms. Reading."

Taken aback by Jennifer's stance, Channing hesitated, unsure of how hard to push his own purposes. "Ms. Watson, it's common practice to record discussions with suspects."

"If Dave is truly a suspect in Willard's death, this meeting is over." She pushed back her chair. "And you'll need more evidence to charge him."

Channing relented. "Okay, I'll agree not to tape our conversation, but I will take notes."

"That will be fine," Jennifer said, pulling back to the table, knowing notes could be challenged if Channing attempted to use anything they said as admission of wrong doing.

Channing said, "To start, Mr. Randle, we know you had an altercation with Hank Willard late yesterday afternoon. Tell us about that."

Dave glanced at Jennifer who nodded.

"I went to the apartment occupied by Billy Cranford and Willard to determine the whereabouts of Miriam Reading. She has been missing for three days now and given the past history between Cranford and her, I suspected he was holding her. Hank attacked me, tossed me on the ground, tried to kick me in the head but hit my shoulder instead. I defended myself. The last time I saw Willard, he was on his feet and entering the apartment. Before I drove away I called Detective Rasmussen and requested the police initiate a search for Reading. I don't know if that happened. We heard the news about Hank on the local television station last night."

"Your testimony is that you had nothing to do with Hank's death. Is that correct?"

"Yes."

"And you are sure he was okay when you drove away from his apartment following your little set-to?"

"He walked on his own into the building. I drove away immediately."

"Why your interest in Miriam Reading?"

"We represent her in an spousal abuse situation involving Billy Cranford. When her employer called about her absences from work, I became concerned about her safety, especially after Cranford abducted her previously in defiance of a court order."

"Did you try to force Hank to reveal her location?"

"I asked him twice, once before he jumped me, and again after he gave up the battle. I didn't go beyond that." In retrospect, he wished he had. Hank might still be alive.

Channing scanned a paper, than said, "I have a theory about what occurred based on your reputation of forcing people to yield whatever you desire at the moment. I suspect this happened with Hank and you killed him. Then you called Rasmussen to divert attention from your actions."

Remembering Jennifer's advice about maintaining self-control, Dave said, "I didn't force Hank to give up anything. And if I'd killed him, I certainly would not have notified the cops I'd been near him." He wanted to add that with their hands-off approach to the Cranford issue, they'd likely have never made the connection, but held back.

"So, if you didn't kill Hank Willard, who did?"

"I don't know."

"Do you have ideas?"

Over breakfast Jennifer and Dave had discussed what he might say if this question were posed. They didn't want to give away Monk and have his operation closed down. And having the cops questioning Monk's could lead to Gibbons, and explode that relationship. Dave said, "Perhaps, but it'd be a guess."

Channing looked at Rasmussen, then asked, "Are you refusing to give us the names of the person or persons you suspect?"

Dave stared at Channing. "Yes. I depend on that person as a source of information not to be violated."

"So a snitch?"

"Not in the usual sense, but I've learned things that solved cases neither the cops nor I could get a handle on. Detective Rasmussen can verify this."

"We could throw you in jail until you think better about that response."

Jennifer broke in. "But you're not. First, you don't have enough evidence to tie him to the crime. Second, if you people had done your jobs and not caved in to political influence, we wouldn't be listening to your accusations and Miriam Reading would not be held captive by this guy protected by the very people who should be concerned about her well-being."

Channing flushed and muttered, "That's a bit high-handed, Ms. Watson."

She smiled at Channing and said, "You haven't seen high-handed until we inform the press of this protective scheme you people have concocted. There'll be a field day and I suspect some of you will be looking for new jobs, if not in the slammer yourself."

Channing stared at her for a moment as though wanting to challenge her, then closed his folder. "Mr. Randle, be aware you are under watch. And we may yet indict you for the murder of Hank." As though he'd delivered the final word, he stood.

Rasmussen left with Channing, but he nodded to Dave.

An hour later, Rasmussen called Dave at the office. "Just in case you want to call me back, I'm at home. Frankly, I don't trust that my phone at the office is not being monitored. I'm sorry Channing brought you in and threatened you, but I couldn't persuade him otherwise. Stay under the radar for a few days. Don't give him reason to move toward an indictment."

"What can you tell me about Hank Willard?"

"Whoever killed him had also broken both knees, several ribs and his shoulder. He'd been whacked him around badly. He might have died from internal injuries even if they'd not shot him."

"It's obvious he didn't tell them where Miriam was being held or they'd have her by now."

For a moment Dave thought the connection had been broken, then Rasmussen said, "Could be he really didn't know. I'm completely frustrated with this deal. I'm concerned Miriam is being battered and abused while we sit around doing nothing but kow-towing to a politician interested in protecting his hide."

"I may be out of line asking, but is Channing part of this cover for Cranford?"

"I suspect he's caught in the middle between the Mayor and the Chief, but I don't truly know. I've never seen anything like this before, but the Chief is mad as hell."

"Maybe he needs to let you guys do your jobs. The Mayor wouldn't dare can him and be confronted with the backlash. Everything he's trying to hide would come out and his situation would be worse."

"He's not thinking clearly or he hopes this will all go away. But you know, the first reaction by any politician is to cover any tracks that might embarrass him. Nothing else matters."

Dave considered telling Rasmussen about his idea of tracking Cranford on Monday, but thought it might place his friend in another untenable position with his supervisors.

CHAPTER 10

When he rolled over in bed on Sunday morning, Dave's shoulder ached so badly he thought it might be dislocated or some bone had been broken. An involuntary groan escaped from his throat. Bracing himself for the pain, he eased to a standing position. He grimaced as he pulled on a tee shirt. His upper left arm and chest area looked as though it had been spray painted with a black and blue mixture of exotic dyes. Rebelling against his usual response to tough it out until bruises and aches ran their courses, he downed a pain-killer Jennifer had insisted they pick up from the pharmacy on the way home from the visit with Channing. Thoughts that he was getting old or becoming soft ran through his mind. He knew from past experiences that while movement might relieve the tightness, it could worsen the situation to the point he'd be forced to visit a physician.

Downstairs he followed the aroma of brewing coffee and sounds to the kitchen to find Jennifer creating omelets for breakfast. She glanced at him, retied her robe around her waist, and said, "Well, you can still move, but you'd better take it slow today."

"I took one of those pills you bought. I hope it doesn't make me to groggy. I've got to do something to locate Miriam. The longer Cranford has her, the more likely she'll get killed."

"I don't know what you can do. No doubt Monk has his scouts on the lookout. They'll know to track Cranford, if they can get a trace."

"Cranford will be hard to locate on the weekend. Maybe I should go by Monk's. See what he knows. Maybe comparing ideas will lead to something we could do."

Jennifer turned the omelets in a large iron frying pan, a household item passed from Dave's grandmother, although when asked, he couldn't recall how he ended up with it. "I know you're frustrated, but waiting until you can track Cranford is the best you can accomplish. Whatever you do, remember Rasmussen's advice—stay out of sight of the cops."

By the time they'd eaten and put dishes in the washer, the pain medication had kicked in and the ache had subsided to a dull throb when he remained still, but when he moved his arm, a shooting pain reminded him of the damage. Deciding he could tolerate that by limiting his motion, he took off.

At Monk's operation all seemed quiet. Dave rapped on the front door and walked into a small vestibule. Faint sounds of televisions or radios could be heard from rooms near the entrance. Remembering Monk's telling Miriam he had an apartment in the basement, Dave descended stairs lighted by a dim bulb dangling from a cord midway down the flight. There seemed to be only one living space adjacent to a room with a washer and dryer. A gray-haired man was sitting on a metal chair, no doubt waiting for one of the machines to finish the cycle. He nodded toward Dave before returning to his magazine. The door of a utility area was partially closed but he could see tools stacked just inside and a breaker box on the wall. He knocked on the door of the apartment.

Immediately Monk opened the door and peered through the opening. Seeing Dave, he grinned and swung the door wider to let him enter.

Dave said, "Sorry to bother you on a Sunday morning, but I wanted to know if you've found out anything about Miriam."

"No bother. I been up a long time. Went to early Mass. You interested in coffee?"

"Sure."

While Monk rattled in the cupboards for a moment, Dave surveyed the space. Surprised by the tidiness, he realized the furnishings were quite nice and in good condition. He'd expected a run-down, seedy place. Rather he'd found a middle-class living unit maintained beyond his expectations by a single male. Cushions were neatly arranged on the couch. Magazines and papers were stacked on a coffee table. Aromas of bacon mingled with the coffee.

Monk returned and handed Dave a mug, vapor rising from the top. They sat in hard-back chairs around a small maple table in a dining area nestled between the living room and the kitchen.

Monk said, "To answer your question, I haven't found anything about her. I have two guys out looking, but it's a dead end at the moment." He sipped from the mug. "My guys searched Friday night and most of yesterday, but nothing. I'm afraid she's been knocked in the head and tossed in the river."

"I met with Cranford's house mate on Friday, but he refused to tell me anything." Dave hoped Monk would reveal his men had discussed the missing woman with Hank without him asking directly. Monk didn't bite or didn't know about the encounter. Guys who'd been in trouble with the cops seldom revealed anything that might shine any light on their activities, including telling the person who sent them on a mission.

Monk said, "I assume the cops are doing nothing. Your partner told me you'd notified them and they were reluctant to start a search. Maybe the usual crap about being missing forty-eight hours before they initiate anything."

Dave shifted in the chair, prompting a shooting pain in his shoulder. "It's more than that. Cranford is being protected by a directive from the Mayor's office. The cops can't do anything without losing their jobs."

Monk grimaced and shook his head. "So much for law-abiding leaders."

Dave put his empty mug on the table. "My best guess is Cranford has Miriam locked away in some place we don't know about. I'll try to tail Cranford tomorrow when he returns to work. If that doesn't lead to her, I don't have any other ideas."

"I'll keep guys on the lookout," Monk said.

Dave stood, experiencing another pain through his shoulder. "Thanks for the coffee. I'll let you know something by Tuesday morning."

Near the front door of the building, he passed two men who eyed him with suspicion, but he kept moving. He acknowledged any strange face in the building would result in a defensive posture. Everyone in the building was hiding from something or someone.

From the office, Dave called Channel 14. In response to the female voice, Dave asked, "Do you have a roster of who's doing the news on weekends? I'm trying to find an old friend and heard he was now a sports reporter for the station."

"According to the assignments for today, Rusty Hancock is scheduled for both the six and eleven time slots for sports on the weekend."

"Thanks. Guess I have the wrong information." He leaned back in his chair, attempting to relieve the throb in his shoulder. He decided to head home, maybe go against his usual practice and take another pain killer, then take Jennifer's advice to go easy for the rest of the day. He'd get on Cranford's tail tomorrow when he returned for his regular broadcasts. In the meantime, he hoped Miriam was using good sense and not defying Cranford to the point he'd do something stupid. But the inability to rescue her was beyond frustration. He should have maimed Cranford to the point the guy couldn't damage anyone for a long time, but he'd felt reined in by the cops. Channing's threats and Jennifer's advice crept into his thinking.

By Monday Dave's shoulder had improved to the point he could avoid the pills, but he focused on desk chores throughout the day. He talked to a potential client about searching for his adult daughter who hadn't contacted him in several months. The police had conducted a cursory search but had given up since she was mature and had no record of criminal activity nor to their knowledge had she been a victim. They agreed on a time Dave could visit with him, get a photo of the woman, and any additional ideas the father might have about her disappearance.

At 5:45, he parked his Blazer on the busy street leading to the parking lot for Channel 14 employees. Few cars moved for a while, but after the 6:00 o'clock broadcasts, several vehicles left the lot. He didn't recognize Cranford, but didn't know how he operated. Maybe he came in, did the late afternoon sports show, then worked on articles for the late night airing and the next day. Or maybe he'd missed him in the flurry of cars.

At 7:30, he yielded to hunger, picked up a hamburger and fries at the McDonald drive-through and went to the office. He ate the fast food and finished the last of the coffee left from the days batch. He called Jennifer to let her know where he was and his plans to tail Cranford following the 11:00 p.m. newscast.

After she'd listened, she said, "Remember, don't do anything rash. Channing will be thrilled if he can find you doing anything out of line." She paused, "And, how's the shoulder?"

"Not the best, but I'm managing okay." Throughout the day he'd avoided quick movements and positions that seemed to exacerbate the ache.

At 11:15, he parked on the street outside Channel 14 again. He fought boredom, the throb in his shoulder, and the inclination to drop off for a short nap. At 11:45, cars began the nightly retreat from the lot. In the middle of the parade, he recognized Cranford in a sports car when he turned left out of the lot. Cranford gunned the hot vehicle and sped away. Dave followed, pushing beyond the speed limit to maintain sight.

Cranford stopped for a traffic signal at the intersection of Elm and Thirty-fourth street. Dave eased in behind him. He trailed Cranford as he swerved onto a side street and increased his speed. Dave dropped farther behind, but kept the taillights in view. After ten blocks, Cranford braked and pulled into the drive of a small frame house. Dave turned off his headlights and stopped a half-block short of the drive. He waited until Cranford entered the house, then jogged to the yard. In his haste and inattention, he kicked a discarded plastic bottle sending it against the curb, then stopped for a moment between two parked cars in case a neighbor's dog came out to investigate the noise. He edged closer to the Cranford's hideaway, hoping he could overhear voices rather than crash the place. The threats of Channing, Rasmussen's warning about a low profile, and Jennifer's reminders resurfaced as he considered his moves. And he didn't wish to have a physical encounter with Cranford with his shoulder at half its usual flexibility.

Dave eased toward a window, the blind partially lowered. No one was in his view, but he heard voices. After several seconds, he could discern Miriam's voice, pleading to be released from this prison, then Cranford bellowing for her to cease complaining or else. A few seconds later, Miriam screamed.

Resisting the urge to break through the door and confront Cranford, Dave returned to his car. Using his cell phone, he called Rasmussen at his home.

A drowsy voice responded. 'What's up?" No doubt the detective's typical question when the dispatcher or a patrol called late at night.

Dave said, "Sorry to get you up, but I know where Miriam Reading is being held by Cranford. I'd like you to send a patrol to get her out of there. If you can't do that, I'll either get her myself, no matter what Channing threatens. Or I could alert those guys who discussed the issue with Cranford's buddy."

"Did you call the dispatcher?" Rasmussen sounded awake and alert as he considered the alternatives. Dave recognized his friend had limited options. Anything he did could be deemed out of bounds by those above him.

"No. I figured he wouldn't do anything under the current climate. Look, I know this is impossible for you without stirring up a hornet's nest. Maybe forget I called and I'll go from here."

"No, the right thing to do is send a patrol. I'll worry about the consequences tomorrow. Give me the address. And I'll warn them not to come in with sirens and lights. Let's do this as quietly as possible."

"The address is 946 Peacock Lane. It's off Elm Avenue beyond the city park. And I'll wait for the patrol in case Cranford takes off before they get here."

Ten minutes later, two black-and whites pulled into the driveway. Two officers went to the front door; two others took positions allowing them to see any back and side doors of the house.

After repeated banging on the door, Cranford responded. The officers pushed in.

Dave heard arguing, but couldn't discern the words. No doubt Cranford was irate, thinking he was protected by his political friends or believing he was secure in this new location. And without doubt he was threatening firings and loss of pensions.

Five minutes later Cranford was led out, arms handcuffed behind his back, to one of the patrol cars. They sped away. He expected Miriam to appear immediately with the other two, but five minutes passed and he suspected they'd called an ambulance.

He was right. With a siren blaring and lights flashing, the hospital ambulance pulled into the drive. Two attendants in white coats jumped out. One grabbed a stretcher from the rear compartment.

Ten minutes passed and Dave had begun to think Miriam had been killed, but then the emergency personnel brought her out on the stretcher. She seemed to be connected to an apparatus leading into her arm. She wasn't moving, and he couldn't tell how badly she'd been hurt. He wanted to get closer, but didn't want the patrol cops to know he'd been involved.

By now neighbors had emerged from their homes to see what the ruckus was about. Dave slipped lower into the car seat. Stamping down the urge to doze off, he waited until the ambulance left with the cops following and the onlookers had returned to their houses. He drove home, vowing to take things into his own hands. Enough of this crap with Cranford. It was time to change the odds.

Jennifer had gone to bed when he arrived home. Trying not to wake her, he eased into the bath, rinsed the grime off his hands and face, downed one of the pain-killers, and pulled on his pajamas.

She roused when he pulled the covers aside. "Dave, did you find her?" She sat up and pushed hair out of her face.

"Yeah, but I don't know how she is. The cops called an ambulance and she was taken to the hospital."

"Good Lord. She's lucky you found her." She snuggled closer and put her arm across his stomach.

The next morning Dave visited Miriam in her private room at Chester General. Monitors hooked to her arms beeped their readings of vital signs. She appeared pale and drawn as Dave approached her bed. She opened her eyes.

Dave asked, "How're you doing?"

Her usual smile was absent. "I've been better, but they tell me there are no broken bones, except a rib has probably been fractured. They're doing another x-ray to be sure. Deep bruises and maybe some kidney damage where Billy hit me. The doctor wants to keep me for twenty-four hours to monitor everything."

"Then what?"

"I don't know yet. I thought I'd be safe around the station, but Billy waits for me, manhandles me into his car, and hauls me to some hide-away. It's been awful and the authorities seem not to care. They arrest him, but he's out within minutes to do it all over again. I've begun to think I must leave Chester if I'm going to survive."

"It's time for a different approach," Dave said. "I'll check back with you later today." In the doorway, he passed two grim-faced hospital personnel with charts in their hands.

Dave wanted to confront Cranford and threaten him if he didn't stay away from Miriam. He could goad Cranford into throwing a punch, then he would damage him so badly he couldn't walk for months, if ever again. Then he remembered Channing's desire to toss him in jail, no doubt spurred by former battles when the City Attorney had been forced to yield because Dave had critical evidence they'd overlooked. Plus, rash actions could jeopardize the image of the partnership and Jennifer herself. He concluded his inner struggle and went to the office. But deep inside, he hoped Cranford gave him the opportunity for physical revenge. He'd had enough of this tip-toeing around the fringe.

CHAPTER 11

As Jennifer and Dave were putting away the dishes and left-over food from dinner, the telephone rang. Holding a storage container of vegetables, Dave picked up the extension in the kitchen to greet Rasmussen calling from home.

His voice sounding tired, Rasmussen said, "I wanted to let you know I've been placed on administrative leave as a result of my sending a patrol to pick up Cranford."

"The Chief did this?"

"Yeah, but I've no doubt the order came from either Channing or the Mayor. I don't know how long this may last, but if it goes long, I may retire and give it up. I've enough years in, but I don't know what I'd do except drive Nora crazy."

"What can we do?"

"Probably nothing. But if I challenge the order by asking for a review, it'll only be worse. My wife and I have decided to disappear for a couple of weeks. We're going to visit my daughter in Seattle and do some sight-seeing around the northwest for a while."

"Bill, I'm sorry I got you in this mess. I should have taken action on my own rather than get you involved."

"Then you'd be the one in trouble. Channing is itching to charge you with Willard's murder, in spite of all the evidence indicating you couldn't have been the culprit. Plus, arresting Cranford was the right thing to do. If we hadn't, Miriam Reading could be dead."

"So can you tell me anything more about Hank Willard's murder?"

"What I tell you can't get back to Channing or the Chief, but Willard was shot once in the head with a 0.45 caliber weapon. Ballistics traced the gun to other murders committed over the past five years, but not to any user we can identify. He probably picked up the gun at one of these shows where dealers sell everything from machine guns to pistols, ammunition, knives, etc. Most often there is no way to trace these things. And Willard's murder has all the characteristics of a mob-style killing."

"You mean the beating and broken bones?"

"Yeah. The Medical Examiner is reasonably certain Willard would have died because of internal injuries. Could be he had died and the attackers made sure by a bullet to the brain."

"Maybe they were sending a message."

"Maybe, but I doubt anyone will heed it or even make the connection."

"Listen, have a good trip. Somehow all this will work out okay. I promise to do something to get this in the open, but I don't know what yet. And I feel badly for getting you into this mess."

"I'll call when we get back."

Dave replaced the receiver and turned toward the refrigerator. He felt guilty about Rasmussen's situation. He should have employed a different tactic in dealing with Cranford in spite of the threat from Channing. The itch to do something to end this crap with Cranford and the politicians surfaced again. He felt like the a person caught between two lousy choices with no obvious solution to his dilemma.

The possibility of generating publicity about Cranford's protectors came in a setting Dave would not have anticipated. He visited Miriam in the hospital the morning after talking to Rasmussen and found her sitting up, sipping juice through a plastic straw, breakfast dishes still on the tray by her bed. She was alert, watching the morning programs on television. Monitors blinked from a cart near her bed. Two flower sprays were arranged on the window sill.

When she acknowledged his knock on the door by waving a hand, he walked in and said, "Looks like you're doing better." He held her hand for a moment.

She turned off the television using the remote by the bed. "I am, although I have a badly bruised kidney and a fractured rib. The physician is coming by soon to talk about my being released and precautions I must take."

"Anything we can do? You know where you're going?"

At that moment, the doctor showed up. Without knocking or acknowledging Dave, he approached Miriam, asking, "How the pain?"

"I can tolerate it using those pain-killers."

He placed his stethoscope against her chest, moved it around a couple of times, nodding to himself. Then he checked her pulse.

Releasing her wrist, he asked, "How's the tape around your torso, too tight?"

"No, it seems okay. I can breathe okay."

"You'll need to leave it in place for several days until that rib knits some and avoid any pressure on that side for the next month. Let's make sure it heals properly."

Then he stepped back and said, "Ms. Reading, I'm very concerned that you continue to put up with this abuse. I believe this is the third time in the past two months you've been in here. Next time you may not be so fortunate."

Miriam grimaced and said, "I've tried to avoid my husband, but he's defied a court order to stay away. For some reason, the police refuse to charge him with anything. Maybe my friend here, Dave Randle, can fill in the details." Her facial features had gone from smiles to frowns as she considered the situation.

At the physician's gesture, Dave followed him into the hall. The physician stuck out his hand. "Dave, I'm Dr. Schofield."

Dave said, "She's correct. Her husband, Billy Cranford, has kidnapped her on three separate occasions, and each time she's been brought in for treatment. The Police Chief and the City Attorney have protected Cranford. Rumors are the Mayor has threatened to fire them if they press charges. Judge Chandler issued a court order for Cranford to stay away from Miriam, but he's been sheltered by the Mayor's order."

"Does the judge know about his ignoring the court order?"

Dave nodded. "My partner has alerted her to the situation. There's never an official record of Cranford's actions because of the cover-up so I think it's difficult for her to do anything until the cops report the abuse."

"Strange, strange world in which we live. I'm going to let Miriam go home tomorrow, but she must be protected from further battering. If you can, find her a secure place where Cranford can't get at her."

Dave nodded. "I'll give it a shot, but she's uncomfortable with people tailing her and watching her every move."

A woman was waiting for Jennifer and Dave when they returned from lunch. The small-framed blond dressed in a navy pantsuit and white blouse stood immediately and said, "I'm Wanda Easley from the *Register* and I'd like to talk with you about Miriam Reading. Dr. Schofield suggested I contact you." She extended her hand toward them.

Jennifer glanced at her watch and said, "Let's go into the conference room. We can talk a few minutes, but we have clients coming at 1:30."

As soon as they were seated, Easley opened a notebook. "Dr. Schofield gave me some information, but indicated you would know more about Billy Cranford's abuse of his wife and his protection by the authorities."

Jennifer said, "We can give you our version of the issue. However, we prefer not to be quoted or identified. City officials have let it be known we'd suffer the consequences of any accusations against them."

Her eyebrows raised a bit, Easley said, "I'll not identify you as a source, although Dr. Schofield seems willing to confront those breaking the law." A definite challenge rang in her voice.

"He's not as vulnerable as we," Jennifer smiled. "We need to remain out of the limelight for a time."

Within fifteen minutes they'd given her the gist of the series of abductions, beatings, visits to the hospital, refusals by the City Attorney and the Police Chief to hold Cranford accountable even though he'd ignored a restraining order. Dave added the most recent episode that led to the placement of an experienced detective on administrative leave.

Easley scribbled as rapidly as possible, asked a couple of questions to clarify statements, then asked, "Any ideas why Mayor Ridley is going to bat for Cranford?"

Dave said, "Initially we suspected an official at Channel 14 where Cranford works had some dirt on the Mayor, but recently we've learned the President of the station and the Mayor were fraternity brothers at Missouri. I've not attempted to confirm either of those possibilities. Both may be incorrect, but we know with some certainty the Mayor has called the Chief about Cranford."

When Helen Knight knocked and stuck her head in the door, Jennifer said, "I'm sorry, I have a client waiting. Perhaps Dave could continue."

Easley stood and closed her notebook. "I think I have enough and thanks for all the insights. I'll not reveal my source, but I may call to confirm things. I hate to print the wrong information. It results in the entire piece losing any credibility." She smiled and added, "Not to mention my boss screaming about getting the facts straight."

Easley's story merited the headlines in the Monday morning edition of the *Register*. Jennifer and Dave scanned the paper spread across his office desk.

Jennifer said, "She was certainly thorough, even questioning the action against Rasmussen, and quoting an unnamed physician and other witnesses to the affair. But Channing will know we were involved."

Dave grinned. "He can't prove anything. Plus, he'll be so busy defending his tail, he won't have time to look for sources."

"Let's hope that's true. I still have to deal with him on an almost daily basis."

Jennifer's and Dave's anxiety level jumped when Judge Chandler's clerk called at 4:15. Without explanation, the clerk relayed the Judge's message Jennifer should be in her conference room at 9:30 the following morning for a hearing on the Cranford case. Details were not communicated. Jennfer envisoned their firm being questioned about their participation in the cover-up or perhaps other questions she could not speculate about.

Judge Chandler entered her conference room in the City Courthouse at 9:30 on Tuesday morning. She seemed to take stock of those present for the hearing—Billy Cranford and his lawyer, Hiram Bixley; an accompanying executive, Arthur Zabrisky, from Channel 14 Television; the Mayor's Executive Assistant, June Skinner; Stuart Channing, City Prosecutor's Office; and Jennifer Watson representing Miriam Reading. Chandler took the chair at the head of the table and opened a folder.

Again looking at everyone, she said, "The article in yesterday's paper confirmed the rumors I'd heard about Mr. Cranford being shielded by city officials. I talked with several people in city government, including the Police Chief. Those sources validated the information in the paper. As a result of those clarifications, I've asked you to meet in this rather unusual session. I'm disappointed Mayor Ridley has been called out of town, but I'm sure Ms. Skinner can ably convey my thoughts about the issue before us."

Chandler paused, her eyes focused on Skinner for a moment. "If he has questions or concerns about my opinion, he is free to contact me for any clarification. Ms. Skinner, let him know that also. Okay?"

Skinner responded by shaking her head and saying, "Yes, Your Honor."

Chandler continued, "Two months ago at a court hearing, I determined based on evidence presented by opposing parties and supported by other witnesses, that Miriam Reading was a victim of abuse by Mr. Cranford. I issued an order banning Mr. Cranford from further contact with Ms. Reading. However, he has chosen to ignore that order and has on three different occasions abducted her and abused her further. She was released two days ago from Chester General hospital because of his latest act.

"For reasons beyond my comprehension, both the City Attorney and the Chester police have ignored the law, my restraining order, and their responsibilities and have allowed

Mr. Cranford to walk away without penalty. Somehow the Mayor has caused these escapades to be erased from or never entered into the books. Mr. Cranford has felt free to do as he wishes, knowing he was shielded by elected officials sworn to protect the citizens of this county.

"After the news article and additional confirmation of these actions through various channels, I have called you together to tell you they will no longer be tolerated by this Court. Many of the transgressions are beyond my reach at the moment, but I am fining Mr. Cranford ten thousand dollars and confining him to the local jail for ten days. There will be no appeal or additional hearing about the matter by my court. Further, I have requested the Chief of Police to arrest him immediately after these hearings. If the local police cannot do that, I intend to notify the State authorities."

Cranford and his colleagues shifted in their chairs and looked at each other as though they would challenge the Judge. Cranford whispered into Bixley's ear who nodded understanding.

Chandler ignored the shuffling and whispering, continuing, "Further, if after he has time to consider his actions and chooses to abduct or threaten Ms. Reading again, the punishment will be severe. By that I mean a minimum of five years in the state prison system."

She paused seemingly to let her warning sink in. "And for those of you who have protected him, I am putting you on notice effective immediately. Further interference with Court directives will not be tolerated. Moreover, I have notified the State Attorney General and the Superintendent of State Police about this mess."

When the Judge stopped, Bixley said, "Your Honor, my client needs time to get his responsibilities in order. I request that he be given three days to accomplish that."

Zabrisky chimed in. "The punishment is too severe."

Chandler stared at them long enough to effect an eerie quiet in the room. "Do I need to remind you that Ms. Reading has been in the hospital because of your client and employee? I think not. My order stands."

Chandler stood. "This session is adjourned. Officers will escort Mr. Cranford to the city jail. I trust you will convey my thoughts to others who may be involved with this sorry affair." She picked up the folder and disappeared through the door behind her. The group sat in stunned silence for several seconds, each waiting for someone else to make the initial move, then they shoved back chairs and collected papers.

As Jennifer left the room, Bixley and Cranford huddled with Zabrisky. Two uniformed officers stood near. She overheard them as Bixley said, "I warned you guys, but you thought she was too weak."

Cranford muttered, "What a bitch."

"We'll get her out of office as soon as possible," Zabrisky declared.

Stuart Channing caught up with Jennifer in the hall. "I hope you guys were not involved in these disclosures."

Jennifer stopped walking and faced him. "Stuart, are you threatening me? If you are, be prepared to defend all of your actions in the courts. I promise I will charge you with obstruction of justice, threatening an officer of the court and everything else I can muster evidence for. Further, I intend to discuss your actions with the Bar Association. You will have to answer to the State Attorney General. You are not beyond the reach of any of those bodies and neither is Mayor Ridley."

"You'd never charge me and get away with it."

"Try me. I'm tired of your skirting the edges of the law, ignoring evidence and throwing your weight around. This episode with Cranford is the last straw."

She walked away, leaving Channing standing alone in the foyer, but feeling good she'd not allowed Channing to intimidate her. He'd either not heard Judge Chandler's warning or still believed he was above it all.

Dave picked up his ringing telephone on his desk. "This is Edward Stafford. I'm responding to your request and with Donald Givens assistance, I've tracked down four other women who delivered deformed children after taking the Frasier medication. I'd sent a letter to local Medical Associations around the state asking that anyone who knew about such events to get in touch with either Givens or me. Thus far, those four have responded, but there may be more. As everyone else, physicians are slow to react to such things. Unfortunately, some won't make the connection between the medication and the outcome of their patient's pregnancies."

"I'll discuss this with my partner, but we'd like to follow up on those."

Stafford said, "I'll fax their names, addresses, and the relevant data for each, plus the names and addresses of their attending physicians. They're all in the Kansas City area. Givens will help get them together if you like."

"That's good news. We'll follow through and appreciate your efforts," Dave said.

Hanging up the phone, he headed for Jennifer's office.

CHAPTER 12

Jennifer and Dave flew into Kansas City on the early morning shuttle from Chester. A ten minute drive in an Avis rental car through moderate traffic brought them to the Regis Hotel, a smaller but well-known establishment that catered to business clientele who flew in, used the facility as a base, and departed the same day or the next morning. Donald Givens, Stafford's friend from medical school, had recommended the site and had made a reservation for a single room for Dave and a conference room under Jennifer's name. As expected, there would be a charge for a conference space and refreshments.

Parking in the hotel garage, Dave said, "Let's hope they'll all come. I'd hate to waste a trip Our expenses for this case are getting out of hand."

"We're a bit early. But I expect most will be here. It's in their interests we're doing this."

When they entered the second floor room, they were pleased to find four women waiting, chatting about common experiences. Coffee, juice, and muffins had been brought in and each had helped herself. Rather than the typical conference table, soft-back chairs were arranged against the walls. A podium had been shoved against the wall opposite the door.

Jennifer took charge, introducing herself then Dave and explained about their partnership. She invited them to move chairs into a more intimate semi-circle. The potential clients, women in their twenties or early thirties and seemingly healthy, rolled their chairs closer. Then at Jennifer's request, they introduced themselves.

From her position in the group, Jennifer said, "Through your physicians, and I trust with your permission, we have obtained copies of your records detailing the progression of your pregnancy and the disastrous outcomes. We have not had time to review those yet, but will in the next few days.

"At this point, I'd like to explain how our firm, Watson and Randle, became involved. A client of ours in Chester went through the identical ordeal and with the same outcome as each of you. While we are still gathering information and background materials about the drug marketed by Frasier, it seems reasonably clear that the medication was the primary factor in the deformities and deaths of all the children. Our client intends to file a suit against Frasier for malpractice and wrongful death of her child. We believe our case will be stronger if you and others unite in a class-action suit."

A blond woman in a black pantsuit asked, "What does class-action mean?"

Jennifer explained the basis, saying, "A class action suit is filed on behalf of a group of individuals who have suffered the same abuse or have been damaged in some way by wrongful or negligent acts of an individual or a company. It avoids multiple suits by the individuals and usually gives strength to the case as the defendant, in this case Frasier, is less likely to convince a jury or judge that it was sheer happenstance that the condition occurred in any one of you when there are several with the same problem."

Again, the blonde asked, "And you're recommending that we join with your client?"

Jennifer nodded and sipped from her coffee mug that Dave had handed her. "I am, but you must be completely satisfied with this approach. You may wish to discuss the issue with your own attorneys, physicians, and family members before you commit."

"Would we have to testify in court?" The query came from a small brunette, sitting somewhat out of the circle as though she had concerns about mingling with the others.

"Perhaps. We'll need to work through the details after we've obtained all the pertinent information and decide who among you should testify. It could be none of you, but you must confront the possibility. Again, talk with family, physicians, attorneys, ministers, and feel comfortable about doing this. Please don't commit, especially agreeing to testify, then drop out. It only weakens the case by making the defendant believe you have reservations about going forward. It hurts you and the others who have joined with you."

The blonde smiled and said, "In short, once in, always in, until the end."

A larger woman, hints of gray in her black hair, said, "I'm prepared to join with you and hope the others will also. After talking with my physician, I'm convinced what Frasier did was negligent, maybe even criminal."

Jennifer said, "I can't stress enough the benefits of your joining in the common cause. I also want you to be committed. If you have any doubts today, think about the situation for a few days, then give us a call to give us your decision. For those of you who believe you wish to join today, we'd like you to complete a brief questionnaire that focuses on the progress of your pregnancy, the complications suffered by your child and several other questions about yourself and your physician. We will discuss each of your situations with your physician and learn as much as possible about how they came to administer the drug that we believe caused the damage."

"If I fill out the form today, I assume I could still drop out." This came from the small female who didn't look old enough to think about having children.

"Of course. But we will reach a date when I will ask that none changes her mind. We cannot give the any hint of wavering after the suit is filed with the court."

Dave handed out the forms. "If you have questions, talk to either of us. Anything you tell us will be held in confidence. The more details you're able to give, the better. We have pens if you need one."

Each of the women completed the form, a set of questions devised by Jennifer and Ellie, and designed to reveal the treatments and symptoms each had experienced, their history of child-bearing, a brief medical background, and identification of the physician who had prescribed the drug. Dave had taken a draft by Stafford for his modifications and additional insights.

As they completed the questionnaire, Dave paged through them for any gaps or handwriting he couldn't decipher.

With all the forms completed, Jennifer said, "Thanks for coming and we'll be in contact with you. In addition to our client in Chester, there may be others that have not yet been identified. And there's one more thing I should tell you that may or may not become an issue.

"When the Food and Drug Administration approved this drug, they had evidence of successful usage, thus not every woman who's been placed on the drug has experienced the same outcome as you. Still, there should be a plausible explanation for those who responded differently."

The blond asked, "What could be different for us?"

Jennifer said, "The most likely possibility is something in your genetic makeup. To try confirming that possibility, we may at some point ask that you give a sample of blood to your physician so we can check for any common genetic traits that are different than those who did not have problems. Again, anything we find of that nature will be confidential to be shared only with the individual and perhaps her doctor."

The older woman asked, "Have you reviewed the histories of those who participated in the preliminary trial as a basis for the FDA action?"

"We are in the process of obtaining those records."

"If you fail to detect differences, will you go forward with the case?"

Nodding, Jennifer said, "Yes. There are too many of you to ignore the issue. But being able to demonstrate the primary reason behind the problems will strengthen our position. We will argue the company should have looked for those or should have known about the possibility based on preliminary tests."

The small woman sitting to one side asked, a faint smile across her face, "I suppose one of us should ask about the amount of damages we should seek and what percentage will you take?"

"Both are reasonable questions," Jennifer said. "Like most others, our firm usually takes one-third of the settlement, but sometimes we've reduced our fee because we felt the people needed the funds more than we. In this situation, I'd think about twenty-five percent and our expenses would be a reasonable division. As to the amount you should ask, I'd recommend something in the range from five hundred thousand to one million each. After all, each of you sacrificed a child because of Frasier's failure to adequately test the drug or outright negligence. At some point before we file the suit, we will determine an amount for each plaintiff."

"Will you ask our opinion?" The same woman who initiated the discussion about damages.

"Yes we will, likely by telephone or e-mail."

"But you can't really know, can you what a judge or jury will do?"

"True," Jennifer smiled, "but we will present some number as a starting point in our submission to the court. You are likely aware that judges often hold down the awards if a case seems frivolous in any way. I doubt that will happen here. After all, the loss of a child cannot be described as lacking merit and we will do our best to seat a jury who understands that and what it means to lose a newborn."

When the group seemed content, Jennifer said, "We appreciate your coming today and we'll remain in contact with you as we move forward." She stood and the women shook her hand, then Dave's hand.

After they'd cleared the room, Dave said, "That went well. Now you have five, including Miriam, but we'll find others."

Dave rolled the chairs back into the original positions. Jennifer collected the completed questionnaires and stuffed them into her briefcase. "I'm going to the airport, but I hope your session with those physicians goes okay."

"Remember, I'm doing some checking for that client, Roger Ebert, who's last contact with his daughter was in Kansas City after I meet with the physicians Givens is getting together. That'll take a few hours."

She smiled and leaned against him. "I remember. I wish I could have rearranged this meeting tonight with the Bar Association committee but it couldn't be done."

His arm around her waist, Dave said, "You could come to my room and relax for a bit."

"I know what you have in mind, but I'd better get going. Plus, we're getting too old for hanky-panky in the middle of the day."

They walked down a flight of stairs from the mezzanine to the lobby and through the front door where several taxies were waiting for potential riders.

Jennifer reached to kiss Dave on the cheek. "Take care. See you tomorrow."

Donald Givens had arranged a meeting at the downtown Marriott with other physicians whose patients had experienced pre- and postnatal complications or losses after using Plertex. He'd warned Dave that although they'd agreed to come, any one of them could be delayed or called away for some emergency.

Dave arrived fifteen minutes ahead of the scheduled noon meeting and found the small conference room where lunch would be served. A waiter had placed water glasses at the table and was in the process of laying out napkins and utensils on a rectangular table with a dozen chairs around it. Reminding Dave to alert him when to bring in the food, he disappeared through a side door.

Donald Givens arrived with two others precisely at twelve. Givens said, "Westlake called to say he couldn't make it, but if you wish, he could meet you privately tonight. He suspects his experience will match ours."

Dave invited them to have seats and rapped on the door for the waiter. Taking a chair, he said, "I appreciate your coming and Dr. Givens' help in setting this up. We've arranged for a set lunch, and the waiter will show up soon for drink requests."

After drinks were placed, Dave wasted no time in starting. "As you know, we're representing women who used a drug from Frasier Pharmaceuticals with disastrous results. We've discussed the situation with Dr. Stafford in Chester and with Dr. Givens to the extent we know each of their physicians prescribed the drug based on information given to them by a representative from Frasier. In each case, the treatment seemed effective, but each child was born with severe deformities. Earlier today, we met with the women who are interested in filing a class-action suit against Frasier. To the best of my knowledge, none intends to file against you."

Givens said, "That's good news." They all chuckled in agreement.

Lunch plates were brought in and the discussion lagged for several minutes as they ate salads and half-sandwiches. Two neighbors asked about families. Givens and Dave talked quietly about the session with the women.

As plates were pushed away, Dave asked, "If you would like dessert and coffee, let me know." None took the offer but looked at watches, his clue to move forward.

Dave said, "If you don't object, I'd like to record our conversation. This will aid us in keeping our facts straight." He turned on the small recorder in the center of the table.

"One of the issues we believe may be important is the manner in which you learned about this experimental drug and the way in which Frasier courted you."

Givens said, "As I told you before, a sales rep from Frasier brought samples and information pamphlets by the clinic. I scanned the material one evening and thought it was worth trying in this patient experiencing severe cramping and bleeding during the second trimester. Nothing else had alleviated the problem and my experience was that such conditions led either to a miscarriage or spending the rest of the pregnancy in bed. The information sheet indicated the drug had been tested on a sample of pregnant women and had been approved for wider use by Food and Drug. I gave the medication to this patient and her symptoms cleared immediately. However, a scan during the third trimester showed malformation of the fetus. She decided to give birth but the child died within two weeks."

He paused, sipped his iced tea. "Some time later, Dr. Stafford in Chester and I happened to discuss our patients during the state medical convention and realized the cases were essentially identical. In some way, I take responsibility for not doing more checking about the drug, but when FDA gives its blessing, I take that as an okay signal." He placed the glass on the table.

The others had nodded agreement throughout Givens revelation. Then another, Dr. Appleton said, "I had the same experience." The third one agreed by nodding.

Dave said, "It seems each of you has a similar story. Now elaborate, if you don't mind, about your experience with Frasier prior to this drug. Were you courted, taken to dinners, things like that?"

Dr. Appleton grinned and said, "My experience with Frasier is almost unbelievable. My wife and I were invited to take a cruise at Frasier's expense. We spent five days on this luxury liner, dined and drank to our hearts content. During the trip, the Frasier representative made sure everything was fine, but at every opportunity, dropped information about the company and the good things they were doing. Of course, by the end of this excursion, I was a Frasier convert."

"Were other medical people on the same trip?" Dave asked.

Appleton nodded. "I met at least four other physicians, one of whom I'd interned with, but there may have been others I didn't meet. There was never a session for those being sponsored by Frasier."

Then Dr. Nelson spoke up. "I didn't get the cruise treatment, but my family and I were taken to this resort in the Ozarks for a three-day outing. Everything was paid for by Frasier—meals, plush rooms, drinks, golfing, swimming lessons for my son, you name it and we could do it. Much like Appleton, I came away with a feeling somewhat akin to indebtedness to Frasier."

Knowing time was running short, Dave said, "So each of you had received favors from Frasier and would you agree, you were more likely to use their products and give them less scrutiny than before?"

Appleton responded, "I'd agree with that." The others nodded agreement.

Dave said, "Obviously, we suspect such special treatment by Frasier played a huge role in the willingness of medical personnel to prescribe their products."

Givens said, "That's true to some degree, but the fact is all those companies do the same thing. I could spend at least a month each year on cruises or golf outings supported by companies dealing in medicines or equipment. They're pervasive and aggressive. I've taken the position I'll not take any of their freebies."

"We all should have done that with Frasier and since that experience, I've made a practice of not accepting any freebies from now on," Appleton said. "If you think it helps your case, I'd be willing to testify about the prostitution of the medical profession, although I don't believe it influences our work with patients, except when we fail to thoroughly investigate some new product they're pushing."

"But it gives the impression that it could," Givens said, "and I suspect in some instances when we're confronted with decisions about which medication to prescribe, we tilt toward the one who most recently provided some favor."

Nelson, who'd not participated much, said, "You're right, but it's hard to stop when these companies become our foremost link to new products. To their credit, they provide a service by keeping us updated on recent research and innovations."

When Givens looked at his watch and shifted in his chair, Dave said, "I'm willing to talk more, but I know you have busy schedules. But we may want to contact you again as we get closer to the actual trial."

Nelson stood and came to shake Dave's hand. "Don't let the bastards buy you off."

CHAPTER 13

Dave's mission to satisfy the client searching for his missing daughter proved to be a dead end. Following directions given him by the concierge and armed with a city map, he found the address given him, but the site was an empty lot. He called the telephone company and the utilities department of the city. Neither had the name of the daughter or a close facsimile of her last name. Finally, he checked with postal service without success. He gave up the hunt, frustrated he'd wasted several hours on a wild goose chase. He drove back to the hotel.

From his room he called Jennifer to let her know he'd not make it back tonight. They talked about his meeting with the physicians and her trip to Chester. Feeling the need for exercise after a long day of sitting, he wandered up to the workout facility on the top floor, rented gym clothes and worked through all the machines available. Back in his room, he practiced martial arts stances, thrusts and jabs for a while, expecting his shoulder to react with a throbbing pain at any time. When he stressed the muscles, nothing happened, causing him to feel relieved and back to normal. He paced for a while, cooling his system, showered, dressed and found the restaurant on the main floor.

* * *

The Wednesday morning edition of the *Register* highlighted another article under Wanda Easley's byline. Her interview with members of the Chester City Council indicated their dismay and deep concern about the actions of Mayor Ridley in his abuse of power in protecting Billy Cranford. Neither were members pleased with the involvement of Stuart Channing, the City Attorney. A long-time member was quoted as recommending both resign and he promised he would press for that outcome at the next Council meeting. Neither Ridley, Channing, nor Arthur Zabrisky, the President of Channel 14 Television, would comment. Cranford, from his jail cell, refused to talk to Easley.

Easley provided a sketch of the actions of Cranford in his continuous harassment of his wife now separated and seeking a divorce. She revealed the Mayor's involvement and the caving in by Channing and the Police Chief. She speculated that the Mayor had been either bribed or held hostage by some past event Zabrisky threatened to reveal. True to her promise, she'd not hinted at the sources of her information.

On page three a short blurb indicated the police had exhausted clues related to the murder of Hank Willard, but made the connection between Cranford and Willard. As usual, the Chief promised a continuing investigation until they solved the crime.

Looking over Jennifer's shoulder as they scanned the paper, Dave said, "They won't solve it. Those mob guys seldom leave any clue worth looking into."

Jennifer said, "We have a good idea. Should we tip the cops to talk with Monk?"

Walking away a couple of steps, Dave looked at her. "I have mixed feelings. First, we don't really know Monk's guys were involved. And if we give them his name, it will destroy Monk's operation that we may need again. Plus, it would likely lead to Gibbons and I don't want that to happen. He's been off the screen for three years now."

She grinned. "As far as we know. We have no idea about who he deals with from that dungeon he calls an office. Not to mention his home."

Dave said, "I'd be more inclined to drop a hint if they hadn't screwed Rasmussen. There was no reason to do that other than Channing and the Mayor throwing their weight around."

Jennifer folded the paper. "Let's keep it to ourselves, but you know if Channing ever found out we had a lead or even a suspicion, he'd come after us big-time."

Dave grinned in return. "Then maybe I'll alert Monk about Channing's actions in putting Miriam in danger."

"If he reads the paper, he knows now."

"Monk won't do anything unless either Gibbons or he become targets."

"To get back to another facet of Miriam's case, Tom Ware called late yesterday. I have another session with Congresswoman Womack on Saturday. She obtained more definitive information about those FDA hearings. I hope that includes the names of the women who were subjects in the Frasier trial, but Tom didn't know."

"And Helen has set up an appointment for me with Rose Mitchell at Biological Assays to talk about a DNA analysis for some common gene shared by the women in our class-action suit. I just hope I can understand enough to know where we should go with that idea." Dave shook his head. "I've read a couple of articles about DNA and the genetic code, but it's still fuzzy stuff for me."

"It's coming together," Jennifer said, picking up the ringing phone.

Dave sat across from Mitchell, a Ph.D. biologist, in the small conference room at Biological Assays, an organization he and Jennifer had come to rely on for a variety of tests. Solvent odors from the adjacent laboratory reminded him of earlier visits. As usual, Mitchell had on a white coat, the international uniform for lab workers, and a name tag on the pocket. He explained the issue with the women and their desire to investigate a commonality in their genetic makeup, then added, 'We're really over our heads with this, but a genetic difference has been suggested as a possible explanation."

Mitchell's lips, tinted light red, curled into a semi-smile. "Unless Frasier cooked the tests, but you'd think FDA would catch on to that. However, the hypothesis that genetics is involved may have merit. We know certain problems during pregnancy run in families. If the mother had difficulty, the likelihood is increased the daughter will experience the same condition. There's no way to know about this specific situation until we conduct tests to compare those who had favorable outcomes against those who didn't. What we'll need are DNA samples from both sets of women. And remember, these are not inexpensive assays to run."

Dave asked, "Can we be certain we'll find anything through this approach?"

Rose shifted in her chair and leaned forward, putting her elbows on the table. "There's considerable risk we'd strike out. Comparing DNA's is somewhat like looking for a needle in a haystack when you're not certain what you're looking for. We could find it quickly or we might not find any differences at all. But, if those attending physicians are able to indicate some basis for what went wrong, it could give us a starting point."

"So your advice is give it a try."

Rose seem to ponder the possibilities for several seconds, her brow furrowed as she contemplated the best approach. "We could start with samples from a woman who delivered a normal child and from your client with the ill-formed child. We could work on those two and see if we get anywhere. If we fail to detect any difference, you could decide to press ahead or give it up, depending on the finding. To be certain of our findings, we'll need to run checks on several women. There'll be numerous differences for sure. To be on solid footing we'll need to isolate the gene common to all of those affected by the drug. Then compare that to women who experienced no difficulty."

Dave said, "That seems a reasonable approach. I'll do that. I'll ask them to have their doctors obtain sample or come directly to you in the next few days." He stood and reached across the table to shake Mitchell's hand, adding, "It's good to see you again and thanks for your advice."

"Give my regards to Jennifer and remind her we must get together for lunch one of these days."

"I will but she stays busy."

From his conference with Mitchell, Dave went to Stafford's office, hoping he could squeeze in a short visit among the doctor's patients for the morning. But his luck didn't hold. The receptionist shook her head, saying, "I'm sorry. He's filled for the day and as usual, he's running late."

Before turning away and giving up, Dave asked, "Does he ever stop for a drink on his way home? Maybe we could meet that way."

She smiled. "I think he does at times and he'll need one after today. Tell you what. I'll raise the question at the next patient change and give you a call. Okay?"

"Thanks for your help. If that doesn't work, maybe I need to get sick and make an appointment."

"Or come in early before he starts with patients."

S. J. Ritchey

When they met at the front door of the downtown Marriot per instructions left for Dave, Stafford said, "Sorry I couldn't work you in for five minutes today, but it's been a rush. Never seen so many pregnant women before."

They were led to a small table in the middle of the large bar area. Both ordered draft beers, then Stafford said, "So how're things with Miriam Reading?"

"I haven't seen her since she got out of the hospital. I assume she's okay with Cranford locked up for another few days. The reason I wanted to meet was to pick your brain about an idea we're exploring." He explained the possibility of a genetic difference in responders to the Frasier drug. "Actually, you planted the seed the first time we met when you thought Miriam's problem might be a combination of drugs, genetics, or some other factor."

"My friend Donald Givens had the same thought when we first discussed the similarities in our patients, but I haven't thought much about it or tried to find any background references."

Dave told him about his visit to Rose Mitchell and the need to locate a woman in good health who'd had a successful pregnancy and a normal child after using the Frasier medication, then said, "I thought you might put us on the lead to someone or perhaps you'd had a patient who fit the criteria."

Stafford sipped his beer. "I haven't. Miriam was the only one I placed on the drug. After her experience, I didn't want to chance it again. I could scout around, ask at the next meeting of the local Medical Association. There must be one in the immediate area with all the efforts Frasier had put into marketing the concoction."

"When will they meet? We're trying to push this as quickly as possible."

Stafford dug out of his inside coat pocket a small appointment book, looked for a moment, then said, "Next Tuesday evening. I'll make sure to go, although I miss a lot of those."

Dave had hoped it would be sooner, but he said, "Good, and your friend Givens was a huge help in getting those physicians together in Kansas City. We had a good session."

As they talked further about random subjects, Stafford said, "I read in the paper some time ago about your history with special forces. I think it was related to your dealing with those thugs at the retirement home."

"I try not to think about those days, but I fall back by instinct on the training and experience that were so deeply ingrained into my very being."

"I was impressed. You know only about one-tenth of one percent of those in the armed services can meet the requirements for those duties."

"I've heard that figure before. I always causes me to think about the demands put on those personnel and their capacity to respond under severe circumstances." He swallowed the last of his beer and shoved the mug aside.

Stafford glanced at his watch. "Dave, I need to go. One of my kids has a school function tonight and I must show up. But I'll get back to you after the meeting next week. And I'd like to talk more about your service time. My dad was a career Army officer who spent most of his time in intelligence, primarily behind a desk in the Pentagon."

As they moved toward the door, Dave said, "He probably sent orders for my unit, though we never knew the source. We were told not to try finding out."

"Even if you'd tried, no doubt you would have run against the brick wall of bureaucracy inherent with those departments of the federal system."

Congresswoman Womack's schedule seemed to be less hectic on Saturday when Jennifer arrived for her 9:00 appointment. They sat at the conference table with coffee mugs in front of them. While Womack arranged papers, Jennifer glanced around the room, realizing all the wall photographs and art had been changed since Womack had taken over. The Governor's portrait had been moved from the side wall to the front.

The papers now positioned in front of her, Womack said, "Well, I've been successful in finding out more about those FDA hearings. They were contentious and ended up with the scientific panel voting against release of the drug, but as you heard, the Commissioner overrode their recommendation and permitted Frasier to move forward. The person who keeps minutes of those hearings met with me and a person in my office. However, she was unable to find the names of women who participated in the initial trial. Those were retained by Frasier on the grounds of protecting their privacy."

"That's disappointing but understandable," Jennifer said. "We were hoping to contact some of those participants and discuss their experience as part of our case against Frasier, especially if some had unsatisfactory outcomes."

Womack said, "I'm sorry I couldn't obtain those for you, although I can't argue too much against their protection of private records. Nevertheless, I was able to do a couple of things that might be useful."

Womack opened a second folder, retrieved a sheet and handed it to Jennifer. "There are two names there. Dr. Rosalind Peters is on the FDA panel and led the debate against release. My office called her and she would be willing to talk with you.

"The second name is Dr. Russell Ardmore who worked for Frasier for several years as an employee and then as a consultant and has some knowledge about that trial. He recently retired but I believe he is credible as well as irritated with the company.

He may, according to Peters, know a lot about how Frasier treated the data from those women. She's interacted with him at scientific meetings and thinks he'd be willing to share his insights with you."

Jennifer asked, "I hope he's not one of those disgruntled employees trying to exact revenge on the company?"

"I can't be certain of his feelings, but he had a niece in the Frasier test group. From what I could decipher, she had the same experience as your client. I'd recommend you meet him, as well as Peters. Their addresses and telephone numbers are in the file I'll give you."

Jennifer glanced at the information, than said, "I see there are both in the Washington area, so we can likely accomplish our goal with one trip."

"If you like, I could get my assistant to set up a session with both of them. Maybe in my offices would be as good as any place."

"That would be most appreciated," Jennifer said. "I'll look forward to your call."

CHAPTER 14

At 5:00 p.m. Dave waited for Miriam as she completed her work day and came out the side door of the Channel 14 building. She smiled when she saw him and increased her pace. To his surprise she hugged him close, the feel of her sensuous body reviving old memories. He pushed aside the urge to pull her even closer.

Removing his arm from her waist, he said, "I came by to see how you're doing and to make a request."

"I'm good, but Billy gets out tomorrow." The look in her eyes changed from happiness to dread as she considered the possibility of another ordeal.

"Where are you staying?"

"At my new place on Melrose. You and Jennifer will have to come by sometime."

"Are you secure there?"

She shrugged and shifted her purse from one hand to the other. "It's a gated community. You have to insert a pass card to open the entrance, but my concern is Billy snatching me as I leave here or as I leave the grocery store or wherever. That's what he's done the last two times."

Dave said, "I'll work on that so you are safe. But you must not leave alone. Wait for other people. And stay in crowds when you're shopping."

Frowning, she said, "I know, but I hate to go through life running scared. Anyway, what do you want me to do? I know you didn't come by just to check on me."

He explained the process of comparing DNA samples and said, "Either go by Biological Assays, or have your clinic take a swab from your cheek and take that by. Rose Mitchell will know what it's about."

"I'll do it tomorrow."

"How are your ribs? I know first hand how painful that can be."

"Much better. I was able to take off the binding two days ago, but I'm careful about what I do. I still feel pain when I'm in certain positions." She edged away as though she had to be somewhere.

Dave watched her get into her car and leave the parking area, his thinking about how to protect her. Even when she didn't wish to be sheltered.

From the office Dave called Monk. After identifying himself, he said "I wondered if you can help Miriam for a few days starting tomorrow? I'd like one of your guys to watch when she leaves work. If Cranford grabs her, have him follow."

Monk growled, "We won't follow, but we'll protect her."

Dave hung up hoping he'd done the right thing. He could visualize Cranford with a slug through the head like Hank Willard and he'd feel some responsibility. But he didn't have a better plan to protect Miriam. The cops wouldn't bother and he didn't have the time to be available every day. But perhaps the recent publicity would restrain Cranford. He probably wouldn't risk another confrontation with Judge Chandler. And the chances of being arrested and charged had increased now that Cranford's protectors were on notice to cease and desist. But the history of control freaks didn't bode well for him to act in a responsible manner. At some point the would snap and do something rash.

Jennifer flew into Reagan National airport and following instructions from an aide in Womack's office, took the Metro to the stop nearest the Rayburn Office building. Most seats on the car was were taken but no one was standing in mid-morning, the rush hour having passed.

Washington weather had taken a distinct turn toward summer. The heat and humidity baked her as she trudged along the concrete emitting waves of heat. The slight breeze failed to dampen the impact. She recalled earlier business trips to the D.C. when she'd worked in New York but those ego laden lawyers wouldn't stoop to ride the public transit and insisted the cab drop them as close as possible to the door. She stopped under the shade of a tree and slipped off her jacket.

At the entrance to the huge building, a guard asked for an identification and opened her purse and briefcase after she'd walked through the metal detection apparatus, a significant change in protocol since the terrorist threats had changed the existence of everyone who worked in places likely to become targets. The guard, a sturdy dark-skinned male, smiled and directed her toward the elevators. She deviated her path into a rest room to straighten her blouse, replace her jacket, and run a comb through her hair.

The young red-haired receptionist in Womack's suite led her to a small conference room. She said, "The others are present, but Ms. Womack is unable to join you at the moment. Coffee, tea and soft drinks are on the sideboard." She spoke in a monotone as though she delivered the same greeting numerous times during the day.

Sitting next to each other at the rectangular table with coffee cups in their hands, Dr's Rosalind Peters and Russell Ardmore were talking as she entered. They both stood as she came to shake their hands, saying, "Thanks for coming. I know this is an inconvenience for you."

Peters, a gangly woman, gray-hair combed neatly around a long face with minimum makeup, said, "We trust what we know will be useful to you. Congresswoman Womack has explained your case."

Ardmore, gray-haired and balding, slender but shorter than Peters, echoed her thought.

Jennifer found a soft drink on the side table and sat across from them. "I'll get down to my questions as I know you have busy agendas." She rummaged in her briefcase and handed them business cards.

Ardmore grunted and smiled, "Not any more. Retirement allows me to set my own agenda, but I say no to a lot of requests."

"I'd like to record our conversation for future reference, if you don't object." She placed the small machine in the middle of their grouping.

When both nodded acceptance of the intrusion, she turned on the instrument and recorded the date, place, time and names of participants.

"If I may," Jennifer said, "I'll begin by asking Dr. Peters about the hearings before the FDA panel. I've learned the group denied Frasier's request to release their experimental drug, AK-427 P or now marketed as Plertex, but the commissioner didn't heed your recommendation."

Her voice strong, causing Jennifer to visualize her lecturing to a room of students and daring anyone to fall asleep, Peters replied, "That's correct. In fact, I was the one who first questioned the data shared by Frasier. They had twenty women in the preliminary trial, but shared the information from only sixteen. That was a tip-off that everything was not quite as rosy as Frasier wanted us to believe. When we pressed them for the data from the missing four, they responded with a bevy of excuses—miscarriage and didn't complete the test, dropped out, moved away and lost her address. In my mind they were all pretty lame if the company is expending thousands of dollars to verify the safety and performance of this drug. Bottom line, I didn't trust them and convinced a majority of my peers to vote down their request until they brought in all the data."

She paused, sipped from her coffee, and continued, "You know, Ms. Watson, any scientist worth their salt wants to see all the numbers. Sometimes it's the negative ones that open your eyes to additional questions and eventually to the truth. Ignoring those so-called outliers is not acceptable to me or to most of my colleagues."

"Did you know why the Commissioner overturned your recommendation?"

Peters smiled. "Politics. I'm truly disappointed in this administration. Every decision comes down to pleasing some friend, most often because they have given big money to campaigns or can sway some constituent group to support these politicians. It's democracy at its worst. But of course, the commissioner never met with us to explain his rationale."

Jennifer turned slightly in her chair. "Now, Dr. Ardmore, I believe you worked for Frasier and may have a different version of what occurred."

As Ardmore opened a folder on the table, Peters walked to the side table and refilled her coffee cup.

Ardmore said, "You're right, I worked for Frasier for twenty-five years in their research and development department. My background is biochemistry and I'd worked at Michigan State before joining Frasier. It was an exciting place to work because they were willing to explore those areas ignored by most companies because the problems were too complex. Frasier was not big in comparison to others, but it did some nice work. And their products had a solid reputation. Their drugs did what Frasier said they'd do with little or no downside for the patient."

He grinned as though thinking about the good times. "Of course, because they tackled the difficult, they didn't make as much money as others. But five years ago, Frasier was bought out by a larger firm. New management came in and the focus of the company changed."

Jennifer checked her recorder and asked, "How do you mean?"

"Our research focus became more routine and we focused on variations of products already on the market, gave it a new name, and sold it to the public. We sought the quick answer and began to ignore those areas we'd worked in for years. I was disappointed and frustrated because I'd done research on a potential drug for seven years, but was forced to drop that work."

"Were you involved in the development of Plertex?"

Shaking his head, Ardmore said, "No, but colleagues in an adjacent lab were the primary scientists in formulating the drug. I'd known them for years and knew they were concerned about the sudden rush to finish the product."

"Did they talk to you about it?"

"No, but little hints of frustration came through at times— you know, over lunch or riding the Metro together. Once I asked a question and this buddy whom I'd known for years just shook his head and said he was told not to discuss the progress with anyone outside the immediate lab. That was almost unbelievable in an organization that had thrived on open communication as a way of getting insights from as many co-workers as possible."

Ardmore stood and refilled his coffee cup. "Fortunately, I was able to retire two years after the new people took over. I wasn't there when this drug was tested but my experience after that point became personal. When Frasier sought volunteers to be subjects in testing the drug, my niece called me about enrolling. She was pregnant with a first child and was having difficulties early in her pregnancy and wanted my advice.

"Based on my past work with Frasier, I recommended she do it. My experience with Frasier had always been good, although I was not directly involved with the product testing phase. I'd never heard of short-cuts or cooking the data so to speak, to get the outcome you desired. The reluctance of those involved to discuss the situation caused me to think seriously about the possibilities of something going wrong, but my faith in Frasier overrode those issues. I didn't raise objections.

"So Andrea became a subject. The symptoms of her problem disappeared immediately, but the child was born severely malformed and died within ten days. Frankly, I was devastated, thinking I had led her into this trap."

He sipped coffee, making Jennifer think they would need a rest room break soon. But Ardmore continued, "When I learned the drug had been approved for general distribution, I was floored, called a couple of colleagues still with Frasier, but they wouldn't discuss it with me. But this woman, a friend of ours through our church, who is on the staff at FDA called me to tell me there were others who had the same problem as Andrea and that some lawyer in the Midwest was exploring the potential for a suit against Frasier. She also suggested I call Congresswoman. Womack's office."

Jennifer nodded. "That's because I'd contacted Ms. Womack to check on the hearings. But did Andrea ever know others in the test group or receive a list of the group?"

Ardmore pondered the question for a moment, then said, "I'm not sure, although she did mention, sort of in passing one day, that a person she knew had been given the Frasier medication and had a normal delivery with a healthy child. She had encountered this woman during one of Frasier's routine check ups of the participants and while waiting their turn, compared notes. You know, like all pregnant women tend to do," he grinned, "and sometimes pregnant fathers."

Jennifer said, "The reason I asked is a couple of physicians have suggested the basic problem in those who had deformed children could be genetic in nature. Some way the drugs and her genes weren't compatible and thus the problem. They didn't really know but were speculating. We would like to check out the possibility if we can locate enough women to make our comparisons credible."

Peters jumped in. "It sounds like a shot in the dark, but that's why you don't discard information from those who don't fit your original theory. I don't know enough genetics to be helpful, but a colleague of mine at Hopkins has been involved with the Human Genome project. She knows as much as anyone about those things."

"If you could give me her name and telephone number, I'd like to discuss it with her."

Peters said, "I'll have to look up the number, but I'll e-mail it to you tomorrow."

"I'll get the name of this woman from Andrea and send that to you," Ardmore injected. "And if per chance she has a roster of the participants in the Frasier test group, I'll fax that to you, but I doubt that's available to anyone outside the immediate scientists doing the tests and the top administrators."

Jennifer asked, "I've learned it's typical to test a new drug in a small number of subjects, then if everything seems okay, conduct a larger trial. I've heard Frasier ran a trial using two hundred women. Did either of you ever know that to be true?"

Ardmore shook his head. Peters blurted, "Why do that? They had the go-ahead to market the product."

Jennifer said, "You've both been helpful and I understand you could be reluctant to testify if this ever goes to trial, but I'll ask about your willingness anyway."

Peters jumped in. "I'd do it without reservations. You can call me as a witness or whatever."

"I'd have mixed feelings," Ardmore said. "I want to support Andrea who, by the way, might be interested in your class action suit. But I still have residues of loyalty to Frasier. They were good to me for many years and I dislike employees who turn on their organizations at the least bit of provocation."

Peters stood and placed her coffee cup on the sideboard. "Ms Watson, I must leave because of a late afternoon lecture, but if I can help you further, let me know."

Her decision prompted Ardmore. "Likewise for me."

Jennifer asked, "Did you drive here?"

"I drive to the end of the Metro system and take the train downtown," Ardmore said. "Parking is too expensive and difficult."

"I took the shuttle from Baltimore to Reagan, then used the Metro to here. It's more costly than driving, but it saves me time." Peters added, "And I can use the time on the plane to do some work."

Jennifer shook their hands, thanking them again and feeling as though she'd been in the company of keen minds who knew their subject matter as well as anyone. After they departed, she reviewed her notes, and listened to the tape. At the present she didn't know the extent of the usefulness of the information, but she'd learned quite a bit about the process of testing new products and the political influence often brought to bear on what should be a scientific endeavor. And she'd confirmed her suspicion that Frasier had not followed through with a larger trial which might have caused them to modify the formulation before rushing to market.

She was thinking about food when an aide came in. "If you have the time, Ms. Womack would like to have lunch with you. She usually walks to the cafeteria, but if you'll join her, we'll pick up food and bring it here. That would give you some privacy."

"Thank you. That would be nice. Now can you point me to the nearest restroom?"

Womack came in shortly after Jennifer had returned. She looked exhausted, her eyes rimmed with dark circles, her shoulders seemed to sag under the weight of her black suit jacket. She dropped into a chair, and mumbled, "It's been a rough couple of days. I was in St. Louis last night for a political party activity, after hearings and committee meetings all day, then hearings again this morning. I haven't had much sleep in the past three days."

"But you are accomplishing some important things. Getting Dr's Peters and Ardmore together for me was wonderful."

Womack smiled, a faint upturn of her mouth. "Thanks for a bright note in my day. It helps to have a few of those among the constant arguments based for the most part on party lines rather than seeking compromises for the betterment of our citizens."

She hesitated as though uncertain of how to broach the issue on her mind, then almost blurted, "I had a personal reason for wanting you to meet in my offices. I need a smart attorney on my staff and hoped I could persuade you to come to Washington for the next year. Just see how life is and what you can get done. Then if I am reelected, your appointment could extend."

Caught completely off-guard, Jennifer couldn't respond for several seconds. Images of Dave and their growing partnership raced through her thoughts, their remodeled house, their garden project, their jogs along the creek, and the clients who depended on them. It would go down the drain.

Finally she responded. "I'm flattered, but my place is in Chester. I've lived in New York and while all the hustle and bustle is exciting, I've settled in where I am and hope to stay there."

"Think about it. I know this is sudden, but you would be a true asset to both me and your fellow citizens. Let's talk again the next time I'm in Chester. Now let's find out what the staff had brought in for lunch."

CHAPTER 15

Jennifer's return flight to Chester was filled with whirling thoughts of the day's events. She'd hoped to doze, but her mind was too restless with the additional insights into the Frasier suit, knowing that there were four failures in the preliminary trial and that one of them, Andrea, would likely be joining the litigants. While the genetic-drug interaction possibility seemed remote, there were still leads to that end. And perhaps it didn't matter, if she could demonstrate Frasier's failure to reveal all the data and basically conceal the failures. That in itself would persuade a jury that the pharmaceutical company was not quite honest and women had suffered because of their devious behavior.

But the offer by Womack had floored her. At one point in her career when she'd concluded that the huge New York law firm was not in her best interest, she'd considered working for a Senator with the belief she could make differences in the formulation of new legislation and in the interpretation of current statutes. The chief aide to the Connecticut lawmaker had made a persuasive case for her potential influence. But her home area presented it's own attractions and the possibility of establishing her own firm had been part of her dream in choosing to go into law. In spite of the slow startup, the firm in Chester was now thriving and she was being recognized for her work in the legal profession. She couldn't give those up for the glamour of the Washington scene. And she couldn't put Dave in the position of looking for a new position if the firm folded. After a gin and tonic and the so-called dinner meal, she knew she would reject Womack's offer.

Dave's smiling face and firm hug when she arrived at the airport cemented her decision. She wanted in this partnership and marriage for the long haul. She wouldn't tell him about Womack's tender knowing he would insist she give it full consideration and begin to look for ways to make it all work.

Two days following the Chester Medical Association meeting, Stafford called Dave at the office. "I've located a control case for your test. She used the Frasier drug and had a normal child. She's coming in tomorrow to have me obtain a DNA sample and I'll have my assistant run it out to Biological Assays."

Dave said, "We'd like to talk to her if she's open to that."

"I'll ask her when she's here. I don't even know her name yet but she was a patient of Bob Hastings who practices in Mims. He is contacting her today to set up the appointment. He's certain she's willing to do that much."

Dave ended the connection realizing Stafford had become a real advocate for their case, doing things to foster their collection of information useful to their suit. He called Rose Mitchell to alert her to be on the lookout for the sample from Stafford's clinic.

Then Miriam called. "Dave, I wanted to update you on a couple of things. First, I gave a blood sample to Biological Assays. Second, yesterday afternoon as I left work, Billy approached me. He said he wanted to talk and asked that I go for a drink with him. I was suspicious and said no, that I was concerned he had some scheme to grab me again. Then he yelled and grabbed my arm. That's when these two hoodlum-like guys rushed from their car parked near the exit from the building. One of them pointed a gun at Billy and told him the next time he touched me would be his final act on this earth. They scared him badly enough he rushed away. It's the first time I've ever seen him back down from a confrontation."

"Were you concerned they'd harm you?"

"Initially I was, then I recognized the one with the gun. I'd seen him around Monk's place and talked to him at dinner a couple of times. They didn't say a word to me, just turned and left when Billy scampered away."

Dave said, "So you know why they were there, I asked Monk to look out for Cranford as you leave work and go about the routine things you have to do for a few days. He took my request seriously."

"Those guys are scary. They might start shooting and kill people who are passing by."

"The flip side is Cranford won't bother you near the station. They mean what they say. It's not an idle threat."

"I guess I should thank you. Lord knows what would have happened if they'd not been around."

Three days later, Jennifer responded to a request from Hiram Bixley, Cranford's attorney, to meet with the two of them and Arthur Zabrisky, the President at Channel 14 Television, to discuss the pending divorce hearing before Judge Chandler. They, along with Miriam, met in their conference room. She had alerted Dave to be around in case Cranford pulled one of his macho stunts.

The atmosphere in the room was tense as they found chairs, aligned across the table in opposition to each other. Cranford glared at Miriam then at Jennifer as though trying to intimidate them. Zabrisky couldn't sit still, constantly shifting in his chair.

Giving up on Bixley to begin, Jennifer said, "Mr. Bixley, we're open to your suggestion regarding the divorce proceedings. On the phone you had hinted at attaining some settlement rather than go to court."

Zabrisky jumped in by saying, "I haven't been able to understand why Billy and Miriam can't get back together. It's his desire to do that, but she refuses any overtures from him."

Jennifer placed her arm on Miriam's and said, "It's fairly simple, Mr. Zabrisky. His overtures have been in the form of kidnapping, battering, intimidation and threats on her life. My client has ended up in the hospital on three occasions and is too frightened of Billy Cranford to get near him, much less try to reconstitute the marriage. From her perspective divorce is the only option. She wants him out of her life."

"I called Bixley to arrange this meeting," Zabrisky said, "and avoid a nasty court hearing open to the press. The station doesn't want the publicity that will emanate from that process and neither does Billy."

Bixley shuffled through papers in front of him. "I'm proposing that Mr. Cranford and Ms. Reading seek a settlement and avoid the court process. He is agreeable to that and is prepared to move forward as rapidly as possible to conclude the separation."

"On what terms?' Jennifer asked. She and Miriam had discussed various options by telephone earlier. Miriam wanted out. Terms were meaningless to her at this point.

"I'm recommending they split their common assets, establish separate residences, sign a no-fault divorce agreement with the court, and go their separate ways with no payment of alimony or damages."

"That's acceptable to Ms. Reading," Jennifer said. "And I believe the only common holding is the house and some furniture. Since neither of them reside there, I suggest the property be sold and the proceeds be divided equally. The furniture can either be sold or divided as they can agree."

His hands balled into fists on top of the table, Cranford muttered, "I don't want any of that stuff. She can have it."

Jennifer ignored Cranford. "If we are agreed on the terms, I'll draw up the legal documents and have both parties sign with a notary present. We can file the papers with the Clerk to finalize the divorce. I will notify Judge Chandler regarding the outcome."

Miriam said, "And I want it clear that my position at the station will not be jeopardized."

Zabrisky nodded. 'I'll put that in a letter to you. In spite of all this fuss, we value both of you in the organization. My goal in getting involved is to prevent negative publicity that only hurts the operation."

"And Mr. Cranford must remember the court directive from Judge Chandler remains in effect," Jennifer added. "Further contact with Ms. Reading is out of bounds and violation of that ruling will lead to punitive action by the judicial system. Understood?"

Cranford nodded and Bixley said, "He understands and intends to abide by that order."

"If the parties like," Jennifer said, "my office will contact a realtor and oversee the sale of the house. When there is an offer, I will contact you both and obtain your agreement to the terms of the sale."

"That would be okay with us," Bixley said. "And we will look forward to concluding this deal." He stood, followed by Zabrisky and Cranford.

As the door closed behind them, Miriam said, "Thank you for bringing this to an end. Now I can get on with my life."

"But be wary for a while," Jennifer said. "It's well documented that abusers like Cranford never fully get past their urge to control and dominate others who they believe is their property. You read in the papers frequently about former husbands and sometimes wives who just cannot let go with the final outcome being murders of one or both, including any one else involved in their lives. I'm concerned Cranford is one of those who allows their rage to boil over. If you noticed, while he was shaking his head in agreement, he had his fists showing."

"I know. He can't control himself."

"The issue we let slide with Cranford was any damages because of past abuses. If you wish, we can bring that back to the table."

Shaking her head, Miriam said, "No, let's get it over with. It's not worth the hassle. My insurance has covered most of my medical expenses and seeking damages would take too long. I want to move on as quickly as possible."

Jennifer brought her up to date on the Frasier suit. "So we have a lot of pieces of the puzzle to be examined, some of which will not work out. Nevertheless, I hope within another month we'll be ready to file with the courts."

Dave found the address for Hazel Turner in Mims without a hitch. Past cases had brought him this small community north of Chester enough he knew his way around.

Turner, a late twenty-year old, with brown hair and a pleasant smile, answered the door on the first ring of the bell and invited him into the living room of the moderately priced home. She said, "I'm glad you called rather than take a chance. Most mornings I'm out doing things in the community."

Dave said, "I appreciate your giving a sample for our review. It may be important to our case or it may not lead anywhere, but we have to be certain."

"My doctor explained the reason. I was surprised because I'd not had any difficulties and my little boy is wonderful." A smile creased her face as she thought about him. "But I got thinking about the drug because a friend of mine took the medication and her girl was so badly damaged, she didn't survive the first week. On top of that her husband left her and she became so depressed she's going to therapy on a regular basis now."

"And you're sure she was given the same drug?"

"She showed me the container once when we were having lunch after our aerobics class for expectant mothers. Of course, then neither of us knew how things would work out. And I'd forgotten about it until my doctor called me about giving this DNA sample."

"Does her physician know about the other women who had problems/"

"Don't know, but I doubt it. He's an older man who is slowly giving up his practice by not taking new patients, but he's been their family physician forever. I suspect he doesn't keep up with recent findings in the medical field as well as he once did."

Dave said, "I'd like to talk to your friend if she'd be willing."

Turner stood and straightened her tan slacks. "Just a minute. I'll call her and maybe you could go there from here." She disappeared through the door and after a brief interval Dave heard her talking.

Within three minutes she came back, smiling as she walked toward him. "She'll see you now. She's Katherine Mosby. She's in the brown house with the big maple in the front yard, middle of the next block."

"Thanks for your help," Dave said. "I'll walk from here."

Katherine Mosby was standing in the front door of her home when Dave walked toward it. Her slim figure, further enhanced by her tight-fitting blue and white sun dress, hemmed above the knees, captured his attention. She asked, "You must be Dave Randle?"

"Yes, and you're Katherine Mosby?"

Inside Dave told her about the deformed children from women who'd used the Frasier drug and said, "Mrs. Turner indicated you'd had the same problem."

"That's correct. Our child didn't live but ten days. My husband blamed me for not taking care of myself and we separated three months later."

"You still have a sample of the medication?" Dave wanted to verify she'd used the experimental drug from Frasier before he delved further.

"I think so. Let me look." He watched her disappear into the next room, thinking she was one of the more attractive females he'd been around in a while.

Katherine returned in a minute with a bottle and handed it to Dave. "This is it. Frasier Pharmaceuticals. My doctor prescribed it when I had problems early on in the pregnancy, and you know the outcome. I didn't think much about the drug as the culprit and neither did my doctor. We chalked it up to fate, except my idiot ex-husband who blames someone for everything."

Dave explained the testing being done by Biological Assays to try connecting the drug with some genetic characteristic. "We'd like you to participate in that as well as the class action suit against Frasier. We believe they should be held responsible." Throughout his discourse, he was aware of her staring at him as though examining his innermost character and crossing her slim legs to reveal knees and thighs.

"I'll do both. I can go by today to give the sample while I'm in Chester. I'm starting work next week as a sales person in Penney's and have to complete payroll information for them."

Dave stood. "I'm pleased you're willing. The more who join the suit, the better our chances of success. I'd appreciate your completing this form which gives us information about your experience with the drug and related things. You can mail it to the address on the top."

She came near him, almost touching, to take the form and envelope from him. "Would you be interested in coffee?"

Pushing down the temptation posed by an attractive female obviously interested in him, he said, "Thanks, but I'd better keep moving. I'll let you know how the testing turns out. And don't forget the form."

He was aware of her staring at him as he turned onto the sidewalk along the street.

CHAPTER 16

Two days after her return from Washington Jennifer received the fax from Ardmore with his niece's name and address and to her surprise, the list of women who'd participated in the Frasier preliminary trial for Plertex. He was unable to identify the four who'd had problems. Neither did he reveal how he'd come up with this information, but he asked that she not disclose him as the source. She surmised he'd wrangled it from some friend associated with the actual field trial and who would lose his or her job, or worse, if identified. Now she had to determine how best to use this data without revealing her knowledge of the participants or her source.

Later in the morning she received an e-mail from Peters with the name and address of her friend working on the Human Genome project. She forwarded that name to Rose Mitchell, thinking Rose would know better what questions to ask the experts deeply involved in the science.

The office settled into the normal routine of handling problems of clients as they waited for a break in the Frasier suit. Dave visited with Roger Ebert to tell him his daughter, Margaret, was not at the address he had given Dave.

Dave suggested the police would be better able to mount a search than a one-man investigator. "Mr. Ebert, what I'm saying is I've done what I can do. I'm sorry it didn't work out."

The old man stared at his shoes for several seconds. "I guess you have. Send me my bill and I'll pay you for your efforts."

Dave left, feeling sorry for Ebert and thinking how he could reduce the fee they'd normally charge for a portion of the plane fare to Kansas City, mileage on a rental car, and other expenses, plus the hourly rate for services.

They'd weeded their garden for an hour after work. Soon they could harvest some of the vegetables and reap some benefit from their efforts. Tomatoes were appearing on the vines now requiring staking or the fruit would drag in the dirt. They'd harvested some lettuce already and green beans were coming soon. After dinner they'd sat around reading the papers, scanning magazines, and giving scant attention to the television.

Then at 9:35 the announcer broke in. "We have received word of a serious altercation at the Chester Country Club. We know few of the details at this time, but a man was badly hurt when he was attacked by another during a social function. His female companion was thrown to the floor but other than minor bruises seems to be okay. Police were called but the attacker, identified by witnesses as Billy Cranford, the sports caster for Channel 14, had disappeared. The injured man, not identified yet, was taken to Chester General but we don't know the extent of his injuries at this moment. We will bring you more details as they become available. Now we return to our regular program."

Jennifer said, "Well he didn't restrain himself very long. I'd bet the woman was Miriam."

"That'd be a good guess. If Rasmussen were here, I'd give him a call. But I'll see what the morning news has to say."

"Surely Cranford just won't disappear. Channel 14 depends on him."

"But Cranford doesn't think about consequences. His temper overwhelms any constraint. He might just hide out for a while, hoping the cops will forget and and the injured guy doesn't press charges."

"Maybe we should check on Miriam first thing tomorrow. Plus, we need to get a phone number for her new place."

They had just entered the office the next morning when the telephone rang. Ellie, always early, called to Dave, "It's Chief Drummond."

Dave picked up, thinking it might be news about Rasmussen, but the Chief said, "Dave, I'd like to talk with you about Billy Cranford. Can you come over in a few minutes?"

Thinking about his recent confrontations with the city officials, Dave asked, "This is not some ploy to tie me into Cranford's disappearance, is it?"

"No, but it's something I hope you help us with. It involves Billy Cranford."

Fifteen minutes later in the Chief's office, Dave said, "I heard about the set-to at the Club. I assume you haven't found Cranford yet."

Drummond, heavy set, graying on the sides, shook his head. "We've issued a APB, but I thought you might have ideas about his hide-outs."

For a moment Dave considered walking out after the way Drummond had caved in and mistreated Rasmussen, but he thought this might be a way to mend some fences with the Chief. "I know the locations of the two residences where we've found him previously, but you know those as well as I."

"We looked at those last night without success. Plus, we posted lookouts at both in case he returns."

"Chief, all I can tell you is keep your spotters out. I'd guess he'll show up around the TV station pretty soon. And you might have someone tail Miriam Reading. He's hung up on her and all his problems stem from his desire to control her. If nothing else, she needs protection until Cranford is brought in."

Leaning back in his chair, Drummond nodded. "We're doing that. She was the female involved at the club." He continued, "Apparently Reading and Bill Jackson were talking at this reception for Channel 14 advertisers. Cranford approached and asked, witnesses say demanded, she leave with him. She refused. Jackson suggested Cranford quit bothering her. Cranford slammed Jackson in the face, knocked him down, kicked him in the side. In the scuffle Reading was knocked to the floor. At that point Cranford seemed to realize what he'd done and ran through a side door leading to the parking lot. No one has seen him since."

"Who's Jackson?"

"He an executive with Mason Auto Parts. They run ads continuously on the station."

"I've seen those. How is he?"

"Broken nose, fractured ribs, but he'll recover and I'm sure will file assault charges."

Drummond stood from behind his large oak desk, piled high with papers. "I'd like you to keep an eye out for Cranford. I realize we've been on your butt for other things, but that's in the past."

"Sure, I will and let you know if I happen to see him."

Drummond's face contorted into a tight grimace and he shook his head. "What I'd really like, if you will, is to actively search for Cranford. According to Rasmussen, you seem able to locate people when we can't. We'll pay your hourly rate for the time you spend and any expenses." The police had done this rather unorthodox thing in the past, but it'd always been through Rasmussen, but Dave figured the Chief had to agree to any expenditure of funds and had tacitly agreed to the arrangement.

"I'll work on it," Dave said, "as I have time. By the way, when is Rasmussen back?"

Drummond shuffled a pile of papers and frowned as though trying to erase an unpleasant subject. "Next Monday."

Wanting Drummond to know how he really viewed the situation, Dave said, "He got a bum deal, you know."

Eyes on his desk top, Drummond responded with a shake of his head and, "I feel badly about what went down, but the Mayor gave me no choice."

Dave turned away, but at the door stopped to say, "I'll let you know how it goes with Cranford."

After several days of no news about the Mayor's involvement with Channel 14 and Cranford, the morning edition of the *Register* headlined a long article under Wanda Easley's byline about the City Council meeting. They had voted to ask for Ridley's resignation, the most surprising part was they had agreed unanimously against him. Of course, the Mayor was making all kinds of excuses for his action and swearing it was all a misunderstanding.

Easley had uncovered information about the relationship between Ridley and Zabrisky revealing they had indeed been fraternity brothers, but in addition, Ridley had married Zabrisky's sister. The reporter suggested without any direct statement that the Mayor's tendency to cheat on his wife had raised Zabrisky's ire to the point he'd threatened to reveal the several affairs, the latest of which was with a close associate in the administrative offices of the city. Anyone on the inside would know that to be June Skinner but Easley had not identified her.

The City Council had, as per Easley's article, scheduled a meeting with Stuart Channing to hear his version of the cover up. That his position was in jeopardy went unstated.

Jennifer handed the paper to Helen Knight. "Looks like it's all coming to a head. I bet Ridley resigns within a couple of days, then Channing will follow in a week, just after his session with the Council."

Still scanning the article, Helen said, "Could be, but politicians have a way of squirming out of bad situations and hope the voters will forget by the next election. It's almost a game with some of them."

Dave met Miriam for lunch at Gibbons the day after he'd talked to Drummond. Following his custom when Dave came in, Gibbons wandered by as they settled into a booth and scanned the menu. The old man said, "Good to see you both but I won't squeal to your wife you've been seen around with this other woman." His face broke into a crooked grin, discolored and disfigured teeth showing in his creased face.

Dave introduced Miriam to be sure Gibbons knew who she was, although she been in the restaurant several times. They talked briefly about the business when she suggested he advertise on Channel 14. Then Gibbons shuffled away when the waitress came to take their orders. As usual Dave had the daily special of clam chowder and a roast beef sandwich. Miriam settled for the Chef's salad with a vinaigrette dressing on the side..

Dave said, "In addition to finding out you're doing okay, I wanted to pick your brain about Billy's typical pattern of activity. What did he do when he wasn't working? Any favorite bars? Any buddies he hung out with?"

Miriam sipped her iced tea, her face without expression. "He wasn't very open about what he did and where he went, but he wasn't around home much. I recall taking a message to meet some friends at a place called Dizzy's. It's on the outskirts of the city near where Joplin Street approaches the interstate."

"Were you ever there?"

"Once with Billy we stopped in coming back from a road trip. It's better inside than outside. Bunch of guys, mostly truckers I thought, sitting around, drinking beer and watching television. Waitresses in short skirts and low-cut blouses. But overall, pretty quiet the night we were there. I thought I heard pool balls crashing together in a back room, but we didn't go in there."

Dave tried the chowder, stirred it again to cool it a bit more. "If Billy were hiding out somewhere, where would it be? Any special buddy who'd risk alienating the cops?"

Miriam laughed softly. "He has several who'd do that. One who called him a lot at home was Rod Wilson. They'd played ball together in college. Now Rod is a manager with an interstate freight company, but I don't recall the name."

"So you know why I'm asking these questions is Chief Drummond would like me to help the police find Cranford. For some reason Drummond believes I have this ability to locate people the cops can't find. Truth is, they don't work at it."

She grinned. "And you have connections they don't, like Gibbons and Monk."

Dave let her comment pass without a response. "Have the police talked to you since the altercation at the country club?"

"Some uniform cop took my statement at the scene, but they've not asked about Billy." Shaking her head, she said, "I see what you mean about not working at the task."

Dave shoved the plate aside. "Rasmussen is the person who drives any investigation. Since he's been put on leave, no one has taken up the responsibility."

They finished their meal in silence, both thinking about Cranford and the possibility he'd skipped the country and would never be found. As they laid aside utensils, Dave asked, "I assume you're doing okay. You look great."

"It's good at the moment. I'm getting back in the groove at work. Been working out at the little gym in the apartment complex. I'm careful where I go. Keep to the busy places where there are crowds." She smiled, "And I see Monk's boys around at times."

"Should I ask him to pull them off?"

"Not yet. I feel more secure knowing they're close, especially with Billy running free and not working. But they probably scare the daylights out of others who see them lurking around."

Dave picked up the check. "I plan to search for Cranford as I can work it in to my other cases. I'll let you know."

"How's Jennifer?"

"Doing great. The suit against Frasier is coming together, but we have some important pieces yet to fit into place."

Miriam reached into her purse and handed Dave a slip of paper. "Here's my telephone number at the apartment—it's unlisted. I don't want Billy or one of his buddies calling me. I've given it only to Monk and the secretary at the station."

Rose Mitchell phoned Jennifer. "I've compared those samples from the women. As you'd guess, they have numerous genes that are different, so I've had some difficulty in knowing where to look for that specific one associated with the problem during pregnancy, if it exists at all. But this morning I received a fax from Dr. Peters. She'd discussed the possibilities with her friend on the Genome project. And after some digging and consideration, they suggested I concentrate on chromosome fourteen. Based on her understanding of the genetic code, she thought that if there are differences I'd locate them there. So we're plowing ahead to compare those pieces in the next couple of days."

Jennifer said, 'At least you've narrowed the search."

"Let's hope so, but it's still a huge puzzle."

CHAPTER 17

Dave parked between two vans in the lot on the west side of Dizzy's. At 9:15, the neon sign shone brightly, partially illuminating the graveled area. The street lamp atop a high pole at the corner of the intersection added more light. Assorted type vehicles filled most of the marked spaces and had spilled onto an adjacent grassy area. He waited a minute for a pickup with two men to park and for the occupants to walk into the front door. Dave followed a few paces behind, thinking he wouldn't be so conspicuous behind the two who were likely steady customers. He eased onto a bar stool at the end of the long fixture. His jeans and tee shirt, a baseball cap pulled down across his forehead, matched the prevailing dress code.

The bar was crowded with a mixed group, primarily males unwinding after a long day on the job or others just killing time as they watched the Cardinals and Giants on the large screen TV. Several women mingled with males at tables for four. The bartenders and waitresses rushed about filling orders with a minimum of talk, only stopping when someone asked for a refill or their check. Idle chatter between the staff and customers seemed out of place.

When the bartender approached, Dave ordered a draft beer. The brew came immediately, foam bubbling over the top, moisture gathering on the icy stein. Dave sipped the beer for a few minutes, then looked around the room. No one he recognized. He guessed most of the customers were either truckers or salesmen staying overnight in motels near the interstate. After thirty minutes, he walked through the crowd into the rest room. Conversation focused on highway conditions west of Chester. Apparently, there'd been a downpour that resulted in a crash and subsequent blockage of the interstate for a couple of hours. While rinsing his hands in the men's room, one guy was muttering to a buddy about lost time and the need to make it up tomorrow.

Back on his stool, Dave requested a second draft. By 10:45, the establishment had emptied except for three men who'd come in late and yelled for beers before reaching a table. When the bartender came close, Dave asked, "You this busy every night?"

"This is pretty typical." He looked more closely at Dave. "I haven't seen you in here before."

"This is my first time. I was to meet a buddy, but he didn't show. I'm going to give it up and try again later in the week."

"Is he a regular? Maybe I know him."

"Could be. Name is Rod Wilson. He's with a trucking organization that does a lot of business along the interstate."

Wiping spillage on the bar, he grinned. "Yeah, he comes in here once a week or so, usually with men he's doing business with. His office and truck park are a half-mile down the road. Last time he was with some big man who looked familiar, but Rod didn't introduce him."

"You recall what night that was?"

The middle-age man scratched his jaw, wiped the towel across the surface of the bar. "I think it was last Thursday, but you know, it's easy to not remember exactly."

Dave slipped off the stool and dropped bills on the counter. "I'll try again, but it's too late for him to show now. Maybe I got the signals crossed."

"Take care. Better luck next time."

Jennifer was dressed for bed but watching the downstairs TV when he arrived home. He touched her cheek, saying, "Well, some progress. Cranford has been at the place with Wilson in the past few days. I'd guess they'll show again."

"That means Wilson is sheltering Cranford somewhere near."

"That'd be my guess. On the drive home I thought about alerting Drummond and let him put his people in Dizzy's. I could spend a lot of time and never hit the same night they show." He put his cap in the closet near the front door.

"Drummond will press you to continue the vigil for a few days or until he runs out of money to pay a hired hand."

He sat on the couch and pulled her legs into his lap. "So I'll give it another couple of nights. If I strike out, maybe Drummond can put a scout around Wilson's place." He caressed her knees and lower thighs.

Jennifer said, "I take it you're ready to adjourn to the upstairs."

"If you are."

"I was hoping you'd be in the right mood."

"You know I am most of the time." To her surprise, he picked her up. As they moved up the stairs, their lips met.

* * *

Suspecting Wilson would stick to some routine, Dave entered Dizzy's on Thursday evening at 8:45. He found his stool at the end of the bar available and perched on it, ordered a draft, and nodded recognition at the bartender when he placed his drink.

The place was as busy as before with a steady hum of talk and the constant movement of the waitresses and customers pervading the room. The baseball game had been rained out and replaced on the TV by a rerun of an old movie no one seemed particularly interested in watching. The sound had been reduced. Most of the patrons sat quietly, nursing a drink and talking to others at their table. Some stared into space, apparently thinking about the next day's work, getting home, or nothing.

Dave felt the draft of air when the front door opened, but didn't look up. Two men passed him as they headed toward a table in the rear. Suddenly, a hand grabbed his shoulder and spun him on the stool. Cranford rammed his face close to Dave's, almost yelling, "You tailing me, you bastard."

Wilson clutched Cranford's arm and tried to pull him along. "Come on, stay out of trouble."

Cranford shrugged off his friend's hand. Still close to Dave, he poked him in the chest and grabbed his tee shirt.

The bartender yelled, "No fighting in here."

Cranford ignored him and balled his fists, ready to crush Dave. But he wasn't prepared for the quick thrust of Dave's flat hand across his throat.

Cranford stumbled backward, his hands holding his throat, his mouth gasping for air, his eyes blinking and watering. Before he could recover, Dave rolled off the stool and kicked him in the gut, dropping him to his knees.

The room had gone quiet as the people tried to see what was happening. People at the nearby tables moved away, not wanting to be caught in the melee. Dave said, "Don't get up. Stay down."

His eyes on Cranford, Dave barked to the bartender, "Call the cops—now."

Wilson reached down to help his buddy to his feet, but Dave shoved him away. "Let him stay down." But knowing Cranford wouldn't yield so easily, he moved away to avoid a kick or sudden rush.

When Cranford put his hands on the floor, Dave prepared for some new attack. Cranford suddenly sprang toward him intending to tackle him or jam him into the bar stools. One huge arm hit Dave across the shoulder, but Dave moved too quickly for him to grab and hold. Dave thrust a stiff hand into one of those vital places in Cranford's mid-section below the rib cage. Cranford dropped to this knees again, his face white, obvious pain racing through his entire system.

Dave pulled Cranford's arms behind his back and shoved him to the floor, his face against the grimy tile structure.

Wilson yelled, "What have you done to him? He looks crippled."

"He is, but he'll recover. As for you, stay put. The cops will want to ask you about harboring a known fugitive."

Cranford moaned in pain. Wilson dropped to his knees so he could see Cranford's face. "He's going to die, you bastard. What'd you do?"

Dave said, "He'll be okay but it will take a few minutes."

Cranford showed signs of recovery after several minutes. He struggled to sit, then almost collapsed again, but Wilson held him in a sitting position.

Dave was preparing for the next onslaught when two uniformed cops burst through the front door. One yelled, "What's the problem here?. His nightstick was in his hand.

Dave pointed to Cranford and Wilson. "The one of the floor is Billy Cranford. His buddy is Rod Wilson. Chief Drummond wants them both."

The cops looked at each other. The leader shook his head. "Yeah, we've had a search going for Cranford, but nothing about Wilson."

"Take them both," Dave said. "I'll meet you at the station and explain it all. You probably should notify the Chief or whoever's in charge of the night shift."

Dave met with the Chief the next morning. Drummond said, "Finding Cranford didn't take you long. You must have known something we didn't."

Unsure of what Drummond was pressing for, Dave said, "No, just usual detective work. Ask a couple of Cranford's acquaintances about his habits, buddies who might shelter him, and likely hideouts. Then wait and watch at the most likely spots, hoping luck will be on your side. In this case, it came pretty rapidly."

"What do you know about Wilson other than he operates this trucking company and is a friend of Cranford?"

"Not much else. They were football teammates in college and one of my sources thought Wilson might be a person to watch since they hung out together at times."

The Chief came around his desk. Shaking Dave's hand, he said, "I appreciate your quick work with this deal. We'll charge Cranford with assault and battery and other things. As for Wilson, I don't know yet. But send me your bill."

Dave reached in his coat pocket. "Here it is. Eight hours, twenty miles of travel, three beers and lunch for two will cover it." He decided the city should pay for his lunch with Miriam. She had been his source of information leading to Wilson and then to Dizzy's.

On the way out of the station, he detoured by Rasmussen's office. His friend was at his desk, his feet propped on a partially open desk drawer, staring at a sheaf of papers in his hand.

Dave rapped on the door and asked, "You remember how to do this stuff?"

A grin spreading across his face, Rasmussen got to his feet. 'I'm learning all over again. This is my first day back. I'm still not settled into any routine." They shook hands.

"How about lunch. Bring me up to date with your travels."

"I'd like that. Bring Jennifer and I'll call Nora to join us— Gibbons at noon."

"Sounds like a party."

As they walked along Main Street returning from Gibbons, Jennifer said, "Rasmussen seems pleased enough with the way things turned out. An apology from the Chief and full reinstatement of responsibilities. But I'm somewhat surprised the City Council is now inquiring into Drummond's behavior." Rasmussen had dropped the nugget during lunch. He wondered aloud what it all might lead to but quickly dismissed any rumors he could replace the Chief.

"They should, "Dave said. "If he'd done his job, he would have resisted Ridley's threats about firing. He should know the Council wouldn't go along with that."

"Maybe he's insecure with all these politicians."

They waited for the traffic light to change amid a crowd of pedestrians returning to work after the lunch break. Dave lowered his voice. "I'd like to see Rasmussen become chief but I doubt he'd take the job if offered. He doesn't like all the political crap the top dog has to put up with."

"Don't blame him." She put her arm through his. "And your special relationship could disappear."

Rose Mitchell called mid-afternoon. An edge of excitement sounded in her voice. "Jennifer, I believe I've made progress with your gene testing problem. I discovered a segment of the DNA along chromosome 14 different in the women with deformed children from the normal birth mothers. But I don't have confidence in my results because of the few numbers involved."

"What should do we do then?"

"Two things. First, I'm faxing my data to Dr. DeVries, the one who worked on the genome project. She can tell me if my supposition makes sense. Second thing is, if she thinks I'm on the right track, I'd like to run the analyses on more subjects."

"How many more?"

"The more the better but if I could get information from eight or ten of each, I'd feel fairly confident in telling you you're on solid ground before a judge and jury."

"Any suggestion there is a difference could influence a jury," Jennifer said, thinking about how confusing all this scientific stuff was to lay people. And to the legal profession as well who tried to deal with a different jargon.

"I know, but I'd like to know our data are reliable. Who knows, it could influence the way drugs are tested in the future. Or make drug companies examine those negative responders."

"We'll work on locating other women and getting samples to you," Jennifer said.

"It should go faster now that I know where to focus my search."

"Let me know what DeVries thinks."

Jennifer replaced the receiver and smiled to herself. Progress had been slow but now there seemed to be significant promise to their theory.

CHAPTER 18

Three days later, Mitchell phoned again. She bubbled out her message. "Jennifer, good news. Dr. DeVries from Eastern Institute is reasonably certain I'm on the right track and suggested I push ahead with more subjects. She will be willingly to check my work using their genome sequencer if she can use the data for a paper in a scientific journal. She'd list me as a co-author."

"Great," Jennifer said, the feeling of an important breakthrough racing through her mind. "With Dr. Stafford's and other's help Dave is lining up additional people for you. They're confident we can find ten of each group."

"Send samples along as you collect them. I'm excited about this."

To give additional impetus to their search, Jennifer, Dave and Ellie divided the list of women who'd participated in the Frazier preliminary trial, but first they devised a strategy to elicit information. They would not reveal the source of their information about the participants. They would not tell about the suit unless the woman was one of those who'd had a deformed child. They would reimburse those who'd had normal babies and volunteered a DNA sample.

Jennifer called a woman in Lincoln, Nebraska. Stella Paige agreed to talk after Jennifer had told her she was asking about the outcome of the pregnancies following the Frazier trial. Paige had been given the drug by her local physician who'd heard about the trial through a salesperson from Frazier and had recommended she enroll in the test. Her symptoms had immediately disappeared and she'd had a normal child, a girl weighing a bit over seven pounds with no apparent defects. She had been more than pleased with the outcome. Jennifer could detect the excitement in her voice as she described her child.

A Frazier representative had visited with her on three occasions during the gestation period, asking her a series of questions focused on her response to the medication and asking about any side effects associated with the experimental drug. Paige had no complaints and congratulated Frazier on producing a medicine that helped women in her condition.

Then Jennifer said, "You probably don't know, but twenty percent of the women who'd been in the trial delivered malformed babies who only lived for a few days."

Paige gasped, "Oh, I can hardly believe that. Everything went so well for me. That's awful for those poor women."

Jennifer indicated they were interested in determining why certain women had reacted so differently and wondered if Paige would be willing to send a DNA sample to Biological Assays. She assured her the results would remain private and confidential. No one, including Jennifer, would be able to tie specific data to the individual.

After several questions about the procedure and concerns she might violate her agreement with Frazier to not reveal her participation in the trial, Paige agreed she would visit her physician who would know how to obtain the sample and send it to the lab.

By the end of the day, they'd been in contact with everyone on the list except one who'd apparently moved with no forwarding address and telephone number. They'd enlisted seven so-called normals and four abnormals. All of those with problem children had agreed readily to join the suit after they had considered the implications and asked questions because none had attributed their misfortune to the medication. Neither had any of their physicians made the connection, always chalking up the outcome to sheer circumstances beyond anyone's control. Information packets and questionnaires were sent to each of them, including a legal document consenting to be a litigant in the suit.

As the three compared notes, Jennifer said, "If everyone follows through, we should have a sufficient number for a solid comparison. In a few days, we'll know if they sent a blood sample to Biological Assays."

A long-time City Council member came into see Jennifer. Henry Mason had been around Chester for years and had been on the council for over twenty, always reelected by his constituents because he considered their ideas and needs above everything else. Mason owned a thriving men's clothing store located in the downtown area and was active in civic clubs. Pleasant round face, balding, a bit overweight, Mason was dressed in a brown sports coat, tan slacks, white shirt and tie. Jennifer invited him to the conference room and offered coffee which he readily accepted.

Mason sipped his coffee as he examined the room. "Ms. Watson, you've done well. I recall when you started and most people thought your practice would never get off the ground."

"So did I," Jennifer laughed. "We struggled for about two years, then things took off."

"I won't take much of your time, but I wanted to ask about your relationship with Stuart Channing. So you know where I'm coming from, representatives from City Council are talking to several law firms in the city and our conversations will be held in confidence. The City Attorney is elected by the citizens and reports to the Council through the Mayor, thus we have the responsibility to review the City Manager's assessment of his job performance on an annual basis and to become involved with any investigation of any apparent unethical practices." He frowned and continued, "It's one of the less exciting tasks we become involved with."

Jennifer nodded her understanding, sipped her coffee and waited for the important question.

Mason pulled a pen from his shirt pocket, opened a folder he'd brought in, glanced at it and asked, "How has your relationship been with Channing?"

Striving to give a balanced picture about Channing, Jennifer said, "As you'd guess, the very nature of our responsibilities put us in adversarial positions much of the time. He leads the prosecution of cases for the city and we're often representing the defendant. Stuart is well versed in the law and is well prepared for his cases. In most instances I would say he represents the city in a positive and effective manner."

She paused to sip from her coffee cup and wait until Mason stopped jotting notes, then added, "In one situation we, our partnership that is, thought he acted unethically. Trying to help the police and the City Attorney, we had obtained evidence from a confidential source about a crime. Channing insisted we reveal the source who'd agreed to provide a deposition if he was not identified, but we refused knowing we would lose the confidence of this person who'd been helpful on numerous occasions. Stuart either knew beforehand or guessed who our source was and set out to arrest him, although he would destroy important evidence. To be candid, since that episode, we've not fully trusted him to be straight forward with us."

"As you are aware," Mason said, "Council has been irritated by this protection game the Mayor and Channing have conducted in regard to Billy Cranford. Give me your thoughts about that."

"I have read the account in the *Register*," Jennifer said. "Cranford's wife is our client, thus we've been associated closely with all of the events involving his relationship with her. To say the least, we were baffled and irate when the Mayor intervened on behalf of Cranford, then we learned Channing had become involved also. Our confidence in the City attorney's office nose-dived. From my perspective his actions represented an absolute abuse of authority. I was disappointed in all of the players."

Mason looked up from his note taking. "You mean the Mayor and Channing?"

"And Chief Drummond who caved in to the threats from the Mayor. I wished he would have resisted and brought the issue into the public arena. And Stuart could have done the same thing."

Mason's face creased into wrinkles. "So do I."

"Their actions unnecessarily placed our client in grave danger more than once."

"I understand through talking with other attorneys that you are a member of the Ethics Committee of Chester Bar Association. Has that body discussed taking any actions regarding Channing's behavior?"

Shaking her head, Jennifer said, "Not to this point. Our chair thought it better to wait for Council's reaction. That is not to say the group will not review the situation at some later date."

Mason closed his folder and drained his coffee mug. "Ms Watson, this has been helpful. Your view matches most of the others with whom we've talked." He stood.

Jennifer reached across the table to shake his hand. "I'll be interested in Council's review."

Ever the salesman, Mason grinned and said, "Bring your husband into our shop sometime. We have some nice things he might like."

"I'll try, but he's pretty resistant to new clothes."

The Council's opinion of the situation became evident when Wanda Easley struck again with an article in the *Register*. Stuart Channing had been called before the City Council to explain his role in the Cranford cover up. Easley described his appearance as defensive and evasive as the members had pressed him for details. After a long session, Channing was warned any further such activity would result in his firing and his position would be filled by an appointment until the next election. Easley speculated that Channing, having been publicly chastised, would not stand for election for another term.

While they harvested tomatoes from the flourishing garden that evening, Dave asked, "Were you surprised at the City Council's treatment of Channing?"

"Actually I thought they'd be more severe, perhaps fire him and appoint an interim."

Dave placed a large tomato into the basket. "Channing is lucky. He seems to always slip by some way."

"But, Easley is correct in her analysis. Channing won't stand for reelection in two years. His political aspirations have been demolished. He'll join some private practice, likely a large firm where he can hide away, do background work and retire with a good pension. But if Anita Chandler followed through with the State Attorney General, Stuart will be confronted with another review, actually one that might be more rigorous than that of City Council."

Dave moved across three rows of the plot. Then he called to her, "I'm going to pick a few of these beans while we're here."

Judge Anita Chandler called the group around her conference table to order. "I've assembled you for the purpose of confirming the details of Mr. Cranford's latest explosion and arrest. He seems unable to abide by an order of the court and is continuously in defiance of that edict. I have read the accounts in the newspaper, but I want to hear from people who were present. And this hearing has nothing to do with the pending charges for assault being brought by Mr. William Jackson."

Jennifer and Dave had been asked to attend in case either side had questions regarding Miriam Reading's role in Cranford's problem that went beyond her testimony about the incident at the country club.

Chandler addressed Miriam by saying, "As a starting point, Ms. Reading, please tell the court what happened on the night of July 24th while at the Chester Country Club."

Miriam, dressed in a dark blue dress, her blond hair parted and falling around her face, presented a composed front. "The station was having our annual reception to show our appreciation for advertisers who support Channel 14. There were probably a hundred people present at the reception to be followed by brief presentations by our President."

She paused, as though thinking about the sequence of events, before continuing, "My role was to make sure our visitors were comfortable and included in conversations."

She smiled. "There's nothing worse than being left alone to stand in a corner, so to speak, while everyone else in conversing with acquaintances and meeting new people."

Chandler interrupted. "So you moved around from person to person."

"Yes. I saw Bill Jackson standing by himself. I went over, introduced myself, although we'd met briefly before. We talked some about his business and I inquired if the station was meeting his expectations."

"Did you perceive your conversation as personal in any way? Were the two of you holding hands or touching?"

Shaking her head, Miriam said, "No. We shook hands, then were a couple of feet apart as we talked. Each of us had drinks and small plates of food in our hands."

"Then what happened?"

"Billy Cranford approached, almost yelling, demanding that we break it off."

"Did you or Mr. Jackson respond?"

"I told Billy to leave us alone. He grabbed me by the shoulder and shoved me. I tripped over a flower stand and fell, spilled the drink and scattered food across the carpet. Jackson yelled at Cranford and came to help me up. That's when Billy hit him across the face and knocked him down. Then he kicked him in the side."

"And then?"

"Billy stood there for a few seconds, looking at us, then he dashed through the side door and disappeared. Someone called the police and 911."

"Had you seen Mr. Cranford earlier during the reception?"

"Yes. Before our guests arrived, the staff people were present and waiting to act as hosts. Billy approached me and asked that I have dinner with him after the function. I turned him down because of my past experiences with him."

"Are you referring to the kidnappings and beatings?"

"Yes. I knew the same thing would occur if I left with him."

"How did he react at that point?"

"He stormed away, then seemed to collect himself and became a congenial host to a group arriving at that moment."

"Did you consider Cranford's reactions to you and Jackson as those of a person who'd lost their ability to control their emotions?"

"Billy is always like that—living on the edge. When someone does something he doesn't like, he reacts in the same manner. It's not unusual in my experience with him. Everything becomes confrontational and often physical until he prevails."

"And do you think his seeing you isolated with Jackson was one of those times?"

Nodding, she said, "While we were married he couldn't tolerate my being the least bit friendly to other men. He seemed to think I was double-crossing him or coming on to the other man."

"So you were not surprised at his reaction during the reception when he accosted you and Jackson?"

"In a way I was." Miriam leaned forward in her chair. "We were at a business function. He knew I was doing my job and I thought he'd control himself under the circumstances. But I was wrong and Bill Jackson was badly injured."

"Thank you, Ms. Reading. Now Mr. Cranford, do you care to speak?"

Bixley responded as Cranford shook his head. "He prefers not to."

Chandler stared at Cranford for several seconds, then asked, "Mr. Cranford, have you understood clearly my past orders to stay away from Ms. Reading?"

Cranford nodded, then mumbled, "Yes."

Chandler, continuing to look at Cranford, said, "I've seen you on Channel 14 News. You come across to viewers as a rational, even sophisticated and charismatic, individual, but this continuous activity in relation to Ms. Reading is a mystery. Obviously, your brief stay in our city facility did nothing to get your attention to the point of modifying your behavior. Thus, I am ordering you to do the following along with a jail sentence of one year but will suspend that for the time being. You are to avoid Reading at all times. You are to enroll in anger management counseling sessions approved by the Court psychologist. You are to report to an appointed officer of the Court each month for the next two years. My suspension of additional jail time is dependent upon your abiding by my other conditions. However, one slip and the sentence will be enforced. Understood?"

Speaking for Cranford, Bixley said, "Yes, Your Honor."

Chandler said, "Mr. Bixley, I want you to inform me a week from today about Mr. Cranford's adherence to my orders. There is no room for delay in starting. Understood?"

"Yes, Your Honor."

"Then I trust we will not have to visit this issue again."

Jennifer left the hearing with disappointment rushing through her brain. She had hoped Chandler would come down hard on Cranford by imposing jail time immediately along with a hefty fine for ignoring previous court rulings.

CHAPTER 19

Following a telephone conversation between the two, Rose Mitchell met Jennifer in the conference room at Biological Assays. Rose spread several sheets across the table as she asked about Dave and how the partnership was progressing. Then she said, "To this point I've run seven samples from women with abnormal children and eight from the mothers of healthy babies. Each of the seven have the same combination of nucleotides on chromosome 14. None of those with normal children have that identical configuration." She pointed to the computer generated printouts of the four nucleotides making up the DNA of every individual.

Mitchell said, "See, these are different for this individual, a woman who had a malformed child, than this one who had a normal baby. And the same is true for those seven. This DNA fragment is unique to them."

Understanding Rose's explanation and knowing they'd hit upon a remarkable discovery, Jennifer smiled, "Wonderful. So Stafford's guess turned out to have some basis."

"I called him earlier this morning. He admitted he was just rattling off potential contributors to the problem when he talked with you and is rather amazed we've reached this conclusion. He's coming over tomorrow to examine the data. I think he's as excited as we are."

Becoming pragmatic about the situation, Jennifer said, "I believe we have a few additional samples coming, assuming all of those who agreed to cooperate actually follow through."

"The more we have, the firmer our case," Mitchell said, "but we have solid proof now. The chances of this combination appearing in some random fashion are astronomical." Her hands moved continuously as she talked, pointing, clenching together, waving in the air.

"Have you shared this with DeVries and Peters yet?"

"I faxed both of them the data summary last night. Haven't heard back yet, but they'll be pleased. And they might have additional insights."

Watching Rose's animation and excitement, something rarely seen in this cool scientist, Jennifer asked, "Have you discovered a new gene?"

Rose shrugged. "I don't know, but I expect DeVries will or know how to verify the possibility. Wouldn't that be something for this small lab to be involved with?"

"Indeed. You could be famous," Jennifer touched her friend on the shoulder.

"Let's not go that far." Laughing softly, Mitchell turned back to her records and began reassembling them into an orderly format.

"I'm filing the suit with the Court this afternoon. Things have come together really well. I'm going to ask for one million per plaintiff. That will likely get reduced as we go forward, but it will get Frazier's attention."

"You can't feel lenient toward them. They should have been more open and willing to investigate further. When twenty percent of the subjects in the test run experience problems you must know something is not right. But they were too eager or greedy to assess the real findings and attempt to modify the drug before putting it on the market."

"It's possible they never considered a genetic difference, but you're correct about ignoring the problem women. Had they revealed those data to the FDA panel, one of those scientists might have put them on the track to prevent future problems."

Rose concluded, "If nothing more than warning women whose mothers had experienced the difficulty. I bet if we tracked these women, each of their mothers were bedridden during the latter phase of gestation."

"You're probably correct," Jennifer agreed. "But that's an issue to be taken on by a research investigator. We don't have the time or funds to hire that kind of expertise."

"Neither do we," Rose said, as she stood.

Dave crossed paths with Miriam at Gibbons during the lunch period. She was there with a couple of co-workers. Dave was on his own as Jennifer was involved in a conference call with two lawyers from Kansas City about an issue raging in the State Bar Association. She had been appointed as the Chester County representative to a state committee and noon seemed to their preferred time to check with each other. He could envision them sharing legal jargon while they consumed dry sandwiches and sipped tepid drinks, trying not to have their mouth full when they needed to communicate.

Leaving her colleagues waiting at the door, Miriam stopped by Dave's booth as she left the restaurant. "Just saying hi," she said, her smiling face suggesting she was happy for the moment or masking her concerns.

"Things going well? Have you seen Cranford?"

Her smile faded. "He roams around the hall near my office sometimes probably checking on me. That's a concern and I try not to get isolated in some file room where he might lash out."

"Remind him of the court directives, including the distance he's to stay away from you each time you see him lurking about. If he ignores that, call the cops."

"I've told my supervisor and co-workers to remain alert to any strange behavior by Billy and I avoid saying anything that might trigger his temper. Better to ignore him than to challenge him."

"Are Monk's men still close in case Cranford does something stupid?"

Miriam shook her head. "I ask Monk to stop. Those guys were scary. A couple of my friends asked who they were and thought they were stalking me."

"Maybe Monk could get them to be less visible, but still in position to respond if Cranford threatens you."

"No, it's okay. Billy is too concerned about the Judge's warning to do anything that will get him in front of her again."

Dave wasn't certain she had made the right decision, but he didn't argue. She knew Cranford better than he and knew what might trigger one of his rampages. And if Monk's men were so visible, he could understand why anyone with Miriam might be spooked. He said, "Keep in touch. Let me know if Cranford threatens you or anyone you're with."

"I will," she said, turning away and heading for the front door. He watched her weave through the crowd, her slim figure and long legs enhanced by the dark skirt and white blouse, and remembered their intimate times together. And her insisting Jennifer was the right person for him to marry. At the time he was certain it was her way of breaking off their affair. But she'd given him good advice. It had taken months and another broken relationship for him to realize it. But every day with

Jennifer brought joy and a deepening conviction their marriage was the best thing for him, and he hoped for her as well.

Three days after Jennifer had filed the suit against Frazier, an attorney for Frazier was led into her office by Helen Knight. She'd never seen the very tall man in Chester and his expensive gray suit, polished black shoes, and designer tie, screamed big money.

He waited for her to stand. "I'm Alexander Horn from St. Louis. My firm has been retained by Frazier Pharmaceuticals to represent their interests in this suit about their drug Plertex."

Jennifer shook his hand and pointed to a chair. "I'm not sure we should be talking, but how may I help you?" Her guess was Horn hoped to discover the depth of her information forming the basis of the litigation, although the crux of that was in the documents filed with the court. By now, Frazier had received copies of everything she'd submitted. Maybe he wanted to size her up and obtain a measure of her ability to follow through on such a potentially huge case.

A slight grin across his face, Horn said, "You could help a lot by dropping this silly suit against a reputable company."

"You know I can't do that," Jennifer said, allowing a smile to drift across her face to show she could have a sense of humor, albeit out of context in the seriousness of the issue before them. "People are depending on me."

Horn crossed a long leg, pulled his pants to straighten the crease. "I've read the copy of your document sent to Frazier. The basis of your suit seems more than frivolous. And this stuff about a genetic difference is ludicrous." His black eyes bored into Jennifer's face, looking for any hint of doubt.

Returning his stare, she said, "Mr. Horn, I'm willing to let a judge and jury make that decision. But I'm confident we're on solid ground here. And in case you didn't notice in the papers, reputable scientists with no personal stake in the outcome agree with our conclusion." She started to add that not only did they support the position, they had aided in the formulation, but decided to let their court testimonies confirm that information.

Horn looked around the office for several seconds. "Your operation doesn't have the resources to mount this suit. You're a single lawyer and you'll be battling a team of experienced litigators who've worked on cases with national, even international implications."

"Are you offering to join with me?"

Horn didn't smile this time. "I can't believe you will stand a chance. Maybe you should admit you're over your head and fold the tent now."

Jennifer stood. "I think we've concluded our conversation. I'll look forward to seeing you in court."

Horn took his time unfolding his legs and standing, then ambled through the door as though he resented the treatment he'd just received from this female attorney struggling in a small practice.

As the door closed behind Horn, Jennifer smiled at his efforts to cast doubts on both the evidence and her ability. She liked the odds in their favor. And she liked being the underdog, honed by her years battling for recognition among male competitors with huge egos. Plus, trying this case in a Chester court would play to her advantage if a local jury perceived the arrogance of Horn and colleagues.

Three days later, Jennifer received a call from the clerk in Judge Esther Plunkett's office. "Ms. Watson, the Judge wanted you to know Frasier, through their attorneys, have asked for a change of venue. They have filed a motion to have the trial moved to a jurisdiction in Kansas City. She will get the opposing sides together soon to hear arguments."

Jennifer thanked the clerk and immediately turned her thoughts to the debate about the appropriate site for the court battle. She preferred Chester because she knew the players, would be in a better position to predict the actions of potential jurors and it was convenient for her. She accepted the attorneys for Frasier would take a polar opposite stance. They would attempt to convince the judge that Chester was too remote from which to decide a major case that could establish precedents for other suits. Nevertheless, she had confidence she could make a persuasive argument regardless of the arena. She thought she had an advantage over the Frasier attorneys before Judge Plunkett, remembering Plunkett had complimented her in which the ruling had set a precedent in support of workers judged to be non-insurable because of genetic probabilities they would be stricken with a disease earlier in life than most of the population. Jennifer knew from talking with friends at the Bar meetings that judges, while deemed to be impervious to outside influences, were often swayed toward the position of those attorneys who had a reputation for cutting-edge interpretations of the statutes. Plunkett would be fair, but Jennifer hoped she would recall the cases in which she'd prevailed because of her utilization of little known and seldom used laws.

Two days later Judge Plunkett assembled the attorneys in her conference room. Alexander Horn was accompanied by a local lawyer from the largest firm in Chester, Harvey Ennis, who had opposed Jennifer in others cases.

Judge Plunkett called the session to order, reminded them that minutes would be taken by the clerk stationed to one side of the conference table, then said, "I believe Ms. Watson has seen the request from Mr. Horn but I will ask either Mr. Horn or Mr. Ennis to summarize their motion to change the venue for the pending suit of Reading and others against Frasier Pharmaceuticals."

Horn unfolded his length and leaned forward to look directly at the Judge. "Ms. Watson has requested the case be heard by a jury rather than permitting a judge to render a verdict. From the perspective of Frasier, we believe a fair hearing would be less apt to occur in a smaller jurisdiction than a more cosmopolitan one such as Kansas City or Washington, D.C. We contend there has been excessive publicity about this case and the probability of finding an impartial jury is remote."

Plunkett looked toward Jennifer, in effect seeking her response. Without shifting in her chair, Jennifer said, "Judge Plunkett, selection of a jury panel doesn't consider education, or experience, but depends on citizens on the tax rolls. I doubt Chester is any different than any other metropolitan area. Then it's dependent upon the attorneys to eliminate those potential jurors who they believe might not understand the issues being presented. As for pretrial publicity, there has been essentially none. I have every confidence an impartial jury can be empanelled in Chester."

Horn started to speak, but Plunkett held up her hand. "Mr. Horn, I've read your brief accompanying your motion and find nothing that persuades me to change the venue. The usual reason cited for a change is pretrial publicity and I am not aware of that situation related to this specific case. Unless you can convince me otherwise, I am denying your request and will ask the Chester court to determine a date for the beginning of this hearing. And it's reasonable to utilize the judgment of citizens who could be affected by the outcome."

When neither Horn nor Ennis responded immediately, Plunkett stood, saying, "Thank you for coming today." She moved toward a door at the side of the room and disappeared. The court reporter followed.

Breathing an inaudible sigh of relief, Jennifer stood, placed her papers in her small briefcase and left Horn and Ennis mumbling to themselves.

Harvey Ennis caught up to her at the courthouse door to Main Street. "Ms. Watson, before the meeting with Plunkett, Horn and I discussed the possibility of a settlement and avoid a trial. Could we meet tomorrow to discuss the potential?"

Knowing that most of these type issues were resolved through mutually agreed terms, Jennifer said, "I can do that. What about our conference room at 2:00?"

"That's agreeable," he responded, shifting his briefcase to the other hand. "I'll see you then."

CHAPTER 20

Jennifer and Ellie sat across from Horn and Ennis in the conference room of Watson and Randle. Jennifer acknowledged the sparse furnishings of their small firm couldn't match the upscale accoutrements Horn and Ennis were accustomed to, but they had the basics and in time would improve their decor.

Ennis began. "We appreciate your meeting with us." Both he and Horn continued to survey their surroundings. Neither had accepted the offer of coffee or tea.

"I'd like to introduce my associate, Eleanor Blackwell, who is a paralegal in our firm and who will complete her law degree this summer. She has worked with me on this case."

The opponents nodded. Ennis ventured, "I wish you well with the bar exam and all the stuff that follows the degree."

Ellie smiled at Ennis, glanced at Jennifer, then said, "I'm looking forward to having it all behind me."

Horn, obviously bored by the conversation and eager to get down to the business of the morning, said, "We'd like to propose a settlement figure that we believe is fair to your clients and will avoid spending time and resources in a court battle. Harvey and I have discussed the situation and believe a hundred thousand per client should be satisfactory. After all, no one suffered permanent injury and all have the opportunity to deliver offspring in the future. Furthermore, we know the odds of your clients receiving the amount proposed in your brief are quite unrealistic based on the evidence supporting the claims." Horn stared at Jennifer as though daring her to disagree.

Jennifer looked at Ellie and nodded, communicating that their earlier conversation about the probable offer by Horn and Ennis had been on target. Then turning toward Horn, she said, "I'm disappointed you place such little sympathy on the agony these women experienced as they saw their newborn die from the malformations caused by this drug. These will never recover from the disappointment and frustration associated with this event. They had dreamed about being a mother to a normal, healthy child, but instead were presented with a deformed, perhaps grotesque to their thinking, baby who would not survive. Frankly, your recommendation is ridiculous and I cannot in good conscience even report that back to these women. They deserve more, much more."

Horn and Ennis glanced at each other as Jennifer talked, then Horn asked, "What would be acceptable?"

Suspecting she now had an advantage, Jennifer said, "We believe the figure in the brief is reasonable. Our clients should receive fair compensation for the trauma they've experienced, not to mention the expense of medical treatment of their newborn. And we should be clear about another thing—a precious life was snuffed out before there was an opportunity to live in this world. That is not an insignificant matter."

Ennis jumped in. "Ms. Watson, Frasier is prepared to pay up to a half-million per client—nothing more. We want to be fair about this, but your request is much too high. We believe no jury will award that amount and certainly no judge will sustain such a finding."

"Harvey," Jennifer said, "you might be correct, but there is a good possibility you could be wrong. We'll take our chances with the figure in the papers filed with the court. But we've discussed the potential for a settlement with our clients and they can accept eight hundred thousand each, plus legal fees."

"Too high," Horn snapped. "Frasier will not go above a half-million."

"Jennifer said, "Then we'll take our chances with a jury." She closed her folder while looking at Ennis, thinking he might disagree with his colleague and accept her offer.

Horn shook his head. "See you in court."

As their opponents left through the front door, Ellie said, "Well, that was quick. I was surprised at the attitude taken by Horn or did I read him wrong?"

"No, you're correct. These high priced lawyers from huge firms are usually arrogant, like to throw their weight around and bluff people, but the bottom line is they don't know any more about the law that we do. And they seem to have little or no feeling for human suffering. It's all about the money."

The next two weeks passed swiftly. Jennifer and Ellie lined up their witnesses, prepared questions for each and conducted mock sessions with each, coaching them on their responses, reminding them of appropriate dress and demeanor while on the stand, trying to anticipate the questions the opposition might raise to cast doubt or shake their testimony. Jennifer talked with Miriam at length as she was scheduled to be the first witness and needed to make a solid impression on the jury. They would remember because she was first and they would still be attentive.

Jennifer flew to Kansas City to meet with the two women who would follow Miriam. Ellie prepared the woman from Mims. Initially they'd planned to hold Katherine Mosley in reserve in the case they needed to bolster their presentation, but after Ellie's session with her, they decided to place her immediately behind Miriam, believing Mosley would impress the jury and her local ties might be important.

Jennifer called Dr. Peters who would testify about the FDA hearings. Dr. Stafford would reveal the treatment he'd given Miriam and the information he'd received from Frasier. Dr. Givens would follow with his story about being courted by Frasier. Somewhere in the mix she would put Rose Mitchell on the stand to testify about the gene differences.

During the period Jennifer met with other clients, although she tried to shift their appointments to the time after the trial. But several could not wait or demanded an immediate hearing. She accommodated them, then stayed late at the office, never feeling completely prepared as new ideas and approaches breeched her thinking.

On Wednesday morning, five days before the trial was scheduled to begin, Miriam appeared at Jennifer's door without an appointment, causing two clients to wait beyond their scheduled times.

Dropping into the chair in front of Jennifer's desk, she said, "I apologize for barging in, but you need to know something important. Late last night, a lawyer representing Frasier called to offer a settlement."

"Those bastards," Jennifer muttered under her breath.

Then she asked Miriam, "How much?"

"Four hundred thousand."

Fearing the worst, Jennifer asked, "And did you agree?"

Her eyes on the desk top, Miriam shook her head. "I put him off, saying I wanted to think about it overnight. I was tempted to accept. He made a persuasive argument, four hundred thousand free and clear, while the trial may yield nothing. He tried to make the case that the evidence you will present is not strong enough for any sane jury to buy into an award of any size."

"Was he calling all the women?"

"Don't know, but probably. I thought you should know as soon as possible." She stood from the chair.

Coming around her desk to stand near Miriam, Jennifer asked, "And what will you tell him when he calls back?"

"I'm going to reject any settlement. Remember, you warned us all Frasier might pull some stunt like this and we should stick to our plan."

"Let's hope the others follow your example, but I'm going to have Dave call them all as quickly as possible."

"I need to get going," Miriam said, turning toward the door, "but I wanted to alert you to this deal."

"I'm glad you did. And stand fast by your decision to reject. They may up the offer. And remember, you'll be the first witness for us. That'll likely be Tuesday morning but stay in touch in case the process moves more quickly than usual."

"I'll be ready. Just give me an hours notice."

Dave spent the next two hours calling everyone on their list. They had all been contacted by Frasier's attorneys on the previous day. While most had turned Frasier down, a couple had asked for time to consider. He convinced them to stand firm, even if Frasier upped the ante in the next couple of days. Dave thought Frasier was worried and would elevate the amount trying to avoid the publicity of a public hearing.

He was unable to contact Katherine Mosley at her home number, then remembered she was taking a position at J. C. Penney's the day after he'd seen her in Mims. He walked over to the department store, seven blocks from the office.

After wandering through the large store for several minutes, Dave saw Mosley in the women's department. She was arranging blouses on a rack and didn't notice him until he approached and asked, "How are you today? Job going well?"

Her eyes brightened. "Good and good."

Then her face clouded. "I know why you're here—the call from Frasier."

"You're right. But I need to know your response."

Now standing close, she put her hand on his arm. "I remembered Ms. Watson's advice. I told them to go to hell."

"Good for you. They're playing games that seem to be a bit unethical."

Her hand still on his arm, Mosley said, "But the lawyer who called was persistent. He didn't want to take a no. He said he'd call back tonight, but I suggested he'd waste his time."

As Dave eased away, Mosley asked, "You have time to get coffee next door? There's something I'd like to talk to you about."

Dave glanced at his watch, not wanting to be late for an appointment at the office. "I can spare fifteen or twenty minutes."

Mosley walked to another counter, her figure in the black skirt and lavender blouse drawing his attention. Katherine said something to the clerk behind a display of slacks, then came back, took his arm and led him out the side door. They found a square table in the corner of the small café three doors down the street and ordered coffee from a teenage waitress.

Sitting across from him in old chairs, their plastic covers cracked in places from long use, Mosley said, "I'm having problems with my ex-husband. He left me when our baby was born with all those problems, but now he wants to come around, believing I'll have sex with him with no commitment beyond a little romp in bed."

Sipping the tepid brew, Dave asked, "Is a divorce in the works?"

"Yes, we agreed to a no-fault split but somehow he thinks he still has rights. I've told him to stay away, but he wanders back, telling me some sad story about getting chewed out by his boss for malingering. I feel sad for him, let him inside, we talk for a few minutes, then he insists we do it."

"What happens if you don't allow him inside? Just say no or you can get a court order to keep him away from you."

"I think he might break through the door if I turn him away."

"Then call the cops, charge him with breaking and entering."

A frown creased her face. "I hate to do that." She sipped from the coffee cup. "Then he'll have a record and have more problems getting jobs. Then he'd want money from me. I'd like you to talk to him."

"Your local police is a better avenue. If he doesn't resist or cause other problems, he won't have a record with the cops."

Shoving her mug away, she said, "I'll try that, but I doubt it'll work unless they . . . ." Her voice trailed off and she slipped out of the seat. Standing, she added, "Then I'll call you for help."

As they stood for a moment, Dave asked, "Any chance the two of you can reconcile your differences and get back together?"

She edged toward the door. "I don't think so." But her delay in responding and the tone of her voice suggested it might be something she'd consider if her former husband made proper overtures, gave her attention and stopped making demands.

Dave followed her out, saying as they reached the outside, "I'll see you either Tuesday or Wednesday during the trial."

He watched her push through the door into Penney's, thinking her agenda really was something else, and a bit flummoxed by his attraction to her. He'd not had this feeling toward another woman since he and Jennifer married and he vowed to be faithful to her.

The trial of Frasier versus Reading et al began at nine on Monday morning with Judge Esther Plunkett presiding. The court room was almost empty. A few family members of the plaintiffs were present. One reporter lolled in the section reserved for media.

With no pretrial motions to be considered, the matter of jury selection took center stage. The first person called from the pool was a middle-age woman dressed in a fashionable outfit, suggesting she was active in the community and sophisticated enough to know what was going on around Chester. Jennifer had done background checks on the pool and knew Mrs. Geraldine Robinson would be acceptable to her.

But Horn and Ennis had concerns and set out to question her. Ennis, assigned the responsibility for probing prospective jurors, asked about her background.

Her eyes on Ennis, Robinson told about her experience as a real estate broker following education in the Chester public schools and a business degree from the University of Missouri.

Ennis asked, "Do you have children?"

Her eyes brightened as she responded, "Yes, two adult children, neither of whom lives here."

"During your pregnancies, Mrs. Robinson, did you have difficulties?"

Robinson looked at him for seconds as though asking him to define difficulties, then answered, "Other than days of so-called morning sickness, both pregnancies went well."

"So you weren't treated for pre-eclampsia or other conditions?"

"No."

"But you have heard of women who had those problems?"

"One of my good friends was bed-ridden for the last trimester to avoid a spontaneous abortion or early delivery. She had a terrible time."

"Thus, a medication to relieve those symptoms would be wonderful, wouldn't it?"

"Of course, but there seemed to be nothing her physician could recommend."

"Have you heard of the drug Plertex?"

"No."

"Have you heard about women using this drug with great success?"

"No, I haven't."

"Nothing in the local papers or on the newscasts have alerted you to those persons?"

"No, and I read the papers daily and hear the evening news programs most days."

Ennis stepped back from his position near the box and said, "Judge Plunkett, Mrs. Robinson is acceptable to the defense."

And the selection process continued throughout the morning. Jennifer used her preemptory challenges for three prospects, two of whom worked in the pharmaceutical industry in some way. The third person, a male who had such a belligerent attitude toward the court system, she was concerned he'd hold hostage anyone who might benefit from a favorable ruling. She couldn't take a chance on him.

One man had heard about the malformed children born to Miriam Reading and others. Ennis could not accept him. By noon they had found twelve acceptable jurors and two alternates.

Judge Plunkett declared a noon recess and indicated opening arguments would begin at two this afternoon.

Surprised by the pace of the trial and the Judge's announcement, Jennifer hurried to the office, found Dave at his desk. "This thing is progressing so rapidly, we might be calling witnesses by mid-afternoon. Would you alert Miriam and Katherine Mosley to be at the court house by two-thirty?"

"I'll call them right now, then you want to find lunch?"

She glanced at her watch. "Could you bring me a sandwich. I need to review my notes for the opening. I thought it wouldn't happen until tomorrow morning, but now it's at two this afternoon."

Shortly before one, Dave came back. He placed a sandwich and a soft drink from Subway on her desk. As she wrote on the margin of the paper, Dave said, "Take time to eat. You're ready."

Dave disappeared toward his office as she shoved aside her notes, feeling better about her statement now.

Ten minutes later, Dave returned. He sat across from her, watching her wipe dressing from her fingers. "Katherine will be there, but I haven't found Miriam. I called the station before lunch. The person who answered thought she was out on an assignment and would return soon. I called again when I came back. Her supervisor answered to tell me they haven't seen her at all today. In fact, he seemed peeved because Miriam had missed a meeting with a potential client this morning. I called Miriam's apartment, but no one answered."

"Good Lord, has she been kidnapped again?"

"That'd be my guess," Dave mumbled. "She's known about the date and has always been reliable."

"Keep looking for her. Her testimony could be crucial. Plus, I'm concerned for her safety."

CHAPTER 21

Jennifer couldn't get Miriam's disappearance off her mind even as she heard Judge Plunkett call the afternoon session to order and announce that the counsel for the plaintiffs would now present her opening statement. Jennifer stood behind the table and started, hoping she would not have to rely on her notes and that her demeanor and professional appearance would impress them. She tamped down her concern about her planned first witness.

"Members of the jury, I will be brief, but I trust you will understand the scope of evidence to be presented on behalf of ten women who were victims of a large corporation more interested in money than in their health. Frasier Pharmaceuticals was more intent on gaining wealth than they were in doing appropriate testing of their drug, Plertex. They rushed to market, ignored signals from their test group that all was not right, then used a political appointee to override the advice of a scientific panel who expressed concerns about the safety of the concoction. The bottom line is women and their spouses were damaged and babies were born with life-ending malformations."

As she moved from the security of the table to stand in front of the panel, she outlined the drug-induced problems confronted by the newborn, the difficulties so severe the best efforts of their physicians could not save them. She suggested the women had been devastated as would any new mother seeing the disfigurements even as they could not comprehend the fatal complications associated with vital organs. None of the ten babies lived beyond two weeks.

She concluded by saying, "We will present sufficient evidence for you to hold Frasier liable and responsible for the damages and will ask that you render a verdict that will cause Frasier to compensate these women for their suffering and anguish."

She glanced along the rows of jurors and returned to her chair. Thinking about Miriam again, she turned to look for Dave. He was not in the room.

Alexander Horn made an imposing figure—six-three, black suit, white shirt, red-tinted tie, as he paced across the room, his voice commanding attention. "Ms. Watson has tried to impress you with the agony felt by these women who had ill-formed children. But she failed to mention that the majority of women who used Plertex did so with outstanding results. They were freed from the dread of those symptoms associated with many pregnancies, including hypertension, protein in the urine, sickness, bed-ridden for months as they struggled to maintain a viable fetus. Plertex saved them from all those problems and then they delivered healthy babies. I feel sorry for those who had difficulties, but the overriding evidence suggests Plertex was not the problem. I won't speculate about what went wrong, but will leave that to scientists and medical experts.

"But you must understand that Frasier Pharmaceuticals made every effort to market a safe drug to alleviate the problem, something other companies have given up on because they did not persist long enough. Frasier did all the appropriate testing in animal models, in a trial group of women, then obtained approval by the Food and Drug Administration before releasing this drug for the general market. We contend Frasier did nothing wrong. And if you listen to the witnesses, you will arrive at the same conclusion. You will find Frasier not liable for the problems of those women who for some unknown reason had problems.

"I thank you for your attention and know you will reach a fair judgment." Horn walked in front of the jury, his eyes peering into each face, then returned to his seat.

Jennifer knew Horn had impressed the jury with his brevity and his message. She glanced around the visitors area. Dave had not returned.

Judge Plunkett announced, "The court is recessed for fifteen minutes, then the plaintiff will present their first witness." She disappeared through the door behind her bench.

Jennifer went outside, called the office on her cell phone. To Helen Knight, she asked, "Have you seen or heard from Dave since noon?"

"He hasn't been in the office and hasn't called in. Is there a problem?"

"He was searching for Miriam Reading who is supposed to be in court, but we couldn't locate her. I'll try his cell number."

She got a busy signal when she dialed the cell number. Frustrated, she went to the rest room and returned to the court room, hoping Katherine Mosley was ready for her battle.

Failing to contact Miriam by telephone, Dave left the office and went to the Channel 14 station. At the reception desk, he asked about Miriam. The woman dialed a number, looked blank, then said, 'She doesn't answer. In fact, another person called about her earlier."

"May I speak to her supervisor." He handed her a business card.

The receptionist dialed another extension, spoke for a moment, then pointed Dave toward a door to her left. "Mr. Inman will see you, Room 124 on your right down the hall."

Dave turned off his cell phone as he walked. As he knocked on 124, a burly man dressed in a dark suit motioned to him, stood and said, "I'm Jake Inman. How can I help you?"

Dave introduced himself, handed Inman a card. "I'm trying to find Miriam Reading. She's scheduled to be a witness in court this afternoon."

Inman pointed to a chair, then sat behind his desk, piled high with papers, magazines, envelopes. "I wish I could help you, but we've been looking ourselves. She missed an important meeting this morning and that's not like her."

"When did you see her last?"

Inman pondered the question. "She participated in a marketing meeting at four Friday afternoon. And she was scheduled to meet a couple of clients for dinner that evening. To the best of my knowledge, she did since they didn't call to complain."

"You have any idea where that meeting was to take place?"

Shaking his head, Inman picked up his phone and dialed an extension. "Jane, did Miriam have reservations for that meeting Friday night with those prospective clients?"

He waited, listened, then dropped the receiver into the cradle. "She planned to meet them at Arthur's at seven. Apparently she made that, but she hasn't checked in since."

"Would she typically call in after a session with clients."

"No, she'd report the next morning, in this case today. Sometimes those dinner meetings run late and there's no one here except the broadcast teams and night custodians."

Dave asked, "You may not wish to respond to this, but are you aware she's had problems with Billy Cranford, the sports reporter?"

Inman's face clouded, his slight smile disappeared. "Yes, we all know about that." Then he asked, "You think Cranford is involved with her disappearance?"

"Given his past actions, he'd be the first person suspected if she truly is missing."

Inman said, "Mr. Randle, there's no doubt something is really wrong here. Miriam has been so reliable, she wouldn't skip assignments and miss meetings. And she told me she'd have to be in court today or tomorrow."

Inman held up a hand, dialed a number on his phone. "May I speak to Billy Cranford?"

After a few seconds, he said, "You're sure?"

He dropped the receiver into position. "Cranford flew to San Francisco on a ten o'clock flight this morning. He'll be back tomorrow night."

Dave stood. "Thanks for your help. I think my next stop is the police station."

In his vehicle, Dave phoned the Chester station to make sure Rasmussen was in. He parked in the police lot and walked the three blocks to the court house. Stopping just inside the door to the session, he could see Jennifer in the midst of her opening statement. He watched for a moment, proud of her composure under the threat of a no-show witness.

He returned to the police station and found Rasmussen at his desk. Rasmussen looked up at his knock on the door frame. 'What's up? Thought you'd be in the court room."

"I should be, but I'm searching for Miriam Reading who was last seen Friday night. We haven't been able to find her today."

Rasmussen's eyebrows raised as he considered the possibilities. "I just looked at the reports from patrols for the weekend and this morning. Nothing about her. You called the hospital?"

"Not yet, but I think if she were there, someone would have phoned her work place. I wanted to alert you and have patrols looking for her. Naturally, I suspect Cranford of some crazy scheme to kidnap her again, but he flew out this morning."

Rasmussen stood. "Tell you what. Given the history of her problems, I'll issue an APB now. We'll get search teams out."

"Thanks Bill. I'll stay in touch. Jennifer wants her to testify as soon as possible."

Thinking Jennifer wouldn't need him around the court, Dave drove to Arthur's, an upscale restaurant he'd frequented several times. On the way, he called Inman at Channel 14 to update him on the police plans. He'd heard nothing.

At Arthur's, Dave found the manager, a new person he'd not met previously, at his desk on one side of the large kitchen. Dave handed him a card and asked, "I'd like for you to check your sales receipts from Friday evening. I'm looking for a person who dined here. Miriam Reading is the name."

Standing, the manager said, "I'm Sam, but I don't need to check records. She's a regular and was in for dinner with two males. They left around ten-fifteen. I remember because they were the last customers."

"Anything unusual happen around her table?"

Sam came around the desk. "Don't think so, but let me ask the receptionist if she's come in yet. Come with me."

Dave followed Sam to the station at the entrance to the dining area. A slender brunette woman was inserting typed pages into menu covers and stacking them into a neat pile on the top of a small table. Waiters were busy setting up for the evening meal, replacing table linens and making certain all the lamps worked.

Sam said, "Sandra, this is Dave Randle. He's inquiring about Miriam Reading."

Still holding a group of papers, Sandra stepped closer and said, "She was here for dinner Friday. She and the two men she was with left around ten-fifteen. They were talking about business while she paid the check."

"I guess you didn't see what happened outside? Did they go their separate ways?" Dave asked.

"No, I didn't follow them out. But nothing seemed out of the ordinary. Miriam is here often with clients and there's never been any reason to check on her."

"Did you notice anything unusual near her table during dinner?"

Sandra looked blank. "No. She had asked for that corner table because it's quieter and that's customary for her when she's bringing in clients." She pointed to the rectangular table in the corner farthest from the front door and away from the main traffic stream of waiters and patrons.

Dave handed her a business card. "If you remember anything later, please give me a call. I suspect she's been kidnapped."

Sandra's eyes brightened. She said, "You know, a man asked me who were the men with Miriam. I didn't know their names, but thought it was none of my business to know or find out."

"Can you describe the guy asking?"

She thought, no doubt trying to recall any distinguishing features of a customer mixed in with fifty others during a busy evening three nights ago. "Not much. He was big. Must be six-four and heavy. I've seem him before, but don't know a name. He paid cash which is unusual these days."

"Alone or did he have a companion?"

"He was with another man. They sat at one of those tables." She pointed toward a group of tables intended for couples or singles.

Dave thanked her and reminded her to call if she thought about anything else related to Miriam's time at the restaurant.

Outside, he walked around the parking lot looking for Miriam's car. It wasn't there. If she'd been grabbed by Cranford, it was somewhere else.

He called Rasmussen. There been no sighting of Miriam by the cops and no report of anyone being brought to the hospital because of an accident.

Katherine Mosley grabbed the attention of the jury and the audience as she entered the courtroom. Attired in a pink form-fitting dress, every eye turned to stare as her heels clicked along the hardwood floor. Jennifer was a bit upset Katherine had ignored her recommendation to wear clothing that would not draw attention to her and worried Mosley had diverted attention away from the focus of the day.

After the swearing to tell the truth and nothing but the truth, Jennifer began with the question. "Ms. Mosley, tell the jury about your ordeal during pregnancy."

Speaking clearly, Katherine said, "Early in pregnancy, I began to have cramps and bleeding. My doctor was concerned I'd miscarry and confined me to bed. He discovered I had high blood pressure and kidney problems. At one point he suggested I abort the fetus since I was young enough to try again. But I wanted the baby and so did my husband. We decided to forego abortion and tough it out. Then my doctor prescribed this new drug, Plertex, that had been left by a representative of a pharmaceutical company."

Jennifer asked, "And did this drug relieve the problems?"

Nodding her head, Katherine said, "Yes. Almost immediately, I was able to return to my normal schedule."

"When did you know something was wrong?"

"Not until the baby was born." A deep frown immersed her face. She eased a hand across her brow.

"What happened?"

Her voice became hoarse. "My little boy was badly deformed. His nose was essentially not there. One eye was missing. His arms were too short."

"What," Jennifer asked, "was the prognosis for him?"

"My doctor did a lot of exams. He called in specialists. Their conclusion was the baby would not live because of poor development of his liver and kidneys."

"And were they correct?"

A tear trickled down her cheek. "He died ten days after birth. We never brought him out of the hospital."

"Did your physician think Plertex had caused the deformities?"

"Not until he learned of others who had the same thing happen to them."

"Did your physician contact Frasier or their representative?

"Yes, he and I met with the sales rep. But that man said he'd not heard of any problems associated with the drug. I don't know if my doctor went beyond that. I think not."

"But you hold Frasier responsible for your deformed baby?"

"Yes, I do."

Jennifer yielded to the opposition. Ennis rose from his seat and approached Katherine, standing two feet away from the witness box.

"Ms. Mosley, you cannot know without any doubt can you that Plertex caused the problems with you child?"

Katherine met Ennis's stare. "I can't prove it medically, but with so many other women affected the same way, I am certain the drug is the cause."

"How do you explain the fact that many other women used the drug and had normal deliveries and healthy babies?"

"I can't, but neither can Frasier explain what went wrong with the ones like me."

Ennis ignored her retort, then asked, "Have you considered the possibility that one of your daily habits was the culprit rather than the medication?"

"I don't know what you mean, but I don't smoke or use drugs. I gave up alcohol during pregnancy. No, I can't attribute my child's deformity to anything except the drug."

"Is there a history of deformed children in your family?"

"No."

"What about your husband's family? Any problems in his background?"

"No."

"And you're not willing to accept your child's problems may have been sheer circumstances?"

Shaking her head, Katherine said, "There's always a cause for these type things."

Ennis stepped closer to the jury and asked, "But you jumped to blame Frasier because no one looked for another cause, didn't you?"

"That's not true. Too many others were affected."

Ennis looked at Katherine several seconds, apparently concluded he wasn't going to shake her belief, turned away, saying, "I have no additional questions for Ms. Mosley."

Judge Plunkett glanced toward Jennifer, apparently waiting for a request for redirect, but seeing no signal, she announced the session adjourned until nine Tuesday morning.

Jennifer turned to see Dave waiting at the entrance. He shook his head.

CHAPTER 22

As Dave waited near the door, Jennifer gathered her papers into the briefcase, her mind filled with the progress of the trial and running through the possible whereabouts of Miriam.

Leaving the witness box and hearing the Judge's announcement, Katherine came to Jennifer's table. "I'm glad that's over."

"You did well," Jennifer said, touching her arm. "You didn't let Ennis shake your testimony. I hope the others will do as well."

"Should I be around tomorrow?"

"You don't need to be, but we know where to find you if there's any reason to do so. I'll be in touch with you as this progresses. Or you can come to the trial if you feel it would be best for you."

"I'd better not miss any more work than necessary and Dave knows where to find me if you need me." Katherine angled away and disappeared along the hall. For a moment Jennifer watched her sensuous frame enhanced by the dress and high heels.

Nearing Dave, Jennifer asked, "Nothing about Miriam?"

"Nothing. There are a couple of things I want to check, but I wanted to be here at the end of the day. Things went okay?"

Jennifer nodded. "Think so, but I'm sure Ennis and Horn will make an issue of Miriam's absence with the Judge if she never appears as a witness."

"I'm going to run out to Miriam's residence, then check in with Rasmussen. If there are no leads, I'll come home."

"Let's meet at the office. I need to prepare for tomorrow, then I'd like to eat somewhere rather than making dinner at home."

"Okay. If something comes up, I'll call." He pressed her shoulder before he turned toward the outside door.

Unable to drive through the gate of the controlled community, Dave parked on the street, skirted the barrier, and walked into the parking area. He didn't see Miriam's car, but didn't know where she usually parked. He followed signs to a unit marked 'Office' and pushed the door open. An elderly man jerked alert at the sound.

Clarence, according to a name tag affixed to his shirt pocket, raked a brown hand across his ebony face. "You need help with something?"

Dave showed his identification and said, "I'm trying to locate Miriam Reading and thought I could find her car."

Clarence stood and scanned a chart on the wall. "Her spaces are numbers 67 and 68." He pointed with a twisted finger. "Around that side of the second building. People are pretty good about staying in their slots, else neighbors get riled."

"I'll look there," Dave said, then asked, "I don't suppose you could let me get in her apartment?"

"Can't do that. Against the rules, but maybe the manager could. He's in Apartment 10 on the front side of the first building off the street."

"I suspected you couldn't, but its worth a shot. By any chance, have you seen Miriam the last couple of days?"

"Don't work on weekends. Haven't seen her today."

Dave turned to the door. "Thanks again for you help."

Dave found the spaces assigned to Miriam. Her car was not there, the empty slots foreboding. Something had gone badly wrong. He decided asking the manager for entrance to her unit would be a waste of time. There'd have to be a warrant. His thoughts couldn't leave Cranford as the instrument of likely foul play.

Standing near the gate, Dave phoned Rasmussen. The cops had found no trace of Miriam, but the hunt was intensifying. All patrols were on the lookout for her and her car.

Deciding to try one more possibility and talk with the guys who'd had dinner with her on Friday evening, he called Miriam's office to get names, but no one answered. All had gone for the day. He berated himself for not getting those names on his earlier visit. He headed for the office and dinner with Jennifer.

The next morning Jennifer called as her second witness, one of the women from Kansas City who'd been in the meeting with her and Dave as they sought potential plaintiffs. Josephine Williams, the brunette who'd asked so many questions, was sworn in by the clerk. Josephine had paid heed to Jennifer's instructions and dressed in a somber gray suit and white blouse that masked her female figure.

Jennifer led her through essentially the same set of questions she'd asked Katherine Mosley. The Williams baby girl had deformed facial features, a shortened arm, and the malformed organs which had caused her death nine days after birth.

Concluding her questioning, Jennifer asked, "And you believe the drug, Plertex, was the causative factor in the death of your child?"

"Yes, particularly after my physician had discovered others like me. It seems highly likely the drug was the problem."

Ennis attempted the same scenario of queries he addressed to Mosley. Williams remained steady in her opinion that Frasier should be held responsible.

Following a mid-morning recess, Horn stood and addressed the Judge as the session resumed. "Your Honor, may we have either a sidebar or a brief meeting in your chambers?"

Plunkett waved the attorneys forward to stand in front of the bench. "Your issue, Mr. Horn?"

"The defense is confused by the failure of the primary plaintiff, Ms. Reading, to appear as a witness. We'd like an explanation."

Plunkett nodded and said, "Ms. Watson, Mr. Horn's request seems reasonable. In fact, I've wondered about her absence also."

Jennifer said, "Judge, the fact is we've been unable to find Ms. Reading. She's been missing since Friday night. The Chester police are searching for her as we meet."

Horn probed. "So you don't know if she'll be available at all?"

Looking toward Judge Plunkett, Jennifer said, "I don't know at this point. We're concerned she's been kidnapped or worse."

"Judge," Horn elevated his tone above the whispers they'd employed, "the defense requests a mistrial. When the primary plaintiff is not present, that seems a reasonable action."

Jennifer broke in before Plunkett could respond. "Judge, this is a suit tendered by several other plaintiffs. They should not be denied a fair hearing. It's unfortunate that Ms. Reading's name is first on the docket, but anyone one of the others could be listed as the first plaintiff."

Judge Plunkett leaned forward. "Mr. Horn, I must agree with Ms. Watson's position. Let's continue and trust Ms. Reading will be found."

"And if she isn't?" Horn persisted.

"Then the other plaintiffs will receive their day in court as they deserve. I fail to see what difference the absence of Ms. Reading makes in a class-action suit." She raised her hand, palm out indicting the discussion was over and said, "Ms. Watson, call your next witness."

Rose Mitchell, on the surface confident and composed, took the stand. Jennifer and Rose had rehearsed the set of questions and responses, believing her testimony might be the key element in the case.

Jennifer led her through questions to establish her credentials and experience, then asked, "Have you had experience with genetic diseases and DNA technology?"

"Yes, our lab conducts routine screening tests for local hospitals and clinics. And we've done research into genetic abnormalities employing the most recent analytical tools. To stay abreast of this field, I and two others in the lab have participated in seminars and conferences to maintain our currency."

"Thus, when we approached you about comparing samples of those women who'd had malformed babies to normal births, you felt competent to do that?"

"We knew we were able to conduct the necessary procedures, but we recognized the odds of finding genetic differences were remote. No one had done this previously, but we agreed to try."

"And were you successful?"

A slight smile broke across her features. "After numerous trial analyses and comparisons, we discovered a segment of DNA different in a normal woman versus a sample from a woman who'd delivered a malformed child. I should say here that we received advice from a scientist who'd worked on the human genome project and is regarded as one of the foremost experts in identifying previously unidentified genes."

"What was your next step?"

"Using samples from ten women who had the unfortunate deliveries to an equal number of woman with healthy children, we compared the DNA pieces of the two groups. We found that each of the women with abnormals had the same set of markers. None of the normals had that grouping. We concluded that the drug Plertex functioned as the company advertised in those with one gene code, but did not in those having a different segment. In fact, the outcome was disastrous for those with this particular DNA piece."

She wanted to beat Ennis and Horn to another key question. "What are the probabilities of this finding being an anomaly?"

"From what I've learned and based on the opinions of numerous scientists, the probability of this occurring randomly is astronomical. Thus, I am confident our finding has merit and I suspect we have discovered a new gene."

Jennifer smiled at Mitchell and said, "Your Honor, I have no further questions of Dr. Mitchell. We are submitting for the record a summary of the analyses completed by Dr. Mitchell and her associates." She handed the papers to the Judge who glanced at them and returned them to be passed to the clerk.

Still sitting, Ennis asked, "Dr. Mitchell, isn't this entire business of genetic coding and DNA segments rather unbelievable?"

Jennifer wondered if Ennis were playing a game. He couldn't be so out of touch with all the publicity about genetics and advances in DNA. The daily papers and even the law journals reported on new findings and new interpretations on a regular basis.

Mitchell smiled. "A few years ago, I would have agreed with your statement, but scientific discoveries have laid to rest any doubts about the role of DNA. No, it is not outlandish or unbelievable at all. New genes are being discovered at an increasing pace and lead us to new understandings of how they impact everything we do. Medical personnel and pharmaceutical companies will have to give attention to in the future."

"Has another laboratory conducted the same analyses and found the same results or are you the only one?"

"The team headed by Dr. Julian DeVries at Eastern Institute of Medicine has confirmed my findings. Thus, two labs working independently have obtained the identical results. I'm sure others will check, but I have confidence in our work."

"Where did you locate these so called normals?"

"They were women who utilized Plertex with satisfactory outcomes. Ms. Watson and her partner used physicians who had prescribed the drug and their patients had experienced no difficulties. And the so-called abnormals were found the same way. Both groups had used Plertex."

Ennis glanced toward Horn who shook his head. Ennis said, "I have no additional questions at this time for Dr. Mitchell."

As Rose left the witness stand, Jennifer smiled. Ennis's questions had helped their case.

Dave waited in the Chester Airport terminal coffee shop as passengers from the mid-morning Kansas City flight left the plane. According to the attendant at the counter, passengers from San Francisco should have made the connection for Chester. Dave kept a newspaper raised, partially concealing his face, not wanting to be seen by Cranford if he should look into the shop. As he waited, he scanned the box scores from the major league games played yesterday. The Cardinals had won and had moved within two games of first place in their division.

He was rewarded by the appearance of Cranford moving quickly but talking to a female trying to keep pace with his long stride. Dave gave them a minute, then followed, keeping Cranford's head in sight above the crowd.

When Cranford ducked into the men's room, Dave left the terminal and went to his car, parked in the loading zone near the exit. A Channel 14 van waited four cars ahead.

When Cranford came out the terminal, the van moved forward to facilitate his departure. Dave followed as the vehicle exited the airport and headed for the downtown area. Maintaining the routine he observed before, the station van traveled directly to Cranford's apartment and waited for him to drop off luggage and return with a briefcase in hand. He had not changed clothes nor had he had sufficient time inside to communicate with anyone other than perhaps a cursory hello.

Dave let the van disappear, waited three minutes then knocked on the apartment door and rang the bell. No one responded. He walked around the building. All lights were off, no noise of movement inside. He peeked through a couple of windows, one into a bedroom, but nothing seemed amiss. As he retraced his steps, Dave went up three steps onto a small porch and the rear door. A gas grill took much of the space on the wooden structure. He pushed on the door. To his surprise, it opened and he eased into the kitchen, stopping to listen for any movement.

Making a conscious effort not to touch anything and leave a fingerprint, Dave hugged a wall as he moved down a hall toward the sleeping areas. He recalled freeing Miriam from one of these rooms earlier when he'd confronted Hank Willard. Doors to the two bedrooms were open. No one was there. Beds were made, clothes were hung neatly in closets. None of the usual clutter associated with bachelor quarters was evident.

Pushing his curiosity, he grabbed a wash cloth from the bathroom and opened closet doors. Men's jackets, shirts and pants hung neatly. Shoes were secured on a rack. Nothing to suggest a female had been here. He closed the doors, returned the cloth to the rack, and exited the back door after making sure there were no neighbors eyeing the building.

He drove away, stopped three blocks later and dialed Rasmussen who responded immediately, "Yeah, what's up?".

"Nothing here of promise. How about your end?"

"I'm glad you called in. A patrol just reported a car parked in the back lot of the Holiday Inn located at the next ramp south on the interstate. The desk clerk indicated it had been there since the weekend. Maybe you should go look it over."

"License plates match the ones we have for Miriam's?"

"The plates have been removed. We're getting the vehicle registration number through Motor Vehicles. I'm going to call the patrol guys as soon as I have it, probably within the next few minutes."

Fifteen minutes later Dave wound his way through the traffic around the motel until he saw two uniformed officers standing near the car. He pulled up by them and got out.

Before he could ask, the older guy, his paunch extending over his belt, said, "It's Reading's car. Rasmussen called the registration. It matches."

"Any evidence of what went down?"

"Nope, the inside and the trunk are clean. Almost like somebody cleaned it up recently."

Dave opened the driver side and leaned in. Nothing visible to suggest any activity. The uniform cop was right.

CHAPTER 23

Jennifer met Dr. Rosalind Peters for breakfast in the Marriott restaurant on Wednesday morning. Peters had flown in from Baltimore the evening before and had asked to be brought up to date on the trial and to clarify a couple of questions they had discussed by telephone a week before. In spite of a late arrival and an early start, Peters seemed bright-eyed and alert.

Stirring her cereal, Peters asked, "So did the jury believe the DNA comparisons?"

"Dr. Peters, it's always difficult to know what a jury is thinking, but they were alert and seemed interested. The jury is a reasonably well educated group who keeps up with current events."

Peters smiled, as she put her coffee cup on the saucer. "So you ran background checks on them?"

"I learn as much as possible about the entire panel and use a juror screening professional who helps identify quirky characters who might go against any evidence because of some religious belief or personality trait."

"Will your questioning of me follow the order which we discussed?"

"Yes. I hope to make a strong impression about how Frasier failed to reveal all the test case data to the FDA panel. That will be important in making the case for holding Frasier responsible."

"Will the opposing attorneys go overboard to cast doubt on my testimony or background?"

"Thus far, the Frasier lawyers have been reasonable. They haven't pushed any witness very hard to retreat from a statement they'd made."

"I'm prepared unless there's a huge surprise. Now I'd like to go to my room for a while."

Jennifer stood and said, "I'll see you in forty-five minutes. My associate will come by to escort you to the court house. You will be first up this morning." She watched Peters' square figure as she entered the elevator, thinking about the unique combination of toughness and brilliance melded together in a single personality.

The bailiff approached the attorneys just before opening time for the resumption of the trial. "Judge Plunkett would like to see you in her chambers before we start."

Plunkett was waiting for them, standing behind her desk, robe in place, as they were led in.

She asked, "I wanted to inquire about Ms. Reading. Ms. Watson, any news?"

"She has not been found, but her abandoned car was discovered by the Chester police yesterday. They are still searching for her. Everyone is concerned for her safety."

Horn broke in. "This is most unusual, Judge. I suspect the plaintiffs are playing a game with the court."

"That's absurd, Your Honor. Ms. Reading has been kidnapped on three other occasions in the past few months by her former husband. We believe that is the situation, but the police have not been able to locate her."

The Judge scanned their faces, then looked down at papers on her desk. "Mr. Horn, I believe there's nothing devious in play. Let's continue with the hearing and hope she will be found safely." Plunkett moved around her desk and waited for the attorneys to precede her into the courtroom.

Jennifer led Peters through a set of questions to establish her credentials, summarize her professional experience, and reveal her role on the Food And Drug advisory panel.

"Dr. Peters, were you present when Frasier Pharmaceuticals presented their request for approval of the drug, Plertex?"

"Yes, I was."

"Were you satisfied with the experimental protocols leading to the development of Plertex?"

"I was. I thought Frasier had done a credible job in developing a drug that could be a significant advance for those women who suffer from eclampsia and related complications during pregnancy."

"Are you able to elaborate so the jury understands the process?"

"Certainly," Peters said, her eyes scanning the jury and the audience of several reporters, family members of the plaintiffs and court hounds. "Frasier had done appropriate animal studies in the early stages, then had tested the drug in primates, before the trial test with pregnant women. The hurdle difficult to overcome in the early experiments is duplicating the pregnancy condition in species other than humans. As far as we know, eclampsia does not exist in other species and it is really impossible to set up parallel models. But Frasier had tried and I was satisfied they'd done as well as possible."

"But you had reservations, didn't you?"

"My concerns surfaced when Frasier presented data from the test group of women. They told the panel they had tested the drug on twenty women who through referrals from their physicians had volunteered. But Frasier presented data from only sixteen, all of whom had responded positively to Plertex. Their pregnancies had gone to term and each had delivered a healthy child. However, when we asked about the other four, Frasier hemmed and hawed, giving various excuses for not having that information. Their position on those four gave me reason for pause as I thought about approving this new drug.

"I asked if they would provide the data from the four for our review. When they indicated they could not, I balked. I've been around science long enough to know there are often subjects in a test who don't respond as you predict or as the majority have, but these so-called non-responders are worthy of further examination. Why they react differently is reason to think something is not quite right."

"What did you do?"

"I took the position that we should not approve release of Plertex onto the general market until we could see the information from all the test subject or until we could review the results of the wider trial being planned at that time. My colleagues, all scientists, agreed and we voted to table Frasier's request until they provided the complete results, including the outcomes of the two hundred Frasier intended to conduct a test run of Plertex."

"Did Frasier subsequently submit the missing data?"

"No, but the FDA Commissioner overrode our recommendation and gave approval. After that, Frasier had no reason to follow up on our demand nor to follow through with the larger trial. They had gained what they needed to move forward."

"But you remained skeptical, didn't you?"

"I did," Peters testified, shifting in the witness chair, "and subsequent and unfortunate events proved the panel's position to have merit. Numerous women have delivered deformed children, none of whom have survived. I learned later that the four women in the test group had babies who did not live because of their response to Plertex. Those were the four Frasier did not report on."

Horn objected, standing at his full-height. "Dr. Peters' conclusion has not been proven. It is pure speculation at this point and I move to strike from the record."

Before Jennifer could respond, Plunkett stepped in. "Mr. Horn, you have a valid point, but I believe the trial is about proving the question. I'm letting the testimony stand."

Jennifer smiled at Peters and said, "Judge Plunkett, I have no further questions for Dr. Peters."

Horn approached, his imposing presence looming over the witness box.

"Dr. Peters, you seem to harbor conflicting opinions about the Frasier drug. Am I correct?"

"Initially I believed it was the answer to those problems confronted by many women, but my initial impression has changed because of the problems caused by Plertex."

"But you admit the drug benefited most of the users?"

"Apparently, it did. But I'm not persuaded women should use it until we know why there are non-responders who suffer grave outcomes."

"Can't you accept that eighty percent of the users were elated? Most of the life-changing decisions in this country are decided by much closer majorities."

Peters eyed Horn for a few seconds. "I acknowledge that, but when great damage is done, the minority must be protected. In this specific situation, Frasier might be able to modify the composition of Plerplex to avoid putting the minority at risk or determine what went wrong and advise physicians about the risks. It's doesn't have to be all or nothing."

"Then you are willing to deprive the majority of potential users the advantages of this drug?"

Peters nodded, a few strands of gray hair wafting across her face. She wiped her hand across her forehead to put them back in place. "Yes, I am, but I suggest it doesn't have to be left that way."

Horn stepped even closer to the witness box. "Dr. Peters, we have talked to several of your close colleagues. You have the reputation for being rather difficult to get along with and always find some detail about which to argue. Isn't this the situation with Plerptex?"

Peters put her hands on the railing of the box, as though to challenge Horn. "I insist on things being clean and straight-forward. I can't abide sloppy behavior like Frasier's . . . ."

Horn cut in. "Have the plaintiffs agreed to reimburse you for your testimony?"

Jennifer stood. "I object, Your Honor. This question is out of line."

Plunkett ruled. "Sustained. Mr. Horn, I'm not clear on what your trying to get to."

Before Horn could reply, Peters said, "The jury should know I've not accepted one penny from anyone for my testimony. Ms. Watson agreed to reimburse me for travel expenses. That's it."

Horn retreated toward his table. "That's all I have for this witness."

Plunkett declared a fifteen minute recess.

After weaving through rows of cars and trucks of every make and model, Dave parked in front of Mitchell's Automobile, a dealer for used cars in the Chester county area. He'd found through Miriam's office that she'd planned to meet two representatives, Gerald Mitchell and his son and co-owner Jeremy for dinner on Friday evening to discuss possible advertising on Channel 14.

A salesman strode out to meet Dave as soon as he opened his door. Dave held up his hand, "Not buying today, but I'm looking for Gerald or Jeremy."

"Through the door there." He pointed to the glass door at the right side of the long structure. "A secretary will help you." The salesman turned to greet another potential buyer.

Gerald Mitchell, a heavy-set gray-haired man with a beaming smile, stood when Dave entered his office. "How can I help you?"

Dave handed Mitchell a card and said, "I understand you and your son had dinner on Friday evening with Miriam Reading from Channel 14 Television."

"We did. It was both pleasant and productive. She convinced us to begin advertising on the air, something we've not done in the past." His smile had disappeared.

"You recall what time you left the restaurant?"

"I wasn't paying much attention, but it must have been around ten-fifteen or a bit later. I was home in time to see a television program that started at eleven. What's this about anyway?" Mitchell sat and pointed Dave to a straight back chair in front of the desk.

Ignoring the question, Dave said, "Did you watch Ms. Reading drive away from the parking area?"

Nodding, Mitchell said, "In fact, we followed her out of the lot. She turned left and I went the other direction. I dropped my son off at his place."

"The reason I'm asking, Mr. Mitchell, is because Miriam has been missing since she left the restaurant with you on Friday evening. She hasn't called Channel 14, missed important meetings, and failed to appear for a court date. We're trying to track her movement since you last saw her."

Mitchell's facial expression changed to a deep frown. "That's terrible. You suspect anyone?"

"There are some possible suspects, but we've not tied her to them yet. The Chester police found her car yesterday and we think it was abandoned either Friday night or sometime Saturday."

"So were we the last people to see her?"

"As far as we know now," Dave said. "But let me ask if you observed other cars leaving Arthur's the same time you did or anyone lurking about?"

Mitchell ran a beefy hand across his face. "Not that I recall. For sure, no one was between our vehicle and her car when we drove away. I can't remember if there were other lights behind us, but the parking area had only a few cars around. We were the last people to leave the restaurant, so I'd guess any other cars belonged to staff."

Dave waited for Mitchell to add other thoughts, but after a significant pause, he stood. "Thanks for your time, Mr. Mitchell, and if you recall anything else, give me a call."

"I will,' he said, coming around the desk to follow Dave through the door, "And I'll check with my son. He might remember something I've not."

Dave left Mitchell's and drove to the downtown area, parked in the office lot and walked to the police station.

He rapped on Rasmussen's door and waited for him to complete a telephone conversation.

Replacing the receiver, Rasmussen asked, "Any progress with Miriam?"

"Eliminated the Mitchell's who had dinner with her on Friday. They don't recall anything suspicious around Arthur's. They saw her drive away, so if she's been abducted, it wasn't there. She must have been grabbed between the restaurant and her home."

"We have a tail on Cranford but nothing unusual. He goes from his apartment to work, then back to the apartment. Regular routine yesterday and this morning, but we'll keep at it. And our patrols have turned up nothing. It's like she was snatched by aliens who cleaned her car, took her license plates for souvenirs, and left for another planet."

"I'll check back this afternoon. But you know Cranford had to be involved someway."

Rasmussen stood. "Unless she was a random kidnapping. It happens, you know."

"Yeah, but what are the odds. Bring him in. Give him a thorough grilling. He might say something to give a lead."

Rasmussen pursed his lips, stood behind his desk. "I'll check with Chief Drummond, but it might be worth a try. You want to be involved?"

"See what Drummond thinks. If he objects, I'll understand his not wanting an outsider involved."

Jennifer had fretted and worried about pushing the envelope too far against Frasier and causing the jury to believe she was on a vendetta. But she'd invited Dr. Barry Nelson from Kansas City to reveal his numerous liaisons with Frasier. Following the recess, she called him to the stand.

After the typical run through of questions to establish background and credibility, she asked, "Dr. Nelson, tell the jury about Frasier Pharmaceuticals' overtures to you."

Nelson, tall and gangly seemed ready to topple out of the box as he leaned forward. "Frasier has over the past five years paid for my family and me in a half-dozen expensive junkets—a five-day cruise in the Caribbean, golf outings, three days at a resort in the Ozarks, and numerous dinners and receptions. They have spent a lot of money, not just on me, but on other physicians."

"Why?"

"It's a form of courting health care providers into utilizing their products. Frasier is not the only company that does this, but they seemed to have stepped up their efforts in the last three years."

"Were you ever pressured to prescribe Frasier products?"

Nelson shook his head. "Never in an overt manner, but you feel some debt, perhaps even a responsibility, to use their products as often as possible."

"Who from Frasier arranges these deals?"

"In my experience their sales representative who visits every month will inquire about your interest. Then someone from their advertising group will make the necessary arrangements and accompany you on the junket. Typically, there are other physicians with you. But all the interactions are one-on-one, never a group seminar or session."

"Could you estimate the amount of money expended by Frasier in support of these activities?"

"Just thinking about what they spent on me and multiplying that by say two hundred, it would approach a million dollars. I'm never certain of the number of people being sponsored on a given trip, so it's difficult to arrive at a number you could have confidence in."

"But it's reasonable to assume, isn't it, that Frasier expends millions annually in courting physicians, not just in these recreational events, but in free samples, publications, and advertisements?"

Nodding his head, Nelson said, "Sure, but you have to admit they perform some service by keeping physicians up to date about recent developments." He seemed to reconsider what he'd said, then added, "But it comes at a cost."

"Let me shift to another topic and ask if you ever prescribed Plertex?"

"I have on four occasions. Three of those were successful in that the woman's difficulties ceased and she delivered a normal child. But the fourth was a disaster. The child was so badly deformed it lived only five days and the woman was so depressed, she is now in a psychiatric facility. I can't judge how she is going to come out of this."

"Did you believe the cause in this fourth patient was the drug?"

"Initially I chalked the problems up to some physiological aberration in the patient. Then I began to hear of others, and have come to believe Plertex is a true danger in certain women."

"Would you prescribe it again, even though it relieved serious symptoms in some patients?"

"No, I wouldn't until we know more about why certain women deliver these horrendous babies. The risk is too great."

"That's all I have for Dr. Nelson," Jennifer said, facing Judge Plunkett, then returning to her table.

When Horn approached Nelson, Jennifer was struck by the physical similarities, both tall, gangly, and with long fingers that seemed unnatural. She knew Horn would attempt to discredit Nelson and make him into a pariah in the eyes of the jury.

Horn started, "Dr. Nelson, haven't you used Frasier by accepting these gifts, then turning against them when the first minor problem occurs?"

Staring at Horn as though wanting to reach out and slap him across the head, Nelson said, "If anything, I've been blackmailed into using Frasier products. I should have said no to the first overture, but I didn't. Now I feel used."

Horn persisted. "You eagerly accepted expensive gifts until the first little thing goes wrong, then you turn on your benefactor."

Jennifer intervened. "Judge, I don't perceive a question here."

"She's right, Mr. Horn. Refrain from making arguments and badgering the witness."

Horn, seemingly unfazed by the rebuke, continued, "Don't you have to give Frasier some credit for developing Plertex? After all, it worked wonderfully well in three of the four patients you treated."

Nelson nodded, crossing his long legs in the confines of the box. "I do, but I wish they had done enough research and testing to know the pitfalls in certain patients. I won't chance using Plertex again until I know the drug has been modified to reduce risks."

"Thus we deny the benefits to the majority of women because of the few who have difficulties. Isn't that your position?"

"I can't speak for other physicians, but I will not recommend Plertex until I know why certain women should avoid it. The consequences are too extreme."

Horn gazed into Nelson's face for several seconds as though examining every detail of his features, then said, "Judge, I have no further questions of this witness."

Judge Plunkett announced the noon recess and reminded attorneys the trial would resume at two o'clock.

Jennifer remained at the table, rearranging papers in preparation for the next session, her thoughts wandering about the impact of testimonies on the jury and the status of Miriam. She accepted it would not be good. She'd been missing too long for any favorable outcome.

CHAPTER 24

Chief Drummond had agreed to have Dave present when they interrogated Cranford about Miriam. Dave sat next to Rasmussen and across a rectangular table from Cranford and his attorney, Hiram Bixley. The space, used for a variety of purposes was almost bare— nothing on the gray walls, no carpet to mask the worn linoleum.

Rasmussen turned on a recorder. Bixley said, "For the record, we object to Dave Randle being present. This should be strictly a police matter."

Holding up a hand, Rasmussen said, "We'll note your objection, but Chief Drummond has hired Mr. Randle on a fee basis to aid in our investigation."

When Bixley didn't respond immediately, Rasmussen continued, "And also for the record, we're questioning Billy Cranford in connection with the missing person, Miriam Reading, because of his previous episodes with her. Now, Mr. Cranford, tell us about your activities last Friday evening. And so you know, we have learned you were at the same restaurant as the missing person and that you asked about her companions. What happened after that?"

Cranford eyed Rasmussen as though ready to challenge his authority to pry into his personal life, then said, "I left the place and went home."

"What time did you leave the restaurant?"

Cranford hesitated. "Around nine."

"Who was your companion that evening?"

"Oscar Thayer. He's a friend who was passing through town."

"And did he go to your home with you?"

"No, I dropped him at his hotel, the downtown Marriott, if you wish to check."

"Can you verify you went home?"

Shaking his head, Cranford, "I live alone. No one can support my actions."

Rasmussen referred to a folder, then said, "You are under court order to participate in anger management sessions, but according to the records provided by the counselors, you have only been present one time. That's out of a possible six sessions. Why?"

"My schedule is too hectic." Under his breath, he muttered, "Plus, I regarded those as a waste of my time."

"We'd like to strike that last statement," Bixley said, "My client does not mean that the way it came across."

"Then how does he mean it?" Rasmussen asked. "He doesn't have a choice about participating or the court will lock him up for an extended time."

"I'll make certain he goes on a regular basis," Bixley said, "but he's correct about his schedule."

Persisting, Rasmussen noted, "Then he needs to rearrange his schedule to comply with a court order. That's his first priority."

"Let's go back to last Friday, the last day Ms. Reading was seen," Rasmussen continued, as he closed the folder. "Why did you care about Reading's dinner companions?"

Cranford rubbed his hands together on the table top. "I thought they were potential clients of the station and that I might go introduce myself, but the receptionist didn't know, so I let it pass."

"And you're sure that's the last time you saw Miriam Reading or did you follow her and abduct her again?"

Cranford responded quickly. "Nope, it's like I told you. I dropped Oscar at the Marriott and went home."

Rasmussen turned to Dave. "You have questions?"

Dave said, "We know you've been nosing around Miriam several times since the last kidnapping. If you followed your usual pattern, you grabbed her in route to her home last Friday and have her locked away somewhere." His eyes bored into Cranford's, challenging him to react aggressively, lose his temper and reveal something he was holding back.

Anticipating Cranford's typical reaction when challenged, Bixley stepped in. "My client has told you about his actions last Friday. That's all we're going to say."

"You should know you continue to be our prime suspect in this apparent kidnapping, so you might save further questioning by telling us anything that would help us find Reading."

Bixley stood and pushed his chair back. "I think we're done here. My client has been forthcoming. Anything else I consider badgering." He stood and turned toward the door. Cranford followed.

To their backs, Rasmussen said, "Remember your court obligations or you'll be back in here or in Judge Chandler's chambers."

After Bixley and Cranford had left, Rasmussen switched off the recorder. "I think he's hiding something. I intend to keep up our surveillance."

"I'm going to check on this buddy of Cranford's. Find out when he checked into the hotel."

"Let me know anything interesting," Rasmussen said, as they closed the door behind themselves.

Dave walked to the Marriott and waited at the check-in counter until an elderly couple signed their credit card slip and received a key. The clerk, a young woman, brown hair, bright brown eyes, perpetual smile, looked at him. "May I help you?"

Dave tried to match her smile. "I'm helping the Chester police on a matter and would like to look at your guest list for last Friday." He showed his identification.

Her face turning sober, Pamela according to her name tag pinned on her blazer, said, "I'll need to clear with the manager, if you would wait a moment." She turned to an office behind the reservation and check-in counters.

A moment later, the stern-faced manager appeared. "What's this about?"

Dave explained his mission and said, "I can get a subpoena if needed to determine the movement of this guy, Oscar Thayer."

"That won't be necessary." The manager began to punch computer buttons, paused, hit another key, then swiveled the terminal so Dave could see. "Here. Mr. Thayer checked in last Thursday evening and checked out on Saturday morning."

Dave asked, "Any unusual occurrences around his stay—visitors, long-distance calls, things like that?"

"Doesn't appear to be. Of course, we don't keep track of our guests comings and goings."

Knowing he'd hit a wall, Dave said, "Thanks for your help."

He exited the front door and turned toward the courthouse. Maybe Thayer helped Cranford grab Miriam, clean her car, trash the license plates, and got out of town. But it seemed more likely Cranford did the deed himself. As he passed the doorman, an idea hit him, but this was the wrong shift to respond to his questions.

Jennifer had decided to use Dr. Stafford to remind the jury again about the severity of the malformations in those children damaged by Plertex. She led him through his credentials and experience, his awareness of Plertex through Jeffrey Short, and his deciding to prescribe it to relieve Miriam of her severe symptoms.

"Dr. Stafford, as the attending physician for Miriam Reading, how would you describe the events associated with her pregnancy?"

"Both Ms. Reading and I were pleased with the initial response to the drug. She was able to resume her normal schedule and we believed the pregnancy would proceed without problems. Then, as I normally do with patients, we ran a scan of the fetus around the seventh month. Obvious abnormalities of the face and head appeared. Ms. Reading decided to allow the pregnancy to go to term. The child was born with deformities and worse, neither the liver nor the kidneys had developed normally. The child died on day ten after birth."

Jennifer picked up a photograph from her table and handed it to Stafford. "Is this a picture of the Reading child?"

"Yes. I took the photograph before the mother and child left the hospital. I typically do that when there are unusual physical characteristics. Those records can assist other physicians and myself with future situations."

. Jennifer turned to the Judge. "Your Honor, I would like to show this picture of Miriam Reading's child to the jury. Ms. Reading has given permission for this." She handed the photo to the Judge.

Horn was on his feet. "I object, Judge, to the picture of some deformed baby being flouted in a public arena. We're not even sure it is Reading's child."

"Dr. Stafford has testified to the authenticity of the photograph, Your Honor, and the jury needs to understand the trauma involved here. I suggest the jury must see this to be able to fully comprehend the nature of the damage."

Her face frowning, Judge Plunkett, said, "I'm going to allow this, Ms. Watson, in spite of Mr. Horn's objection and the nature of the photograph."

Murmurs of conversation broke out among the audience as the jurors passed the photograph along, each staring for a moment, some wiping heir faces as though trying to erase the images, others staring blankly as they passed it to their neighbor.

Her attention now on Stafford, Jennifer asked, "When did you suspect Plertex to be the causative factor in the deformities?"

"I had suspicions when we did the scan because there were no other indicators in Ms. Reading's family history to suggest a problem. My suspicions became factual when I learned of several others much like the Reading baby. "

"Thus, you firmly believe Plertex was the culprit?

"There is no doubt in my mind."

"Thank you, Dr. Stafford. Your Honor, I have no additional questions of Dr. Stafford."

Judge Plunkett waited several seconds as though considering the time, then said, "Mr. Horn, you may cross examine the witness."

Horn and Ennis leaned toward each other and whispered, then Ennis stood. "Judge, we have no questions for Dr. Stafford at this time, but we reserve the right to call him later."

Jennifer stood to gain Plunkett's attention. "Your Honor, this concludes the presentation by the plaintiffs."

Plunkett announced, "In that case, let's recess until two this afternoon."

Jennifer arranged her papers to be prepared for the afternoon session when the defense would call a series of witnesses. She hoped she was ready to cross the experts to appear on behalf of Frasier.

As the courtroom emptied, Dave came forward. "You have time to grab a bite at that café around the corner?"

"And more. I might run back to the office after lunch." She took his hand. "How it'd go with Cranford?"

"Generally a waste of time except for learning the name of his buddy at the restaurant. I intend to explore that lead and I have an idea for follow-up late this afternoon."

During the late afternoon traffic rush in downtown at five-thirty, Dave found the doorman at the Marriott. He approached saying, "Randy, how're you doing?" He had interacted on several occasions with Randy Sanders once they learned both were veterans. Randy had been an front line infantryman during Vietnam, had fought the demons in his memories by using alcohol for years before a rehab program had worked. He'd been at the Marriott almost ten years now as the front man during the late afternoon and night shift.

"Good, busy, lot of traffic these days."

"I wanted to ask about two guys who probably were here on Friday evening?" He showed Randy a photo of Billy Cranford he'd clipped from a news article about the sportscaster.

Randy shoved the Marriott cap back on his head, almost bald with a couple of gray strands. His eyes on the photo, he said, "Yeah, he was around on Friday, maybe about seven, picked up another fellow."

"You recall when they came back?"

"Not certain of the time, but late. Maybe around midnight or later. Not much movement then, so you remember."

"Anything unusual strike you when they returned?"

Randy waved to a car pulling in and yelled at a porter to get out here. He opened the passenger door and smiling and bowing, helped a woman out.

Turning back to Dave, he said, "Yeah, this guy," pointing to the photo, "got out to shake his friend's hand and to talk a couple of minutes. But the odd thing was his clothes were rumpled and dirty as though he'd been in a wrestling match. Just didn't seem quite right, didn't fit two well dressed guys out for a fun evening. I figured he'd gotten into some brawl."

"What about his buddy?"

"I noticed some dirt or dust on his pants, but his clothes weren't as bad as this guy in the paper."

"Did you hear their conversation?"

"No, I was too far away and a city bus passed about the same time."

"Thanks, Randy. You've been helpful." As usual, Dave pressed a bill into Randy's hand.

Ennis called three women in succession to testify that they had used Plertex on the advice of their physicians and had been ecstatic when the symptoms of nausea and cramping had disappeared and they had delivered a normal healthy child on schedule.

Jennifer had asked the same question to each. "Did your mother or sisters experience problems during their pregnancies?"

Each responded in the negative.

Then Ennis called the Research Director for Frasier, Dr. Phillip Armbruster. He testified as having a Ph.D. in Genetics and Physiology from Wisconsin, had been a scientist for Frasier for twenty years, then was elevated to the position of Director five years ago. Armbruster appeared uncomfortable as a witness, no doubt wishing he was still hidden away in a laboratory with a bevy of assistants doing his experiments. Ennis led him through the development and testing phases for Plertex, including the trial with twenty pregnant subjects. He concluded by telling how Frasier obtained approval from the FDA panel without mentioning the arguments that had broken out.

Jennifer approached the witness stand with purpose. Wanting the jury to pay attention, she raised her voice above her usual tone. "Dr. Armbruster, you testified that the FDA panel approved Plertex, but that isn't correct is it? Tell the jury why the FDA panel did not approve Plertex."

Armbruster seemed taken aback by the direct assault. He shifted in the chair and seemed to stutter for a moment before gaining control of his facilities. "There was an debate about a minor issue that was blown out of proportion. Sometimes one scientist will get off on some irrelevant detail and the others will jump on the thing."

"Wasn't the so-called minor issue the failure of Frasier to report data from four women in the test group?"

"A panel member insisted we present those data, although the subjects had not completed the trial."

"But isn't it true that those four women delivered deformed babies and Frasier could not explain why?"

"There are always non-responders in every experiment with live subjects, no matter the species."

"Did Frasier attempt to determine what went wrong with those women?"

"We believed the majority of the women had successful pregnancies was sufficient reason to seek approval of the drug."

"So you did not try to discover the reasons for the deformed children in the non-responders?"

"It was a fluke. That always happens but the eighty percent who responded as we predicted was solid basis for moving forward and obtaining approval for the drug."

"Thus, you suggest Frasier has no responsibility for what went wrong in those women who reacted differently to Plertex than the majority?"

"It has to be something other than Plertex in their background. I don't believe it's the companies responsibility to find out every little flaw in the users."

Jennifer turned toward the jury. "If you believe the testimony of Dr. Peters and Dr. Mitchell, the problem clearly was a genetic difference in those non-responders. Frasier should have searched for that."

Ennis jumped to his feet. "Your Honor, the counselor is arguing the case now."

"I'll withdraw my comment, Judge Plunkett. I have no further questions of Dr. Armbruster."

Dave was in the kitchen when Jennifer got home near six. He had gathered vegetables from their garden and was mixing tomatoes, lettuce, onions, carrots and a radish when she dropped her briefcase on the floor and leaned in to watch his movements, their shoulders touching.

"Looks great. Our efforts at farming have paid off."

He turned to meet her lips. "Maybe check the broiler. Couple of chops probably ready. The trial going okay?"

"Think so," she said, pulling the pan out of the oven and turning off the heat.

"Let's hear the news while we eat." They had fallen into the habit of bringing plates and drinks to the den while watching the evening news.

The first announcement from the local anchor caught their attention. "Breaking news. Chester police have reported the finding the body of an adult female by two boys riding their bikes along the trail in the national forest. Identification has not been released at this time, but according to the teenagers, they believed the body had been there for several days."

CHAPTER 25

The telephone rang. Rasmussen was on the line, 'Dave, I intended to call earlier, but things have been hectic around here. Two teenage boys found a female body while riding their bikes along a trail in the national forest west of town."

"Is it Miriam Reading?" Dave interrupted.

"Yeah, we're pretty sure it's her, but I'd like you to come to the morgue and identify her. If you know of any family living near, we would like them to come also."

"I'm on the way," Dave said.

"Let's shoot for seven-thirty. I'd like to meet you there, but there's something I must do before."

Jennifer watched Dave's face. "What's wrong?"

"That body is probably Miriam Reading. Rasmussen wants me to identify her to be sure." His voice choked.

Dave pulled Jennifer close. They both wanted to yell in frustration and defeat. They remained together for a couple of minutes, neither wanting to let go, seeking comfort and understanding.

Then reality confronted them. Jennifer muttered, "Horn and Ennis will go ballistic and try to stop the trial, but that's the least of our worries now." She moved away from Dave and paced across the room. "When you go, drop me at the office. I want to look up something relevant to a missing plaintiff case and be prepared for what's sure to be a motion to dismiss."

The taste of dinner went from bland to bad as they tried to eat. Their thoughts were too focused on the probable death of a friend and client. After a few bites, Jennifer took her plate to the kitchen sink. "I can't do this now. Maybe we'll be able to eat later."

"I feel the same," Dave said. "I need to change shirts, then we'll go."

On the drive into the city, both were quiet for a bit, then Dave said, "We should have done more to protect her, but I didn't know what else to do, other than shoot Cranford."

"I know how you feel, but other than locking her away, I think we did everything possible. Remember, she dismissed Monk's boys. Had they still been following her, this wouldn't have happened."

Dave paced the foyer of the city building while waiting for Rasmussen, his thoughts on Miriam and how to prove Cranford had killed her or how to find the person who did. He recalled Jennifer telling him about the likely actions of control freaks and abusers like Cranford, that they eventually murdered their victim if not locked away for life. And he thought about how easily he could have killed Cranford on a couple of occasions, just a bit more pressure or in a slightly different location and Miriam would still be alive. The flip side of such action would have been his defending himself in court and damaging his relationship with the local police.

Rasmussen charged in ten minutes late, breathing rapidly and wiping beads of sweat from his forehead. "Sorry to hold you up, but the Chief is stirred up about our failure to protect her."

"That's a switch. A month ago, he didn't seem to give a damn."

They went down stairs to a floor below the main entrance and along a dimly lighted hall through an open door into an office. An attendant looked up from her computer screen and recognizing Rasmussen, said, "The M.E. is waiting for you." She pointed to heavy doors leading into the morgue.

The body was on a slab, still dressed and not yet cleaned, pretty much as she'd been brought in. Her navy dress had been ripped, one shoe was missing, her nylons were torn, and leaves and dirt could be seen on one shoulder. Dave looked at a face he'd held in his hands, traces of dried blood on her cheeks, eyes closed, a deep gash across the side of her head, disheveled blond hair matted with blood and grime. Her fingernails were broken and dirty.

Controlling his desire to scream in frustration, he nodded. "Yes, that's Miriam Reading."

The Medical Examiner, a sturdy middle-age physician, said, "Obviously, we haven't done a thorough autopsy yet, but my best guess the cause of death is blunt force trauma. The back of her cranium is fractured. Probably hit with a tire iron or something like that. I can tell you more by morning."

Rasmussen said, "We'll get out of your way. There's nothing more we can do here."

They walked toward the front entrance to the building, neither voicing their feelings. Finally, Dave said, "I know her parents lived in Chicago, but I don't have an address. Maybe when we're allowed in her apartment, we can locate addresses and telephone numbers."

"We'll have access by tomorrow morning."

The only news in the morning newspapers was a short item on the front page about a body discovered in the forest. Thinking about the court battle sure to come, Jennifer decided to take the initiative, if for no other reason than to prevent Horn and Ennis from criticizing her for not being fully forthcoming. Ten minutes before the morning session was scheduled, she asked the bailiff standing at the door to the chambers to arrange a meeting with the Judge, and to include the defense team.

Judge Plunkett had not yet put on her robes when the attorneys were led in. Plunkett motioned for them to take chairs arranged around the front of her desk. Jennifer started immediately, "I asked for a brief meeting to inform all that Miriam Reading was found dead last evening along a trail in the national forest. I don't have other details at this time but the police are withholding her name until they've notified her kin."

Horn jumped in. "Judge Plunkett, this is cause for dismissal."

"I disagree," Jennifer said . "There are numerous precedents to continue in the absence of a plaintiff who just happened to have her name prominently placed on the court documents. Any one of the others could just as well be listed first. Plus, there are recorded cases when the plaintiff has not been alive and a suit was brought on his or her behalf. If you wish, I can bring in those references for your review."

Horn persisted. "Judge, much of the evidence presented by Ms. Watson has been associated with Miriam Reading, including that hideous photo of the child. I believe that evidence is now null and should be voided."

"Mr. Horn," Jennifer argued, "the findings related to Ms. Reading could just as well have been associated with any of the other plaintiffs. You must remember the testimony of Katherine Mosley who had a similar catastrophe with her child. We could have submitted a photo of her child as well, and if necessary, we will."

Plunkett held up her hand. "From my vantage point, I believe Ms. Watson is correct in citing other cases like this in which the plaintiff has been deceased. Let us continue the trial, but I'd like the jury to not be informed by members of the court about Reading's death. Let's not make an issue of this."

Ennis shrugged. Horn stared at the Judge as though she was out of her mind. Jennifer could visualize an appeal coming if she prevailed with the jury, but she felt secure in her argument.

Horn called Dr. Erich Horvath, a prominent biochemist from a large research institute in the northeast. Horvath's eastern European heritage revealed itself through his dialect and phrasing as Horn queried him about education, background and recent credentials.

After ten minutes Horn honed in on the issue at hand. "Dr. Horvath, tell the jury about your involvement with the development of Plertex ."

"I was a consultant to Frasier Pharmaceuticals throughout the various experiments to develop a medication that would relieve the symptoms of eclampsia during pregnancy. My primary role was advisory in nature rather than in the actual chemical formulation of the drug in the laboratory. I worked closely with Frasier scientists in preparing the initial formula, attempting to respond to the known problems of certain women during gestation. I reviewed the data from the tests with animals, then those with primates, and finally after making minor modifications in the composition of the medication, Frasier conducted a controlled trial with a group of women. I reviewed the information gained from those women."

"In your opinion, did Plertex meet the goals established by Frasier?"

"It did. An overwhelming majority of the test subjects reacted positively and were pleased with the outcome. They all indicated they would use Plertex again and would recommend it to their friends."

Horn scanned the jury to make sure they were attentive, then said, "Thank you, Dr. Horvath. I have no other questions."

Jennifer thought Horvath had impressed the jury. Her experience told her lay people associated certain accents and word phrases with scientists prominent in their disciplines and accorded them more credence than they deserved. She needed to punch holes in Horvath's story.

Near the witness box, she looked directly into Horvath's face. "Dr. Horvath, what was your reaction to the four women who did not respond positively to Plertex and had disastrous outcomes?"

Horvath blinked through his thick glasses and the corners of his mouth turned down into a frown. "I was told by the primary researchers on the study that those four did not complete the experiment. That happens frequently. Subjects tire of the protocol they are forced to follow and just drop out."

"But I understand that Frasier followed up with regular visits to all the participants. Did those four drop out early or were there signals that something was different about those women?"

"I was not involved in that phase. I cannot respond."

Surprised by his apparent lack of what had really happened, Jennifer asked, "Didn't you suspect something other than disenchanted participants? After all, this medication had relieved their problems and they were able to engage in their usual activities. Why would they discontinue the medication and risk a return of eclampsia and all the associated dangers and restraints. "

"I didn't have any suspicions. I truly believed they had dropped out."

"Are you now familiar with the outcomes of those four pregnancies?"

"I was told in getting ready for this testimony that there might be questions about them." He looked toward Horn and

Ennis. "But I don't know any details other than those four women had problems, but likely not associated with Plertex."

"And wouldn't you be suspicious if twenty percent of the group had difficulties?"

"I don't know the statistics of abnormalities or defects found at birth. But I'd hazard a guess it would be in the ball park of the number you cite."

"Dr. Horvath, do you have any idea of infant death rates in this country?"

Shaking his head, "No, I don't keep up with those kind of numbers."

"Do you know of any efforts by Frasier to modify Plertex after the outcomes of those non-responding women?"

"No," shaking his head. "No one has asked for my input into a review of the drug."

Jennifer believed she'd damaged Horvath enough to make him less an expert in the thinking of the jury. She realized she was confronting a scientist who lived in his own sheltered world and while he no doubt made solid contributions to his discipline, he had no idea of what occurred in society around him.

She looked at the jury and said, "Judge, I have no further questions for Dr. Horvath."

Horn and Ennis had on their witness list an associate Director of the Food and Drug Administration. Jennifer had prepared a set of queries for that individual, but now Horn rose and said, "Judge Plunkett, the defense rests."

Plunkett glanced toward the bailiff and then at her wrist watch. "The court is recessed until two this afternoon. At that time, I will ask for closing arguments." She rose and turned toward the door leading to her chambers.

Dave had returned to Rasmussen's office when Jennifer headed for the court session. Rasmussen saw him enter the lobby area and motioned for him to come to his office.

"The M.E. just called. They worked late last night and he has certified the cause of Miriam's death as blunt force trauma. He found numerous other injuries, a broken rib, fractured wrist, a huge bruise on her side. Whoever killed her had knocked her around before or maybe even after the fatal blow."

"Any indication of sexual activity?"

"None. Her clothes were intact, except for the damage you'd expect from being battered. Semen was not found."

"Did he find fingerprints or DNA?"

"He didn't find usable prints, but he'd recovered several foreign hairs and a tiny bit of tissue on a tooth. Her assailant either hit her in the mouth or she bit him in the scuffle."

Dave said, "I'd like to look around the place where the boys found her, if it's okay."

"Sure. We've done what we can do, but we haven't searched very widely away from the spot the body was left."

"I assume you're bringing Cranford in for questioning?"

"As soon as we can find him and go through the usual tussle with his lawyer."

Rasmussen pulled a map from his desk, opened it and scribbled notes on the margin. "Here's the site. It's not far off the well-marked trail used by hikers and bikers."

"I'll find it okay," Dave said. Earlier in the spring, he and Jennifer had hiked along the trail leading to a picnic area where a rushing creek cascaded over huge boulders.

After a stop at the office where he returned a couple of telephone calls to clients with minor issues, Dave drove to the parking area where the trail began. He changed his shoes for boots and his coat and tie for a windbreaker.

Four hundred yards along the trail he sighted the scene, yellow tape still marking off the area. He skirted the boundary, not seeing anything out of order, but the crime scene crew would have collected anything useful in their searches. Thinking about how careless assailants can get when they're concerned about getting away before anyone spots them, Dave widened his search, moving carefully through brush and ducking under tree limbs. He stopped every few feet to survey the area ahead to avoid tramping on a piece of evidence. After fifty yards, he circled back toward the primary scene, taking a different route. Twenty yards from the trail, he walked around a thick growth of shrubs and weeds. A glint of reflected sunlight caught his eye and he edged closer. Peering through the dense growth, he spotted a shoe. Two steps closer, he shoved aside branches of a small pine and stared at the shoe. He thought it matched the one Miriam had on in the morgue. And now he could see a bit of scarf under the shoe.

He trotted to the trail and called Rasmussen on his cell phone. "I think I've found Miriam's shoe, but I didn't want to move it. Maybe you could send someone to retrieve the articles."

"Give me thirty minutes. If you would, wait for them."

When the pair of detectives appeared, Dave showed them the trove. They carefully moved in, taking photographs and placing items in evidence bags, a black shoe, and a scarf partially shoved into the shoe. They continued to search without reward for another ten minutes, carefully shoving aside bushes, and edging further into the growth.

The female crime scene investigator backed out and said, "I think we're done. I'd hoped we would find the tool they hit her with, but it's not here."

Dave said, "Her killer likely tossed it in a dumpster along with all the stuff he cleaned from her car."

"You're probably right and we'll never recover those things."

As the pair left, Dave called Rasmussen. "Have you brought Cranford in yet?"

"We've been unable to find him. He told the television station he would be on vacation for a few days, but they have no idea of where he went. Apparently, his leaving surprised them and left them scrambling for a fill-in. You could tell the manger was irritated by the tone of his voice."

"Cranford's on the run because he knew he'd be the major suspect in Miriam's death. News about the body being found alerted him to seek cover for a while."

"We're putting out an APB and alerting other jurisdictions, including the FBI. He's likely left the state and maybe the country."

"His running only convinces me more he's the culprit."

"I'll let you know as we hear from others looking for him."

CHAPTER 26

Jennifer preferred to follow Horn with their closing statements, but typically the plaintiff was scheduled to lead off. She wore her newest suit, a knee-length black skirt and matching jacket that with a white blouse exuded professionalism but feminine enough to remind jurors they were dealing with a competent woman. But in the end, she knew they would give attention to how she presented her case. Once they retired to the jury room for deliberation, facts along with opinions formed about witnesses would be the central issues of consideration. Attorneys' performances or demeanor might come into play if they had somehow irritated the jurors.

Jennifer reminded the jury, eight women and four men, of the agonies experienced by the plaintiffs when their children were deformed and then died within a few days. "Can you imagine," she stated, "the wonderful expectations associated with a new child, a precious life to be nurtured and loved, only to have all hopes turned into despair as you watched, unbelieving, the tragedy? I hope you will remember the photograph of Miriam Reading's baby. That photo could be replicated for each of the plaintiffs and for numerous other who are not part of this plea for justice.

"These women and their husbands were victims of a promise by a huge company who rushed to market a drug approved by a bureaucratic override of the judgment of scientists with years of experience. Frasier was so interested in making money, they forgot the basis of their enterprise —to create safe and reliable remedies for human ailments. When twenty percent of the women in their test experienced these terrible outcomes, they should have set out to find the reason rather than ignore those data. They pushed aside the concerns raised by the FDA panel who knew there was a glitch and asked Frasier to investigate further. But Frasier did not.

"We don't know yet the basis for the reactions of those women, but preliminary information as shown to you by Dr. Mitchell, suggests a genetic difference. I suggest Frasier can find that biological distinction and then work to provide treatment for all pregnant women who experience symptoms associated with eclampsia. I am more than disappointed they did not do this at the outset when they knew there was a problem.

"I am asking on behalf of these plaintiffs and their unfortunate children that Frasier reimburse them for their agonies. I trust you will find in favor of women who have the right to expect remedies designed to meet their needs. They should be able to place their full trust in the companies that exist to solve medical issues."

Jennifer paused for a moment, then closed. "Thank you for your attention throughout this trial." She returned to her chair and heard the Judge announce the defense attorney would present their argument.

Horn paced across the floor twice before turning to the jury, their eyes following the lanky figure. "Ladies and gentlemen, I too appreciate your attention to the witnesses as they provided their opinions about this conflict between a small group of women and an ethical pharmaceutical company that for decades has provided excellent treatments for a range of illnesses."

He stopped in front of the jury, his hands on the rail of the box, leaning forward almost as though he intended to touch those in the front row. "I don't want you to forget that Plertex met the needs of the vast majority of women who used it. Frasier Pharmaceuticals cannot be responsible for those few who for some reason or another did not respond. As Ms. Watson has attempted to demonstrate, there may be something inherently askew in those few. Neither their physicians nor Frasier understands the mysteries that go on in human reproduction, but they want to hold an innocent company responsible.

"Look carefully, intently, at the facts. Ignore the speculation, but examine the hard evidence as you make your decision."

Horn walked along the front of the jury box again, looking at each one of the twelve. "Thank you. I know you will use your good judgment in finding Frasier not responsible. I believe you cannot do otherwise."

Judge Plunkett reminded the jury of their obligations. She indicated they could request information or clarification of any testimony or document presented during the trial that might be useful in their deliberations. "The bailiff will respond to your needs. I will meet with you if there are questions of the law requiring interpretation."

The stone-faced jurors filed out of the room, led by the bailiff to a private room. Plunkett said, "I ask the attorneys to remain close until the jury reaches its decision. I want you to be able to return to this court within thirty minutes after notification. Thank you." She rose, straightened her robe and moved toward her chambers.

Jennifer breathed a quiet sigh of relief, the ordeal behind her, the pressure now on those twelve citizens she'd hoped could sort through the testimonies.

Katherine Mosley met Jennifer as she exited the courtroom. "I thought you convinced the jury."

"You can never tell," Jennifer shifted her briefcase from one hand to the other. "We should know within a few hours. I understand all of you are anxious about the verdict and I'll let you know soon after I know."

"I read the paper this morning about Miriam Reading." They ambled toward the door leading to Main Street. "I bet her former husband did that to her."

"The police are working hard on the case."

Katherine slowed the pace, causing Jennifer to look at her. "Several days ago I asked Dave to talk to my ex-husband. I'm concerned I'm going to have the same problem as Miriam if he's not stopped soon. It might get really bad if he learns I have come into all this money."

"I'll remind Dave or you could come to the office and put us on a retainer."

Katherine nodded. "I might do that. When I talked to Dave, I didn't think the situation was serious, but it's gotten worse in the past two weeks."

On the street they turned in different directions.

Rasmussen called Dave at the office. "We found a fingerprint on that shoe you discovered, but it's not Cranford's. It matches prints in the FBI database to a person named Oscar Thayer."

"That's the guy who had dinner with Cranford. This shows he helped Cranford in this whole episode. You have an address?"

"No, but he was arrested in Denver seven years ago. He was charged with kidnapping a woman and taking her across state lines. Nothing since then, but often minor incidents don't get recorded. Or this could be an alias and the dots haven't been connected."

"Any sign of Cranford?"

"None. He's off the radar."

"I have an idea and will start looking this afternoon."

Jennifer entered his office as he replaced the phone. She dropped into the chair and said, "Trial is over, now we're waiting on the jury."

"You feel okay with it?"

"We did the best we could do, but the small percentage of women affected by the drug may be a stumbling block for the jury. But on the way out, Katherine Mosley stopped me and told me she'd asked you to talk to her former husband."

"She did but I didn't take her seriously." He frowned and shook his head. "To be honest, I thought she was coming on to me and just wanted some reason to get together."

Jennifer laughed and came around the desk to put her hand on his shoulder. "And you were afraid you couldn't resist."

He grinned up at her. "She's very sexy."

"Not to mention beautiful."

"But so are you." He put his arm around her waist. "I'll call her this afternoon to get his name and address."

"Now, let's find lunch. I'm starved."

They walked onto the sidewalk and turned toward Gibbons. Dave said, "The primary reason I haven't followed up on Mosely's husband is her response to my question about their getting back together. She didn't say no, but left the issue hanging. My suspicion is she'd like to do that if he can be persuaded to approach her differently than he has."

"Maybe you can convince him."

"We'll see."

At one-thirty Dave entered the office of Wilson's Carrier and Trucking. The office fronted a huge warehouse with several semis parked near, waiting their turns to be loaded or drop off their current cargo. Drivers stood around joking with each other and exchanging information about highway conditions, detours, and speed traps.

To the man behind the desk, Dave said, "I'd like to see Rod Wilson."

"And you are?"

Dave handed him a business card. "If he refuses to talk with me, I'll have the Chester police pay him a visit or bring him into the station."

"I'll see what he says." The heavy-set front office clerk disappeared through a door. In a moment Dave heard arguing, then seconds later, Wilson appeared.

"What the hell you want?"

Dave shoved aside the urge to crack Wilson across the head. "I'd like to talk in private."

"If this is about Billy Cranford, I have nothing to say. I haven't seen him in a month, but I'd guess you guys think he killed Miriam Reading."

"Are you hiding him out somewhere like you did before?"

"Nope, haven't seen him since that little run-in at the truck stop."

"You know harboring a fugitive is a criminal act. If you don't want to tell me, call Detective Rasmussen at the Chester police."

"Can't help you." Wilson retreated to his inner sanctum.

Dave thought Wilson was lying, but pursuing him into the back office likely wouldn't pay off. And it could end up in a physical confrontation, something he was trying to avoid.

From Wilson's he drove downtown, parked in the office lot, and walked to the Marriott. At the front desk, he asked to talk to the manager.

The same guy he'd seen before came out, then motioned for Dave to come through the side door into his office.

Dave said, "Thanks for seeing me. I need more information about Oscar Thayer. He was a guest last Friday and Saturday."

The manager ran through the log of check-ins on his computer, then twisted the terminal screen toward Dave. "You can see times he checked in and out. He paid by a credit card under the same name."

"Can you retrieve an address?"

"Maybe, give me a minute." He turned the computer terminal back, punched several keys. "He registered using a Denver address." He jotted on a notepad, then handed a sheet to Dave. "Here is his street address and phone number."

"Thanks for your help." He shoved the note into his coat pocket.

On the street, he phoned Rasmussen and relayed the address for Thayer and described his visit to Rod Wilson. The detective thanked him and said he'd move on getting Thayer extradited to Chester for questioning and assign a tail to Wilson.

Dave walked to the Penny's store and found Katherine Mosley in the women's clothing department. From an aisle away he watched her engaging a customer trying to decide on a blouse. Katherine held the blouse out for the woman to observe, turning it to show the back.

Five minutes later, the transaction completed, Dave approached her. "Jennifer told me to find you." He detected her perfume as she put her hand on his arm. Her eyes bored into his, almost challenging.

"Thanks for coming by. My ex is becoming much more aggressive. Two nights ago he showed up, demanded to come in, but I refused. He left, but not before banging the door so loudly the neighbors came out to see what was going on. I'm afraid he's going to attack me."

"Does he want to resume the marriage?"

Shaking her head, she said, "He just wants to make sure no one else can have a relationship with me. A few days ago, I went to dinner with a friend from work. Nothing happened between us, but Jake was waiting at my house when he brought me home. He stormed out of his car and threatened both of us.

I know my friend was scared silly and probably won't get near me ever again."

"Where can I find Jake?"

At four thirty, Jennifer was called to be told the jury would report at five. Surprised they'd found closure so soon, she went into the restroom, ran a comb through her hair, then walked to the court.

The jurors marched in, their faces expressionless, no hint of their decision, and found their seats.

Judge Plunkett asked, "Have you reached a verdict?"

The foreman, a middle age man dressed in the same suit he'd worn throughout the trial, stood and said, "We have." He passed a paper to the bailiff and waited for it to be returned.

He read, a tremor in his voice. "We find for the plaintiffs and suggest an award of eight hundred thousand dollars to each of them."

Plunkett said, "I will take your recommendation under advisement and thank each of you for your good work on behalf of the citizens of Chester county and in this case, citizens of he nation." She banged the gavel ending the trial.

The bailiff came to the attorneys. "Judge Plunkett would like to see you in chambers."

They followed to find Plunkett still in her robe but seated at the conference table on one side of the room. "I wanted to tell both of you I am leaning toward support of the jury's recommendation for damages. Although less than requested by the plaintiffs, I believe they were not fully convinced because of the numbers of women who had a positive response to the drug. I haven't queried the jury, but that's my impression."

Jennifer, pleased with the jury finding, remained silent.

Horn and Ennis, apparently expecting exoneration, looked at each other, then to the Judge. Horn said, "We are disappointed and may appeal. My concern is that others will hear of this case and Frasier will be inundated with a host of individual suits. We could spend all our time defending Frasier. Just the attorney fees and court cost will be sufficient to bankrupt the company."

Plunkett said, "You may be correct, Mr. Horn, but my advice is for Frasier to find out what went wrong with those women and modify the formulation for the drug. I am not a scientist but I suspect testimonies from this trial should give them a lead. Their own scientists should be able to make adjustments in the composition or discover characteristics of those women in sufficient depth to warn physicians about prescribing the drug."

"We'll discuss the possibilities with Frasier officials," Horn said.

Plunkett said, "And I wanted to commend Ms. Watson for having the insight to begin searching for the reason Plertex failed in certain women. Not often do attorneys go to such lengths. And Ms. Watson, those data should be made available to Frasier."

"I'll make certain that happens," Jennifer responded. She hoped she wasn't promising something Rose Mitchell would object to. No doubt Mitchell would want some payment for her efforts. Frasier should be willing to reimburse her for the information that could move their internal investigation forward. But Jennifer didn't know if the company would attempt to solve the question regarding Plertex and a minority of non-responders.

CHAPTER 27

At eight Dave stopped in front of the apartment building at the address given to him by Katherine. He thought about his approach to her ex, Jake, hoping to avoid a physical confrontation, but prepared nevertheless. He scanned the area, the three story brick building with a parking lot on one side, shrubs screening the front, a trim lawn suggesting a middle class facility that catered to young families and single professionals. The western sun glinted faint rays on the scene as another day moved toward its end.

He climbed the stairs to the second floor, rang the bell at Apartment 216, and stepped back. He could hear faint sounds of a television, then the door opened to reveal a tall, apparently physically fit man in his early thirties.

Staring at Dave, the man said, "Whatever you're selling, I'm not buying." He began to close the door.

Dave put out a hand to stop the closing and said, "I'm looking for Jake Mosley."

"You've found him, but I'm still not buying." Mosley maintained pressure on the door.

Dave had decided not to show his identity early on, but said, "I'm here to talk about your relationship with your former wife, Katherine. I'd like to come in, so this can be private."

"I'm not interested in any message from her, so beat it." He pushed harder on the door, intending to close it, but Dave resisted, shoving inside, forcing Jake to retreat, then closing the door behind him.

Dave put his back to the door. "I'm going to say this whether you wish to hear or not. I've talked to Katherine a couple of times because of the trial in which she testified. She told me about your relationship and wants you to stop harassing her. But I suspect if you took a different approach she could be open to the two of you resuming your marriage. I don't know if either of you is really interested, but you must admit, something still attracts you to her."

Jake looked at the shorter man, seeing someone older than he, but whose gray-blue eyes never left his face. He said, "I don't how to respond to that. Every time I've seen her, she's mad."

"You have to admit you abandoned her at a difficult time and blamed her for the condition of your child. But it's something beyond her control. Recent work suggests the problem is a combination of genetics and the drug the physician placed her on."

Jake rubbed a hand across his face. "She hasn't told me that. She's pissed at my leaving but I truly believed she'd done some stupid thing to cause our baby to be born like that."

"She didn't, Jake. Now if you want to get back with her, other than forcing her to have sex on your schedule, you need to talk to her, take her to dinner, tell her you love her—all the things you did before you were married. It may not work out, but give it a try. And if she isn't interested, you need to leave her alone."

Jake said, "I'll think about it, but you can't tell me what to do."

Dave smiled. "On the surface that's true. But if you force yourself on her again, I'll come back and we'll talk again. But you need to understand, I have been trained to convince people to fall in line or be badly hurt. Give my suggestion a solid try."

"You're an arrogant bastard," Jake yelled in frustration and confusion.

"I hope I don't have to come back." He twisted the door knob.

Dave walked out, pulling the door closed and waited for Jake to rush out after him. When he didn't, Dave descended the stairs. Two minutes later, he drove away, thinking about the encounter. He was concerned he had another Cranford on his agenda, but he vowed to protect Katherine and not allow another bully to become a murderer. But maybe his efforts as a marriage counselor would prevail.

Two days later, Rasmussen phoned Dave at the office. "We're bringing Thayer back for questioning and will probably charge him with either murder or accessory. I'll let you know how it goes. Or you can be present at the interrogation."

"Any sign of Cranford?"

"Nothing, but we're keeping a tail on his buddy Wilson. But the fact is Cranford may have left the country."

"I wouldn't think so," Dave said. "He's holed up with some friend hoping all this will disappear and he can resume his normal life. He's always been able to escape punishment and believes he can do it again."

At three the following afternoon, Rasmussen and Dave sat across from Thayer and Hiram Bixley, the same attorney who'd represented Cranford. The ever present recorder whirred and beeped.

Rasmussen started by going through the routine of getting on tape the persons present, the date and place. Then he asked, "Mr. Thayer, explain how your fingerprint got on Miriam Reading's shoe near the site where her body was left."

"I have no idea what you're talking about," Thayer responded, looking at Bixley.

"Cut the crap," Rasmussen said, his voice taking on a tone Dave seldom heard from the mild-mannered detective. "We're going to charge you with the murder of Miriam Reading and if you're so stupid as to let Billy Cranford get away with the crime and take the rap for him, that's your decision."

Bixley cut in, his hand on Thayer's arm. "You don't have to say anything."

"It's up to you," Rasmussen said, pointing a finger toward Thayer's face. "But you're not walking out of here. We'll hold you for flight risk and charge you with first degree murder. That's life in prison."

Thayer's eyes wavered from Bixley to Rasmussen, then he said, "I'm not taking the fall for Cranford."

"So let's hear your story and quit killing time."

"Okay, here's what happened." Thayer nodded to Bixley and held up his hand as though to stop him from interfering again. Thayer stared at the table top for several seconds as though organizing his thoughts. "I was in Chester for a meeting with a prospective developer for a piece of property I own near Mims. Cranford and I go back a long time and I called him about dinner that evening, just to catch up and remember old times.

"We went to this place, Arthur's, I think is the name. We'd had a drink and had ordered when this woman come in with two guys. I could tell Billy was agitated like it was his wife running around on him, but he wouldn't tell me the connection. He couldn't stop watching them and stopped talking to me." Thayer stopped as though he was thinking about the scene or perhaps deciding what more to say.

Rasmussen prompted him. "So what happened?"

"It was strange. Cranford couldn't stop watching this woman. I tried to get his attention by reminding him of things we'd done together, but it was impossible to maintain a conversation. He'd respond for a moment, then he'd just stop and stare at the three across the room. Then his face would break into a scowl."

"Did he ever tell you who the three were?"

"At one point I asked, but he shrugged and started eating again. He refused to say who she was or why he was upset. Finally, we left. I paid the tab and we went to his car. We started back to the Marriott where I was staying, then suddenly he veered off a side street, muttering he had to do something.

"He drove to this housing complex, the address I couldn't tell you. He wouldn't tell me his plan, but I figured it was something to do with the woman in the restaurant. As we waited near the entry gate, he got out and paced around. He ducked behind a large shrub each time cars passed on the street. I wanted to leave, even thought about looking for a cab, but there wasn't much traffic that late.

"When the woman stopped at the gate to insert her pass card, Cranford charged from his hideout and jerked her door open. Then he hit her in the face and shoved her into the passenger's seat. I could tell they were arguing. She was yelling for help. Finally he hit her hard enough to knock her out. Then he pulled her out and manhandled her into the trunk of her car. She wasn't resisting. I think she was out cold or stunned to the point she didn't realize what was going on.

"Cranford backed her car near his and yelled at me to follow him. He waited until I could get the car going, then raced away. I had to speed to keep up."

Thayer stopped his recounting of events, seemingly thinking about the sequence or believing he'd said enough. He wiped a hand across his face and glanced toward Bixley, who said, "You don't have to say more."

With a new burst of energy, Thayer began again. "No, I want to get this out. It's been a nightmare thinking about it."

He stared at Rasmussen. "Cranford drove to this motel, went in the office and booked a room. I was parked next to her vehicle all this time."

"Where was this motel?" Rasmussen asked.

"Near the interstate, where Route 36 intersects. I couldn't tell you the name, but it was a run-down joint."

"Do you recall the room number?"

"No, but I know it was at the end of this long line of rooms. Hardly anyone else was around. No other cars were parked close."

"Then what happened?"

"Cranford dragged her out of the trunk into this room and yells at me to come in. Miriam, he called her, was sitting on the edge of the bed when I got there. Cranford was leaning over her, a golf club in his hand, yelling about having sex. I shoved him away and suggested he would get in big trouble, but he refused to back away. For a moment I thought he would hit me.

"Miriam got to her feet and screamed she was not cooperating. That's when he hit her across the head with this iron he'd taken from her trunk. She collapsed onto the floor and I shoved him away again, knowing he'd killed her or injured her badly enough she'd need medical treatment.

"Cranford became calm, pacing around the room, looking at her prone on the floor. Blood seeping from the place he'd hit her. I grabbed his arm and said we needed to get away, but he kept staring at her, almost like he couldn't believe she was not moving.

"Then he told me to stay with her and walked out. I could see him through the open door pacing around the cars, maybe thinking about what to do next. He walked to the edge of the graveled parking lot and threw the club into the woods adjacent to the place.

"I bent over Miriam to see if she was breathing. I couldn't get a pulse in her wrist, so I knew she was dead."

Dave asked. "You're sure this golf club was from her car?"

"Yeah, at first I thought it was a tire iron he'd taken from the trunk of her car, but later I could tell it was either a putter or one of the short irons, maybe even a wedge. I don't know if he believed he needed it to subdue her or he intended to hit her with it from the outset."

"Could he have had it in his own car?"

Thayer shrugged. "Don't know for sure. Might have been in the back seat, but I didn't see it until we were in the motel room."

"After he threw the club away and paced around the lot," Rasmussen asked, "what did Cranford do? And what did you do?"

"After a couple of minutes, Billy came back in and said we had to get rid of the body. Without any conversation, he leaned over her, checked her pulse, then picked up Miriam and took her to her car, put her in the trunk. Told me to follow him. We drove to this spot in the woods. He retrieved her from the trunk and yelled at me to follow him. We walked maybe five hundred yards along this trail, then he veered off to the spot he dropped her."

"How did your fingerprint get on her shoe?"

"The shoe and her scarf had fallen off while he was carrying her. I picked them up, sort of stuffed the scarf into the shoe, and tossed them into the brush. I knew Billy wanted any objects belonging to her out of sight."

Without another query, Thayer continued. "We drove both cars back to the motel. We cleaned everything out of her car, rolled everything into a package and tossed it into the dumpster.

Billy said the dumpster would get taken away before the body was discovered and no one would connect it to her."

"I assume," Rasmussen said, "you included her purse with the other stuff."

"Yes, and all the items in the glove compartment and the trunk. Billy grabbed a towel from the motel room and wiped everything in her car, making sure no fingerprints were left."

"What about blood stains?"

"He tried to scrub away those on the floor of the room with a wet towel. There were some on the mat in the trunk, but we threw that into the dumpster."

Thayer continued. "We drove both cars to this other motel. He parked her car in the rear, then he brought me back to the Marriott and dropped me off. I haven't seen nor heard from him since. The next morning I flew out of Chester."

Dave asked. "And you have any idea of where Cranford is hiding out?"

Thayer shrugged. "No idea at all. But he has lots of buddies who would take care of him if he asked. People all over the country."

Rasmussen said, "We've checked the public transportation systems and found no record of his traveling, but he could have driven."

"Does he have a reserve of funds?" Dave asked.

"Don't know," Thayer replied. "He made big money in the pros, but he lived pretty high too. He never talked about investments, things like that."

Rasmussen switched off the recorder. "Mr. Thayer, I'm going to talk with the City Attorney and get a formal statement. I expect he will charge you with accessory to murder and hold you. But that will be up to him and the Judge."

Bixley nodded his head, "That's pushing too hard. For someone who got caught in the middle of this episode."

Rasmussen said, "He could have stopped Cranford rather than just stand around watching him slam her with this iron. He could have run to the motel office and called the police, but he didn't do anything to protect or defend Miriam."

He picked up the recorder. "I'll have your statement typed and bring it in for your review and signature."

Rasmussen and Dave walked out of the room, leaving Thayer to discuss arrangements with his attorney. Rasmussen said, "I'll get people out looking for that golf club and the motel where the murder occurred. We'll scour the room for any evidence."

"If it's okay with you, I'm going to scout around Rod Wilson's place and maybe others who knew Cranford. Maybe the station knows something about his buddies."

"Keep in touch."

Miriam's parents came into Jennifer's office three days after her memorial service. Their dour faces still reflected their loss and sadness. The mother, Teresa, opened the conversation with a question. "I understand Miriam will receive a goodly amount of money from the suit against Frasier."

"That's true," Jennifer responded, "but the precise amount is still unknown. I'd guess she'll receive somewhere around seven hundred thousand."

Fred, the father, said in his quiet voice, almost a whisper. "Ms. Watson, we don't need nor want this money. We're well set financially and would like to donate Miriam's share to some worthy organization."

Teresa broke in. "We've thought about a church, but she was not a member anywhere. And we're not aware of any charity she donated money to. I guess we're seeking your advice."

Surprised by the request, Jennifer thought about Miriam and the organizations and people that had helped her during the crises with her child and her battle with Billy. "One place that stands out is the Chester Women's Shelter. They're always strapped for funds and they provided a secure place for Miriam during a crucial time."

The parents looked at each other. Teresa said, "She mentioned them to us in a couple of letters and how they'd sent someone to the service for the child. It seems like a good idea, but Fred, what do you think?"

"I like the notion and if you're willing, Ms. Watson, we'll leave the arrangements with you."

"I'll be glad to do that for you. Would you like to visit the shelter and perhaps talk to some of the people who work there? They'll remember Miriam."

Again they looked at each other, silently communicating their thoughts, and Teresa said, "No, we're trying to avoid any person or place that reminds us of the ordeal Miriam went through." She reached to take Fred's hand. "Just going through her things in her apartment has been heart breaking for us. Every little thing brings back a memory."

Fred stood and Teresa followed, their hands still clasped together. He said, "Ms. Watson, thank you for your help with all of this. We appreciate what you did for Miriam."

Jennifer came around her desk to hug them both. Tears eased down their cheeks as the memory of their daughter lingered deep inside. As they left, Jennifer watched their slow deliberate steps and remembered her grandmother's last weeks when the once spry woman could not walk at all. She turned back to her desk seeking an item of work to take her mind off the Readings. But her thoughts of a vibrant woman wouldn't disappear. Tears filled her eyes. She pushed aside the papers and walked to the window. She swiped at the wetness with her sleeve, then retrieved a tissue from the desk drawer.

Leaving the office after accepting she couldn't work on anything. Her mind remained focused on the Reading's. She hadn't felt this despondent in a long time and looked forward to a quiet evening with Dave. Perhaps they could gather enough vegetables from their garden to put together a healthy meal.

But she found Dave at home pulling equipment and clothing out of footlockers they'd stored in the attic after the house had been renovated and expanded.

Watching a minute, she asked, "What are you searching for?"

His face was serious, even grim, he said, "I'm going undercover for a few days. I have an idea about Cranford. Rasmussen thinks I'm crazy, but I need to prove to myself I'm wrong. I'm reverting to my days as a hunter, living in the woods near Rod Wilson's place."

"Starting when?"

'Tomorrow night."

"You don't have to do that. Let the cops deal with it."

He came to her, pulled her close. "I have to do this for Miriam's sake."

Jennifer realized this was his way of dealing with Miriam's death. "I can't stop thinking about her and her parents. Such a loss for them."

Dave pulled her close, feeling her shuddering as she let the sorrow overcome her. He swiped at his eyes to erase the mist.

CHAPTER 28

Dave had circled the Wilson property in the afternoon. If fences were an accurate indicator, Wilson had about thirty acres, mostly woods, in the single tract. A small creek skirted the north side, just outside his boundary. The big house dominated the scene from the secondary road a mile from Route 36, but three outbuildings in addition to a garage, could be seen through the trees. He guessed those were a barn and storage sheds for equipment, but you couldn't tell from the distance.

Now near nine and well after the sun had dropped below the western horizon, Dave sat with his back against a huge oak and watched the main house. Lights were on in an upstairs room, he guessed to be a bedroom. Wilson had come home thirty minutes ago, parking near a rear entrance and entering without looking around. Lights came on in a back room. Dave could see movement of two figure, one must be Wilson, the second appeared smaller. Dave assumed it was the wife, getting a meal ready now that Rod had arrived home.

Dave waited, his back comfortable against the bark, a position he'd taken many times in his past. Once he'd watched and waited for three days until his target appeared, but he was out of practice for this kind of deal. He'd gone soft, working in an office and enjoying all the comforts of modern society. The daily grind of training coupled with practice exercises had kept him and others fit for almost any assignment. But he didn't miss the routine associated with being a razor sharp operative. Both Jennifer and Rasmussen had voiced disapproval of his mission. But surveillance by the police had been unsuccessful and Dave persisted in trying to locate Cranford against their advice.

His hunch nagged deeply enough to drive him. He suspected Wilson was hiding Cranford. It was a matter of time and patience for him to appear. He'd told Jennifer he'd give it two days before admitting he'd been wrong. Deep inside he recognized he might need additional time.

Lights came on in other downstairs rooms. Figures moved around, but none that fit the hulking Cranford. Near his lookout spot, small animals scurried about under a cloudy sky hiding the half moon. A gentle wind rustled through the leaves. Dave sipped water from a canteen fastened to his belt. He shifted his position, moved his legs to a different angle, then altered the position of his pistol in the side holster. But his eyes never left the house and movements within.

At midnight all the lights in the house darkened. Dave moved away another two hundred yards and snaked into a clump of shrubs he'd seen on his way toward the house. He'd hidden a knapsack in the bush and now he spread a poncho on the ground among the weeds and roots, pulled a light tarp across his frame and stretched out. He dropped off within minutes, reverting to an ability to relax under extreme circumstances.

Early rays of the sun slanting through the brush and into his eyes woke him. He listened for unusual sounds for a moment then sat up, drank water again, ate an energy bar, folded the poncho and stowed it in the knapsack, covered it all with the tarp, stood and from behind the bushes, then eyed the house and yard. Nothing was moving yet. He returned to his spot by the oak tree.

Just before seven, a teen-age boy emerged from the rear door of the house and trotted to one of the sheds. He stayed inside for five minutes then came out, trotting back to the house.

At seven-thirty, Rod Wilson drove away in the pick-up truck he'd used the day before. The boy left, a backpack slung across his shoulders, walking toward the road, probably to catch the school bus. Five minutes later, the roar of a large vehicle confirmed Dave's guess about the teenager.

Dave settled in for a long day, slumping further down against the tree and fighting off the boredom. He sipped from his canteen and listened to the birds chirping. A squirrel perched on a limb in the next tree, an acorn in his paws. Two hours later, a woman walked from the back door to the garage, them drove away, the door closing automatically.

Dave left his post and edged through the woods until he could see inside the building nearest him. Windows on three sides and a wooden door on one end suggested a spill-over sleeping arrangement. His hunch was confirmed as he peered through a window. A single bed, two chairs, a small TV, and an inside door through which he could partially see a basin and towel rack. Clothes were hung on racks behind the outside door. A pair of shoes were under a chair. He realized someone was staying there, but no one had been there last night.

The building in which the boy had gone to last evening had a lone window through which he could see several cages. Guinea pigs, rabbits and a hamster whiled away the day. This was the kid's menagerie, not permitted in the house itself, but the father had provided him a shelter for his pets.

Dave skirted the out buildings and walked through the woods as a method of overcoming his boredom and keeping body parts flexible. He felt more optimistic after seeing viable signs his hunch had been on target. Those clothes and shoes belonged to a large man, too big for either Wilson or his son. He stopped walking to watch two crows fighting over the carcass of a small animal. The idea of shooting them both crept into his mind, but he dismissed the notion as childish, not to mention an action that could trigger neighbors to call the cops.

By noon he'd returned to his post. He quelled the growl in his stomach by eating another energy bar and drinking water. He thought about Miriam and the first time he'd seen her. He recalled her energy and outgoing personality. He couldn't erase the picture of her lying on the table in the medical examiner's quiet space. Images of Katherine Mosley emerged from the recesses of his mind. He wondered again about her true motive in her interactions with him. He acknowledged he would have reacted differently if not married to a person he loved beyond reason and someone he'd not do anything to damage her trust in him. Those thoughts were replaced by remembrances of endless hours in bringing off assignments just like the one he was now engaged. Seemingly eternal waits, trying to maintain high alert, being prepared for lethal action without warning, then responding with deadly force at the precise moment.

At four the wife returned, stopping her car near the back door and unloading several packages, then moving her car into the garage. The son appeared soon after, dropped his backpack on the steps and trotted to the animal shelter. He brought a cage outside and allowed the guinea pig to run loose for fifteen minutes before his mother called him in.

Dave eased behind the tree and stood, working the kinks out of his arms and legs by stretching and wind-milling his arms. He was back in position when ten minutes later two pick-ups pulled into the drive. Wilson emerged from his vehicle immediately and started toward the house, then looked back. Billy Cranford stepped out of a pick-up truck with the Wilson company logo on the door.

Dave's heart jumped. He eased away from his tree and trotted deeper into the woods, utilizing every precaution his voice would not be heard. He called Rasmussen. "Look, I just saw Cranford. He's in Rod Wilson's house and I suspect he's been hiding out here since Miriam's murder. You know the location."

"I'll send patrols as soon as I can line them up. Give me fifteen minutes to get them there."

Dave returned to his post, stood behind the tree, pulled his gun from the holster and waited. He groaned when he heard the sirens and berated himself for not telling Rasmussen to surprise Cranford.

As the sirens came nearer, Wilson and Cranford scrambled out the back door, their attention focused on the driveway, a two hundred yard stretch to the street. When the cops turned into Wilson's property, Rod went inside. Cranford sprinted toward the woods, almost directly toward Dave's post.

When Cranford was twenty yards away, Dave stepped from behind the oak and yelled, "Stop." He fired a round into the ground near Cranford's feet.

Cranford pulled to a stop, recognized Dave and screamed, "You bastard." He stooped to grab a fallen limb from a pine and shuffled forward, ready to challenge his nemesis.

Dave yelled again, "Stop. Down on your stomach."

Cranford charged toward him. Dave shot him in the knee. Cranford screamed and buckled, his hands grabbing his leg.

Dave turned Billy onto his front, patted him down looking for a weapon. Finding nothing, he bellowed to the cops, now surrounding the house. "I have him here."

As Cranford was helped into the back seat of a cruiser, Wilson was led out, his hands cuffed, to another sedan.

Dave watched them leave, then trotted back through the forest to the spot he'd hidden his equipment and then to the Blazer he'd parked almost two days ago. He wanted to get home. He was too old for these games, but the hunt for a murderer had been successful.

By the time Jennifer got home near seven, Dave had showered and was chopping carrots into a lettuce, onion, tomato mixture. The aroma of broiling meat pervaded the downstairs.

They held each other close for seconds, then she stepped back, her eyes questioning, "Success?"

"We got him." He sketched the events for her as they completed dinner preparations and began eating.

Dave said, "This is great after two days of starvation." He sipped his wine and added, "I missed you, but how's the after-trial dickering going?"

"Essentially over. Frasier has decided not to appeal and we're in a position to work with the court in getting payments to those women who joined the suit. But that will require immediate action by Frasier and the courts."

"Frasier might drag it out."

"Maybe, but there's no reason to delay."

The evening program on television was interrupted to announce the arrest of Billy Cranford and his buddy, Rod Wilson. Neither the police nor Cranford would comment to the reporters. Following an advertisement, the anchor revealed that Mayor Ridley had been forced to resign and was under investigation by the State Attorney General's office for obstruction of justice and interference in the workings of the law enforcement agencies in Chester.

The following morning Dave joined Rasmussen and Stuart Channing in the attorney's conference room. Channing began, "Well, Mr. Randle, we owe you again. Maybe you should become a permanent member of our police force."

"I was glad to help and I felt obligated to Miriam Reading. The truth is if I had followed my instincts and not been constrained by your threats, I would have killed Cranford after the first kidnapping. Miriam would still be alive."

Rasmussen redirected the conversation, knowing what Dave's instincts would have led him to do. "We recovered the golf club from the weeds behind the motel. Cranford's prints were on it. And we found the murder scene in the motel room. Not much evidence there, but a print of Cranford was on the metal door. He neglected to clean that area."

Channing said, "We're charging Cranford with first degree murder and have sufficient evidence to make it stick. Also, we charging Rod Wilson with aiding and abetting a criminal."

"What about Thayer?" Dave asked.

Channing looked toward Rasmussen. "We believe Thayer felt trapped into going along with his friend. Apparently, he didn't participate in any phase of the murder. But he's guilty of accessory."

Dave shook his head. "But he could have stopped Cranford or alerted the cops and saved the department a lot of effort in searching for Miriam. And maybe he even knew where Cranford was hiding."

"He vows he didn't know where Cranford went. And as for giving Cranford up, he was too afraid of Cranford," Rasmussen commented. "But you're right. He shouldn't just walk away free and easy."

Channing said, "I'll talk to the City Attorney. Maybe recommend a suspended sentence or a short imprisonment with suspension of time."

Celebrating the conclusion of a long ordeal and trying to rid themselves of the memories of Miriam Reading, they had agreed to meet Helen Knight and her yet unidentified friend at the Marriott Tower restaurant on Saturday evening. At Dave's request, Jennifer agreed to wear the same dress the last time they were in the place, a sleek, black sheath that enhanced all the right curves. She'd remembered the single strand of pearls and the heels that embellished her legs. She'd insisted he wear his best suit, the one he had worn for their wedding.

Holding hands, they were led to Helen's table by the hostess. Helen and Antonio Gibbons stood as they approached.

Looking at Helen, then at Antonio, Jennifer said, "This is a nice surprise, seeing you together."

Dave shook Antonio's hand. "I haven't seen you in a while. You look different."

Antonio grinned, his usual broken teeth now gleaming white and even. "I'm getting all the parts upgraded. Latest is teeth, so Helen will let me smile at her." They pulled out chairs and settled around the table.

Helen looked beautiful and happy, her smile seemingly etched across her face. She said, "We've ordered drinks for you." She pointed to glasses of champagne at each place.

"So something must be special," Jennifer said, her eyes shifting from Helen to Antonio.

Antonio stood and raised his glass, "Join me in a toast to my soon-to-be bride." He leaned to kiss Helen on the cheek.

They clinked glasses and sipped the bubbly. Jennifer put hers down and said, "This a surprise, but not a surprise. I've seen the looks on your faces for a couple of months and wondered if you had figured out your true feelings."

"It took a while," Helen said, "but we both wanted to be sure."

Antonio turned and waved to a waiter. "Enough of the preliminaries. Let's eat."

THE END

About the Author

S. J. Ritchey has been writing fiction since his retirement from Virginia Tech. He lives with his wife, Elizabeth, in Blacksburg, Virginia. They spend summers at her family cottage in Washago, Ontario, Canada